"Cause of death?" Nick called.

"Nothing visible on the front." Gingerly, Catherine eased the corpse onto its left side and looked at the sheet metal underneath the body, but saw no signs of bugs or any other scavengers. That would disappoint Grissom, who did love his creepy-crawlies. The suit seemed to be stained darker on the back and, moving slowly toward the head, Catherine found what she was looking for.

"Two entry wounds," she announced. "Base of the skull, looks like a pro."

"Firearm?"

"Firearm is my call."

"Anything else?"

She didn't want there to be anything else. The heat pressed down on her from above. Any relief brought on by the cooler soil down here had evaporated and sweat rolled down her back, her arms, and her face. But she forced herself to stay focused on the job at hand.

Then, just to the left of the mummy's head, something caught her attention, something black poking out of the dirt. At first she thought it was one of Grissom's little friends, but closer inspection proved it to be metallic . . . a gun barrel, almost completely buried. Almost . . .

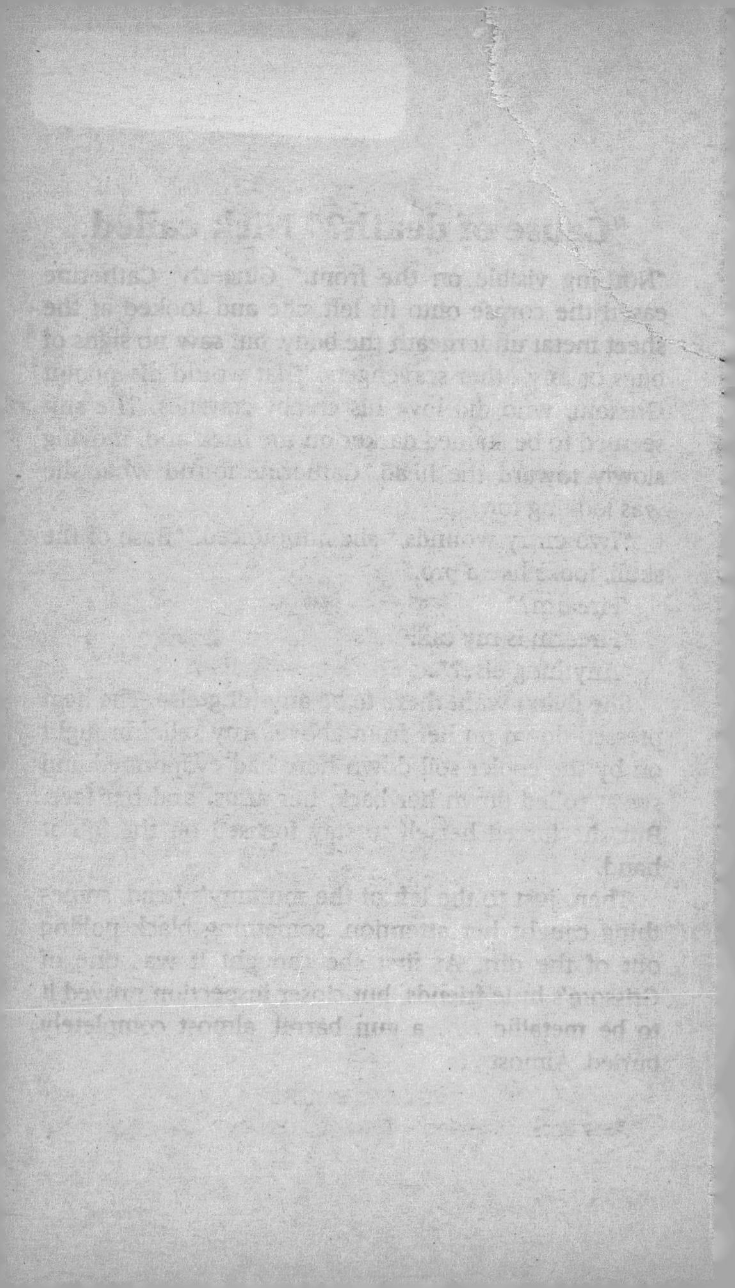

"Cause of death?" Fitz called.

"Nothing visible on the front." [illegible] came [illegible] the corpse onto its left side and looked at the sheet metal underneath the body but saw no signs of [illegible] that would [illegible] wounds [illegible] sign of [illegible]

"[illegible] was [illegible] head.

[illegible] to the left of the [illegible] sometimes [illegible] At first [illegible] closer [illegible]

to be metallic [illegible] a gun barrel almost completely [illegible]

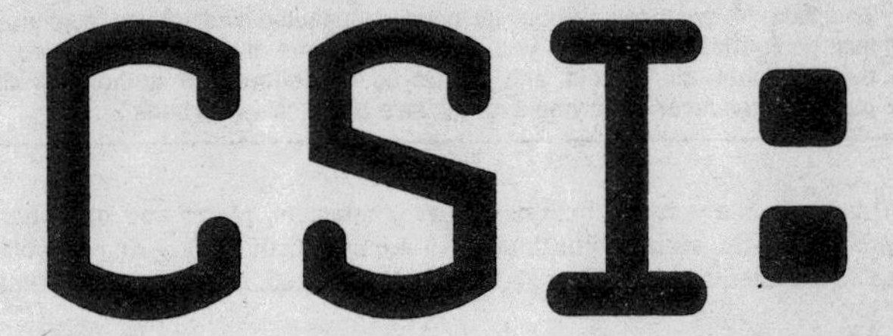

CRIME SCENE INVESTIGATION

Max Allan Collins

Based on the hit CBS television series
"CSI: Crime Scene Investigation"
produced by Alliance Atlantis in association with
CBS Productions
Executive Producers: Jerry Bruckheimer,
Carol Mendelsohn, Ann Donahue, Anthony E. Zuiker
Co-Executive Producers: Sam Strangis, Jonathan Littman
Producers: Danny Cannon, Cynthia Chvatal &
William Petersen
Series created by Anthony E. Zuiker

POCKET BOOKS
New York London Toronto Sydney Singapore

This book is a work of fiction. Names, characters, places and incidents are products of the author's imagination or are used fictitiously. Any resemblance to actual events or locales or persons, living or dead, is entirely coincidental.

An *Original* Publication of POCKET BOOKS

POCKET BOOKS, a division of Simon & Schuster, Inc.
1230 Avenue of the Americas, New York, NY 10020

ISBN: 0-7434-4404-3

First Pocket Books printing November 2001

10 9 8 7 6 5 4 3 2 1

POCKET and colophon are registered trademarks of Simon & Schuster, Inc.

For information regarding special discounts for bulk purchases, please contact Simon & Schuster Special Sales at 1-800-456-6798 or business@simonandschuster.com

Printed in the U.S.A.

In memory of our friend
David R. Collins
author, teacher, mentor

M.A.C. and M.V.C.

With a scientific third degree,
the master criminalist
makes the physical evidence talk,
wringing confessions from blood, guns, narcotics,
hair, fibers, metal slivers,
tire marks, tool marks, and bullets.

—Jack Webb

1

THE SIREN'S SQUEAL SPLIT THE MORNING, THE FLASHING BLUE-then-red-then-blue dashboard light reflecting off other cars as the black Chevy Tahoe weaved its way through rush-hour traffic on US 95. The sun was rising orange and bright, tinting the clouds pink, and the air conditioning within the SUV was already grappling with the July heat.

In the passenger seat sat Gil Grissom, graveyard-shift supervisor of the Las Vegas Criminalistics Bureau. In the driver's seat was Warrick Brown—rank CSI3, just one notch under Grissom—and in back was another member of their team, Sara Sidle, rank CSI2. Warrick sawed the steering wheel right and left as he dodged between cars, his expression impassive. He might have been watching paint dry.

Grissom's boyishly handsome features were slightly compromised by the gray encroaching on his brown hair, and crow's feet were sneaking up on the edges of his eyes, frown lines etching inroads at the corners of his mouth. The politics of this job had taken their toll on Grissom of late. As much as he loved the science of investigation, the constant jousting with day-shift supervisor Conrad Ecklie, the strain on his budget, and the pressures of management had started to age the perennially youthful Grissom. This reality was aided and abetted by the fact that, even though he had never needed much sleep, now he hardly got any at all.

The SUV hurtled toward a small Honda. Warrick slashed to the right, barely missed a FedEx truck, then bounced back left, coming within inches of a blue Lincoln stretch limo.

From the back, Sara yelled, "Geez, Warrick, he's not gonna get more dead. Slow down."

Warrick ignored her remark and jumped into the diamond lane to pass a cab, then hopped back into his own lane.

"Why didn't you let me drive?" Sara asked her boss as she bounced around, her seat belt straining. "Grissom, will you say something to him?"

Ignoring the exchange, Grissom turned his gaze toward the reddish sky. Quietly, without even realizing he was talking, Grissom said, "Red sky at night, sailor's delight—red sky at morning, sailor take warning."

Sara leaned forward. "What was that, Grissom?"

He shook his head as he studied the clouds. "Nothing."

"Please tell me that wasn't an aphorism," she said. "Please tell me you're not spouting quotes while this maniac is—"

"Sailors?" Warrick asked. "Gris, we're in the desert."

"Shut up," Sara snapped, "and keep your eyes on the road."

Warrick shot her a glance in the rearview mirror, twitched a half-smirk, and crossed all three lanes of traffic, jerking the wheel to the right as they turned onto Decatur Boulevard. Seconds later the SUV squealed to a halt in front of the Beachcomber Hotel and Casino.

"Six minutes, twenty-seven seconds," Warrick said as he threw open his door, bestowing on his boss a tiny self-satisfied smile. "How's that for response time?"

As the limber driver turned to jump out of the truck, Grissom gripped Warrick's shoulder, startling him a little. Grissom kept his voice quiet, even friendly, but firm. "From now on, unless I say otherwise, you obey the speed limit—okay, Mario?"

Warrick gave him a sheepish smile. "Yeah, Gris—sorry."

In the backseat, Sara shook her head in disgust, her ID necklace swinging as she muttered a string of curses. As she climbed out, dragging a small black suitcase of equipment with her, she said, "Gonna get us all killed, then who's going to investigate our scene? I mean, we'll all be dead."

Grissom turned and looked over his sunglasses at her, through the open back door. She got the message and piped down.

Warrick grabbed his own black suitcase from the back of the vehicle and fell in next to Sara. Climbing down, Grissom—carrying his silver flight-case-style field kit—led the way. This early, the sidewalk was nearly empty in front of the hotel, the doormen outnumbering the guests. The little group was almost to the front door when Captain Jim Brass materialized to fall in step with Grissom.

Brass said, "The hotel manager wants to know how soon we're going to be out of there."

"Why?"

Brass blinked his sad eyes. "Why? So he can let the guests move in and out of their rooms on that floor."

Shaking his head, Grissom asked, "What'd you tell him?"

Brass shrugged. "As soon as we possibly can."

A rotund doorman stepped forward and opened the big glass front door for them. Sunglasses came off as they moved through the gaudy lobby—Grissom tuning out the sounds of spinning slots, rolling roulette balls, dealers calling cards, the typical dinging and ringing casino cacophony—and Brass led them to the right, toward a gleaming bank of elevators.

"Where's the vic?" Warrick asked.

"Fourth floor," Brass said. "Right there in the hall, outside his hotel room door, shot twice in the head, small caliber, a .22 or a .25 maybe. Looks like a mob hit, might be a robbery got outa hand."

"We'll see," Grissom said, never interested in theories so early. "Is there videotape?"

Most of the resort hotels on the Strip had video cameras in every hall, but not all the ones off the Strip, like the Beachcomber, had caught up.

Brass nodded. "It's set up in the main security room—waiting for you, whenever you're ready."

When they were safely alone in the elevator, away from guests and staff, Grissom turned to Brass. "You tell the manager we'll be done when we're done. I don't care if he has to use a cherry picker to get these people out of their rooms, they're not going to disturb my crime scene. The hotel gets it back when my people have finished with it."

Brass held up his hands in surrender. "Okay, okay, I'll tell him. I just wanted to save the guy for you to alienate."

Taking a deep breath, Grissom let his head drop a little as he exhaled. "Tell him we'll work as fast as we can, but this is not fast work."

The elevator dinged, the door slid open, and it began. Stepping out, Grissom looked to his left where Detective Erin Conroy, stood interviewing a twenty-something young man who wore a white shirt, black bow tie and black slacks—a waiter.

The CSI group paused to snap on their latex gloves.

"Guy's a spitting image for David Copperfield," Warrick said softly, behind Grissom.

"The waiter," Sara said, amused. "Yeah—spot on."

Grissom turned to them. "Who?"

Sara's eyebrows climbed. "Grissom—you live in Vegas and you don't know who David Copperfield is?"

"A Dickens character," Grissom said. "Is this pertinent?"

Sara and Warrick, silenced, exchanged glances.

Moving forward, Brass on his left, Warrick and Sara behind him, Grissom stopped in front of a uniformed officer on watch at the near end of the crime scene. Beyond the officer, Grissom saw the body slumped in a doorway alcove; a large, circular, silver tray lay on the carpet across the hall; and spaghetti, meat sauce, and the components of a tossed green salad lay scattered everywhere. A white carnation, spilled out of its vase, lay at the corpse's feet like an impromptu funeral offering.

"Anyone been through here since you arrived?" Grissom asked.

Garcia shook his head. He pointed to a rangy officer at the other end of the hall. "My partner, Patterson, had the manager let him up the fire stairs down there."

"Good work."

"Thank you, sir."

Turning to Brass, Grissom asked, "Any idea who our victim is?"

"Sure—'John Smith.' "

Grissom raised an eyebrow.

Brass shrugged elaborately. "That's how he registered. Paid for everything in cash too."

"Right. You check for a wallet?"

Brass shook his head. "Waiting for you to clear the scene. I used to have your job, remember?"

Brass had indeed been the CSI supervisor until not so long ago; he'd been something of a prick, in fact, but had mellowed since returning to Homicide.

Grissom asked, "Your people canvassing the guests?"

"They're on it now—they started at either end, so they don't disturb the scene."

"Good call. And?"

"Nobody saw anything, nobody heard anything."

Stepping in carefully, Grissom bent over the body.

Lying on his stomach, head just slightly to one side, his brown eyes open, glazed, staring at nothing, John Smith looked surprised more than anything else. Cautiously, Grissom changed position to better see the wound. Clean, double tap, small caliber; Brass was probably right—a .25. The odd thing was the placement. Two small holes formed a colon in the center back of John Smith's skull, and—if Grissom didn't miss his bet—almost exactly one inch between them.

Grissom felt gingerly for a wallet, found nothing, gave up and rose; then he turned to his CSIs. "Footprints first, you know the drill. If this guy wasn't Peter Pan, he left his mark."

Warrick nodded, alertness in the seemingly sleepy eyes. "All comes down to shoe prints."

"Yep," Sara said.

Grissom stepped aside so Warrick and Sara and their field kits could pass. "Sara, you do the fingerprints. Warrick the photos."

"Good thing I skipped breakfast," Sara said.

"Least there's no bugs yet," Warrick said to her. Bugs and larva were about the only thing that threw the strong-spined Sidle.

"I wouldn't bet on that," Grissom said. "This hotel might not like it, but our little friends are here."

Sara and Warrick began by scouring the entire crime scene for footprints. This would take a while, so Grissom followed Brass over to where policewoman Conroy stood with the waiter.

Flicking the badge on his breast pocket, Brass said to the waiter, "I'm Captain Brass and this is CSI Supervisor Grissom."

The skinny dark-haired waiter nodded to them.

Conroy, her voice flat, said, "This is Robert LaFay. . . ."

"Bobby," the man interjected.

She went on as if he hadn't spoken. ". . . a room-service waiter. He was taking an order to room . . ." She checked her notes. ". . . four-twenty, but he never made it. Ran into the killer."

Turning sharply to the waiter, Grissom asked, "Mr. LaFay . . . Bobby—you *saw* the killer?"

LaFay shrugged his narrow shoulders. "Sort of . . . not really. He was standing over the body, his back to me. Jesus, the guy was already down and he shot him again, right in the back of the head! Then he heard me and turned around, and blocked his face with his arm—you know, like Dracula with his cape?"

"Bobby, did you get any kind of look at his face?"

"No. Not really."

"Was he a big man, small man, average?"

"Mostly what I saw was the gun. It seemed so big and it was the second gun I'd seen tonight."

Grissom and Brass exchanged glances, and the former said, "Second gun?"

The waiter nodded. "Up in eight-thirteen. Big guy, had a cannon on his nightstand. He said he was FBI, but . . ."

"FBI?" Brass said, incredulously.

"You didn't believe him?" Grissom asked.

"Nope."

Grissom gave Brass another quick look, then returned his attention to LaFay. "So, you saw the killer here—and then?"

His eyes widened. "Then I took the hell off toward the elevator and I guess he went the other way."

"Down the hall?"

"Yeah. Anyway, he didn't shoot at me that I know of."

Brass said, "Bobby, wouldn't you know if you were shot at?"

"I'm not sure. That gun wasn't very loud."

Eyebrows up, Brass asked, "No?"

"No. Loud enough to scare the crap outa me, though."

Brass grunted a laugh, but Grissom was thinking he'd have to tell Warrick to dust that stairwell. "Can you tell us *anything* about the killer?"

"I didn't see him good at all."

"Think, Bobby. Close your eyes and visualize."

LaFay did as he was told, his brow furrowing. "White guy."

"Good. What else do you see, Bobby?"

"Older guy."

"Older?"

"Forty maybe, maybe even older."

Feeling suddenly ancient, Grissom nodded his encouragement. "Anything else? Scars? Tattoos?"

The waiter shook his head. "Nope."

"What was he wearing? Shut your eyes, Bobby. Visualize."

". . . Jacket—a suit coat." His eyes popped open and he grinned. "I remember that! 'cause afterward, when I had time to think about it, I wondered why anybody would wear a suit coat in Vegas in July."

"Good, good—anything else?"

"Nope. Mr. Grissom, I can close my eyes till tomorrow this time, and I won't see anything else."

Grissom granted the waiter a smile, touched his

arm encouragingly. "Mr. LaFay, do you think you could identify the killer?"

The waiter thought for a moment, looked at Grissom and shook his head slowly. "No. . . . That good I can't visualize."

Grissom and Brass thanked him, then rejoined Warrick and Sara. They found Warrick kneeling over something on the floor as, nearby, Sara carefully bagged a piece of tomato.

"Got anything?" Grissom asked.

"I've got a footprint in the blood," Warrick said, "but it's smeared, like the guy slipped trying to take off."

Carefully stepping around Sara, Grissom moved in next to Warrick and followed Warrick's gaze.

Warrick was right: the footprint was useless. Turning on his haunches and lowering his head, Grissom carefully studied the hallway. "Look," he said pointing another three feet down the hall, behind Warrick. "Another one."

Warrick got to it, checked it, then turned back to Grissom. "Smeared too."

His head still bent down near the floor, Grissom said, "Go another yard."

"I don't see anything."

"Ever use Leuco Crystal Violet?"

Warrick shrugged. "Yeah, sure, but it's been a while."

Grissom grinned. "Now's your chance to get back in practice."

Brass walked up as Warrick withdrew a spray bottle from his black field-kit bag. "What's that?"

"See the spot on the carpeting?" Grissom asked.

The detective shrugged. "All I see is a dirty carpet."

"There's a bloody footprint there."

"Really."

"Yes—we just can't see it."

Brass frowned. "A bloody footprint we can't see?"

"The red cells have all been rubbed off the shoe, but the hemoglobin and white cells remain."

Warrick carefully sprayed an area of the rug and picked up the lecture. "This is Leuco Crystal Violet—a powder. But here today on the Home Shopping Network, we've added it to a solution of sulfosalicylic acid, sodium acetate, and hydrogen peroxide."

With a small chuckle, Brass asked, "If it's going to explode, you mind giving me a heads up?"

As the solution began to work, Grissom jumped back in. "It's going to work like a dye and bring out the footprint in that dirty carpet."

"No way."

"Way," Grissom said as the spot on the floor turned purple, showing the outline of a running shoe.

"About a size eleven, I'd say," Warrick said. "Now we photograph it."

Brass asked, "Can you match that to anything?"

Grissom nodded. "Once we get it back to the lab, we'll tell you exactly what kind of shoe that print belongs to. After the database tells *us,* that is. Then, when we get a suspect, we'll be able to compare this to a shoe of his and give you an exact match."

"Hey, Grissom," Sara called. "All I'm finding is pasta and a salad. And let me tell you, the buffet at Caesar's is better."

"Keep digging, anyway. And, Warrick?"

Warrick's head bobbed up. "Yeah, Gris?"

"Make sure you do the stairwell—that's the way Elvis left the building."

Warrick nodded.

"So—mob hit?" Brass asked.

Grissom led Brass back up the hall toward the elevators. "Too soon to tell."

"Robbery gone wrong?"

Grissom ignored the question. "Let's go see the videotape."

"Go ahead," Brass said. "I'll join you after I head upstairs and talk to that guy first."

Grissom's eyes tightened. "Our FBI man with the cannon?"

"Precisely."

"The tape can wait. I'll come with you."

"Fine. You interface so well with the FBI, after all."

Upstairs, Brass led the way out of the elevator. Grissom slid in next to him as they moved down the hall toward room 813. Pulling his service revolver from its holster, Brass signaled for Grissom to hang back out of the alcove.

Frowning, Grissom stopped short of the doorway as Brass moved into the alcove and knocked on the door with his left hand.

"Just a sec," said a muffled voice beyond the door.

His feet set, Brass leveled his .38 at the door, which thankfully had no peephole. Peeking around the corner, Grissom watched as the door cracked slowly open. He saw the big man in boxer shorts—and the monstrous automatic in his beefy hand.

And Grissom said, "Gun!"

Brass ducked out of the alcove, plastered himself to the wall, away from the door, and yelled, "Police! Put that gun down, and open the door, and put your hands up—high!"

Silence.

"Do it now!" Brass said.

The door opened and the big man—hands way up—stepped back. His expression was one of alarm, and he was nodding toward the nearby bed, on which the pistol had been tossed.

"I'm unarmed!" he said. "Unarmed . . ."

Brass forced the big man up against a wall.

"Spread 'em."

He did as he was told and Grissom eased into the room behind the pair as Brass frisked the man.

"Why the gun, sir?" Grissom asked, his voice cool.

Over his shoulder, the big man said, "I deliver jewelry. It's for protection."

Brass jumped in. "Did you know a murder was committed downstairs this morning?"

The man looked thunderstruck. "No! Hell no! You don't . . . you don't think *I* did it?"

Grissom moved forward. "Let's slow down for a moment. What's your name, sir?"

"Ron Orrie."

"ID?" Brass asked.

Orrie nodded toward the nightstand. "My wallet's right there."

"Do you have a permit for the pistol?"

"In the wallet, too."

Grissom studied the gun for a moment, a .45. "Is this your only handgun?"

Looking nervous, Orrie nodded. "Only one I have with me."

Glancing toward Brass, Grissom shook his head. "Wrong weapon. Too big. John Smith was killed with something smaller."

Brass didn't seem so eager to let Orrie off the hook. "Why did you tell the waiter you were with the FBI?"

Orrie shrugged. "I didn't want to explain my business. The more people that know what I do, the better chance I'll get knocked over. It was my own damn fault. Normally, I wouldn't have left the gun laying out. But I'd ordered breakfast from room service and he showed up before I was completely dressed and had it holstered."

The detective looked skeptical.

Grissom thumbed through the wallet, finding a New Jersey driver's license and concealed weapons permits from both Jersey and New York. "You are in fact Ronald Eugene Orrie," Grissom said as he compared the photo on the license to the man, "and you have up-to-date concealed weapons permits."

"I know."

"With your permission, I'd like to have your hands checked for residue."

"What . . . what kind of residue?"

"The kind a gun leaves when you fire it."

"I haven't fired a gun in months!"

"Good. Any objection?"

"No . . . no."

"Thank you. Someone from criminalistics will come to see you, within the hour."

The man winced. "But can you make me stay in this room? I don't mean to be uncooperative, but . . ."

A frown seemed to involve Brass's whole body, not just his mouth. His whole demeanor said, *I knew it couldn't be this easy,* and Grissom's eyes replied, *They never are.*

Brass said, "Mr. Orrie, do you have a concealed weapons permit from the state of Nevada?"

Orrie shook his head.

"Then you know you can't leave this room with that gun, correct?"

The man nodded.

"If I catch you on the street with it, I'm going to bust you."

"Yes, sir."

"And don't tell anyone else you're with the FBI."

"No, sir . . . I mean, yes, sir."

"And wait here until somebody from the crime lab comes to see you."

"Yes, sir."

"And if we decide to search your hotel room, will you require us to get a warrant?"

"No, sir."

"Are we done here?" Grissom asked.

Brass still seemed to want to hang on to the only suspect he had. Finally, he said, "Yeah, we're done."

Grissom said, "Let's go look at the tapes."

2

Nick Stokes, at the wheel of the crime lab's twin black Chevy Tahoe, threw a smile and a glance out his window, as if someone on the sidelines of his life might be able to make sense of it—a ref, maybe. "Can you believe this shit?" Nick asked, as he drove up the Strip in medium traffic. "Only fifteen minutes before the end of shift!"

In the passenger seat, Catherine Willows's reddish-blonde hair bounced as she shushed him, her cell phone in hand. Catherine tapped numbers into the phone and punched SEND, then waited impatiently.

The phone was picked up on the third ring. "Hello."

"Mrs. Goodwin?" Catherine asked.

"Yes?"

"It's Catherine. We caught a case. Can you get Lindsey off to school?"

The woman's voice was warm, even through the cell phone. "Sure, no problem."

"How is she?"

"Sleeping like an angel."

Catherine felt a heaviness in her chest and a burning behind her eyes. "Thanks, Mrs. Goodwin. I owe you."

"Don't be silly," Mrs. Goodwin said, "we'll be fine," and hung up.

She'd no sooner pressed the END button on her phone than Nick started again on his litany of woe.

"Do you know who was going to meet me for breakfast after shift?"

"Surprise me."

"A cheerleader."

"Really."

"Yeah, a beautiful UNLV cheerleader."

"As opposed to one of those homely UNLV cheerleaders."

"Now I gotta miss breakfast. This girl was getting out of bed for me."

Despite her anxiety over Lindsey, Catherine couldn't help but laugh. "No comment."

A chagrined smile flickered across Nick's well-chiseled features.

Catherine liked the idea that Nick finally seemed to be coming out of his shell; though the demands of the job kept her—and Nick—from thinking about their own problems, giving them focus, she knew that crime scene investigation was also the kind of work from which you should have at least an occasional break. She'd finally learned as much, and she hoped that now Nick would too.

She asked him, "What do we know about this call?"

Shaking his head, Nick said, "Some construction

workers got an early start today, trying to beat the heat. They found a body under a junky old trailer."

"New body, or junky old body?"

"That's all I know, Cath."

They passed the Mandalay Bay, crossed Russell Road, and turned into the construction site for the new Romanov Hotel and Casino. Supposedly the Strip's next great resort, Romanov would play thematically on the opulence of Czarist Russia, the main building modeled after Nicholas and Alexandra's palace in St. Petersburg, featuring rooms based on those of the actual palace. And if Catherine knew anything about Vegas, the joint would also have dancing Rasputins and Anastasias.

Right now, however, a construction crew had been engaged to clear away debris from the years the lot had stood vacant and become something of a dumping ground. The sun glinted off metallic garbage and presented a rocky, rubble-strewn landscape more suited for Mad Max than Russian royalty. A line of pickups on the far side told her that a pretty good-sized crew was working at the site.

She spotted a semicircle of construction workers standing around the remnants of an old mobile home trailer, staring at something on the ground. Behind them a few feet sat an idling hydraulic excavator, its bucket still hanging over the back of a dump truck where it had been left by its operator. Off to one side, maybe twenty yards away, sat two black-and-whites, the patrolmen leaning against them, sipping coffee, shooting the breeze. Beyond that squatted the unmarked Ford of an LVPD detective.

Nick braked the SUV to a stop near the yellow dump truck. Catherine threw open the door only to be met by a wall of heat that told her she'd be sorry for leaving the comfort of the air-conditioned truck. Nick piled out the other side, they grabbed their field kits, and Catherine led the way to the huddle of men.

Burly, crew-cut Sergeant O'Riley separated from the construction workers and met them halfway.

"Never seen anything like it," he said.

"What?" Nick asked.

"The guy's a damned mummy."

"A mummy," Catherine said.

O'Riley extended his arms, monster fashion. "You know. A mummy."

Nick shrugged at Catherine. "A mummy."

She smirked at him. "Come on, daddy-o. . . ."

The cluster of construction workers split and made room for them to pass.

The rusted hulk of the former trailer looked as though God had reached down and pulled out a fistful of its guts. Through the hole, beneath what was left of the floor, something vaguely human stared upward with dark eye sockets in what looked like a brown leather head.

"Anybody gone in there?" she asked.

The construction workers shook their heads; some stepped backward.

She set down her field kit and turned to O'Riley. Sweat ran down his face in long rivulets, his color starting to match that of his grotesque sports coat. "You wanna fill me in, Sergeant?"

"The crew came in at four-thirty. Trying to get

ahead, work when it was cooler, so they could knock off at noon."

Catherine nodded. It was a common practice in a desert community where the afternoon heat index would probably top 130 degrees.

"They'd only been at it about an hour or so when they found the mummy," O'Riley said, waving toward the trailer.

"Okay, get a couple of uniforms to cordon off the area."

O'Riley nodded.

"We want to make sure that he's the only one."

Frowning, O'Riley said, "The only one?"

Pulling out her camera and checking it, Catherine said, "A lot of stuff's been dumped here over the years, Sarge. Let's make sure there's only been one body discarded."

Nick, at her side, said, "You think we got Gacy's backyard here?"

"Could be. Can't rule it out."

O'Riley called to the uniforms and they tossed their coffee cups into a barrel and plodded toward him.

"Oh," she said, lightly, "and you might as well send the construction workers home. We're going to be here most of the day."

Nodding, O'Riley spoke briefly to the uniforms, then talked to the foreman, and slowly the scene turned from a still life into a moving picture. The workers dispersed, their dusty pickups driving off in every direction as the patrolmen strung yellow crime-scene tape around the junk-infested lot.

"Times like this," Nick said, as the yellow-and-black

boundary took form, "I wish I'd invested in the company that makes crime-scene tape."

"It's right in there with the smiley face," she agreed.

Catherine stepped into blue coveralls, from her suitcaselike field kit, and zipped them up; she was all for gathering evidence, just not on her clothes. She put on a yellow hard hat, the fitted band feeling cool around her head, for a few seconds anyway.

While Nick and the others searched the surrounding area, Catherine took photos of the trailer. She started with wide shots and slowly moved in closer and closer to the leathery corpse. By the time she was ready to move inside the wreck, with the body, Nick had returned and the cops were back to standing around.

"Anything?" she asked as she reloaded the camera and set it on the hood of the Tahoe.

"No," Nick said. "Our 'mummy' has the place to himself."

"Okay, I'm going in." She pulled on a pair of latex gloves and picked up her camera again.

"Careful."

Catherine tossed him a look.

"I'm just saying, Cath, it's rusty metal, unstable . . ."

"I've had my tetanus shot."

Entering through a huge bitelike hole in the trailer's skin, she picked her way through the rubble, slipped through the gash in the floor and slid down next to the body, half of it now exposed to the sunlight pouring in through the wide tear in the roof. The ground felt cooler in the pools of shadow beneath the trailer. She noticed hardly any smell from the cadaver and, judging from the condition of the skin, he'd been dead for quite a long time.

"White male," she said, snapping the first of half a dozen photos.

Outside, Nick repeated her words as he wrote them in his notebook.

Finishing the photos, she set the camera to one side. The body had been laid to rest on top of a piece of sheet metal, probably a slab of the trashed trailer's skin, and slid in under the dilapidated derelict. Though the killer had hidden the body well, he'd also managed to protect it so that instead of rotting, the corpse had mummified in the dry Nevada air.

They did indeed have a mummy of sorts.

Moving carefully, Catherine examined the body from skull to ox-blood loafers. The eyes and soft tissue were gone, leaving empty sockets, and the skin had contracted around the bone, resembling discolored beef jerky. Shocks of salt-and-pepper hair remained and the teeth were still intact. *Good.*

The clothes had held up surprisingly well, though the narrow-lapeled suit had probably faded from popularity well before this poor guy ended up buried in it. She checked the victim's coat pockets as best she could and found nothing. She could tell, even through the clothes, that some of the man's organs had survived. Shrunk, but survived. It wasn't that unusual in a case like this. Moving down, she went through the corpse's pants pockets.

"No wallet," she called.

Nick repeated her words.

In the front left pocket she found a handful of

change and counted it quickly. "Two-fifteen in change, the newest coin a nineteen-eighty-four quarter." She put the coins in an evidence bag, sealed it, and set it to one side.

Again, Nick repeated what she had said.

She looked at the victim's hands and said, "He'll never play the piano again."

"What?"

Shaking her head, she said, "The killer hacked off the victim's fingertips at the first knuckle."

"Trying to make it harder to ID the guy if anybody ever found the body," Nick said.

"Yeah, looks like he used pruning shears or something. Pretty clean amputations, but there's a gold ring that got left behind."

Picking up the camera, she snapped off several quick shots of the mummy's hands showing the shrunken, blackened stubs of the fingers, and the gold ring. She set down the camera and, lifting the mummy's right hand carefully, she easily slid the band off the ring finger.

"Gold ring," she repeated, "with an 'F' inlaid in diamonds."

"Interesting," Nick said, then he repeated her description.

"It would not seem to be a robbery, yes," Catherine said, as she pulled an evidence bag from her pocket, put the ring inside and sealed it.

"Cause of death?" Nick called.

"Not sure—nothing visible in the front."

Gingerly, she eased the corpse onto its left side and looked at the sheet metal underneath the body, but saw no sign of bugs or any other scavengers. That would disappoint Grissom, who did love his creepy crawlies. The suit seemed to be stained darker on the back and, moving slowly toward the head, Catherine found what she was looking for.

"Two entry wounds," she announced. "Base of the skull, looks like a pro."

"Firearm?"

"Firearm is my call."

"Anything else?"

She didn't want there to be anything else. The heat now pressed down on her from above. Any relief brought on by the cooler soil down here had evaporated and sweat rolled down her back, her arms, and her face.

But she forced herself to stay focused on the job at hand. Then, just to the left of the mummy's head, something caught her attention, something black poking out of the dirt. She at first thought it was one of Grissom's little friends, a bug; but closer inspection proved it to be metallic: a gun barrel, almost completely buried! Almost. . . .

She picked up the camera and clicked off several more shots.

"What have you got?" Nick asked.

"At least the barrel of a gun, maybe more."

Maneuvering around the body, Catherine pulled herself closer. Carefully, she dug around the black cylinder and left it completely exposed. Though the pistol was gone, the killer had figured he'd fool the firearms examiners by leaving the barrel with the victim.

More than one way to skin a cat, she thought, as she shot three more photos, then bagged the evidence.

Catherine Willows knew lots of other ways to catch a murderer besides matching bullets.

She glanced back into the hole from which she had extracted the barrel, and saw nothing . . . or was that something? Pulling out her mini-flash, Catherine turned it on and stroked its beam over the shallow hole. A small bump, slightly lighter in color than the rest of the dirt around it, showed at one end of the hole.

Excavating with care, she uncovered the remnants of an old cigarette filter. Part of this murder case, she wondered, or the detritus of a field used as a garbage dump for the last quarter century? Better safe than sorry, she told herself, and snapped some pictures before bagging it.

"One last thing," she said.

"Yeah?" Nick said.

"Cigarette filter. I've bagged it."

Climbing out of the wrecked trailer, she handed the evidence bags to Nick.

"Small caliber," he said, holding up the clear bag, peering in at the gun barrel. "A twenty-five?"

She nodded as O'Riley came up to them.

"Any ID?" the detective asked.

Catherine said, "I didn't find a wallet or anything and his fingertips are gone."

O'Riley frowned. "No fingertips?"

"Don't worry, Sarge. We can still print him."

"It's like Roscoe Pitts," Nick said.

O'Riley looked confused. "Roscoe Pitts? I thought you said . . ."

"No," Catherine said. "Roscoe Pitts was a bad guy back in the forties. Had a doctor remove his fingerprints, then had skin grafted to his fingers from under his arms."

Nick picked up the story. "He walked around like this for weeks." Nick crossed his arms, his hands flat against each armpit. "When he got them cut free," Nick said, wiggling his fingers, "smooth skin."

Getting it, O'Riley said, "No fingerprints."

Catherine grinned. "What Roscoe didn't understand was that, A, with smooth fingertips, he'd made himself stand out even more, and, B, you can get prints past the first knuckle."

"So he got busted?" O'Riley asked.

"Almost immediately."

"And that's how you're going to ID this guy?"

Nick nodded. "If our mummy's in the computer, we'll know who he is before the end of the day."

They turned when they heard one of the EMTs swearing.

"What's the matter?" Catherine asked.

The EMT, a big guy with a blond crewcut, held up one of the loafers with the foot still snugly inside. "I'm sorry. It just came off. It's like trying to pick up a potato chip."

Catherine said, "Nick, let's get the hands bagged first, then help these guys before they dismember the whole body."

With a grin, Nick said, "Sure—I always listen to my mummy."

Catherine tried not to smile, and failed.

Then, two small figures in the midst of a vast, crime-scene-taped lot, they got back to work.

3

The security room took up much of the second floor of the hotel, an anonymous blue-gray chamber where banks of VCRs covered one full wall, a security guard checking off a list on a clipboard whenever he changed tapes. The adjacent wall, constructed of one-way glass, overlooked the casino floor, the frantic universe of gamblers on silent display.

The east wall and most of the middle of the room were taken up by security guards sitting in front of computer screens. Some seemed to be watching one camera feed or another, while several more seemed to be monitoring gauges. One gauge, Grissom noticed, was the temperature inside the casino. A huge console inset with nine video monitors filled the south wall. In front of it sat a young Asian man, in attire similar to a desk clerk, tapping on a keyboard.

"Let's see," the computer tech said. "The fourth floor hall, between when?"

Behind him, Brass checked his notes. "Five-thirty and six o'clock this morning."

Grissom watched as the center video screen went black, then flipped to a grainy black-and-white shot of a vacant corridor, a time code in the bottom right-hand corner, the date in the left. "Can we speed it up until someone comes into sight?"

The guard said, "Sure. Probably not much traffic at that hour." He tapped some more and nothing seemed to happen in the hallway, but the time code was racing ahead. A man appeared and, as suddenly as the numbers had sped up, it slowed to normal.

"Mr. Smith Goes to Vegas," Brass said.

Picking up the narrative, Grissom said, "Heading for his room—practically running. Does he know his killer is coming for him?"

Starring in the documentary of his death, Smith ducked into an alcove about halfway down the hall on the right-hand side. In less than twenty seconds, a second man entered the corridor at the far end. This man stayed near the center of the hallway, glancing from side to side as he went, careful to keep his head lowered so his face never appeared on the video.

"Camera shy," Grissom said. "Stalking his victim—here! He ducks in after John Smith."

The videotape had no sound, so they didn't hear either gunshot. But when the killer stepped back into the hall, they saw the muzzle flash of the second shot. Bobby LaFay entered the hallway, the killer spun to face him, and the tray of food fell to the floor soundlessly as LaFay ran back toward the elevator. The killer turned back this way, head still lowered, slipped in Smith's blood, then ran headlong toward the camera, throwing up an arm to cover his face. He passed the camera and disappeared, presumably down the fire stairs to the first floor.

"Run it again," Grissom said.

Now that he knew what happened, he would be free to hone in on the details.

Again Smith scrambled down the hall wearing a dark suit, a look of fear etched on his face as he fumbled with his keycard until he ducked out of sight into the alcove. Next came the killer, a light-colored sports jacket over a light-colored shirt, dark slacks, possibly jeans, and dark shoes, maybe running shoes of some kind, the small pistol already in his right hand, his left hand also up in front of him, doing something. *What was that about?* Grissom asked himself.

"Run it back ten seconds," Grissom told the tech, adding, "and can you slow it down?"

The tech tapped the keys, the time code reversed ten seconds, and the tape ran forward again, this time crawling along in slow motion. The killer entered the corridor, his two hands up in front of his chest, his right holding a gun, his left . . .

"He's screwing on a noise suppresser," Grissom said.

"Mob hit," Brass said automatically.

"Too soon to say," Grissom said just as automatically.

With the silencer in place, the killer ducked into the alcove out of sight. Then Smith's feet appeared as he fell.

Grissom said, "Impact forced him face first into the door. He hit it, then slid down, his feet coming out into the hall."

Stepping back, the killer pointed the pistol at his fallen victim and fired a second shot, the muzzle flash a bright white light. And at that precise moment came

Bobby LaFay carrying his tray. Once again the killer turned, raising the pistol toward the waiter, the tray of food spilled all over the floor, this time not only silently but in slow motion, and both men took off running in opposite directions. The killer sprinted by one more time, his arm still up, his face still hidden, no distinguishing marks, no rings on his fingers, no bracelet on his wrist, nothing.

Turning to Brass, Grissom said, "You're bringing in all the tapes from this morning, right?"

"Yeah."

"Then I'm going back upstairs."

Brass made some quick arrangements with the tech, then accompanied Grissom back to the fourth floor, where Warrick approached them, a plastic evidence bag in hand.

"What have you got for me?" Grissom asked.

Holding the bag up for inspection, Warrick said, "Five large—money clip in his front left pants pocket."

"Well, the tape didn't look like a robbery anyway," Grissom said.

Warrick asked, "Anything else good on the tape?"

"Looks like a pretty typical mob hit," Brass said.

Giving Brass a sideways look, Grissom said, "Let the evidence tell us what it was. Don't be so quick to judge."

Brass rolled his eyes.

Sara ambled up to join the group. "Found a shell casing under the body, but there's no sign of the second one."

Grissom nodded and led them back to the murder scene.

"I've gone over every square inch of this hallway,

Grissom," Sara said somewhat peevishly. "There isn't a shell casing here anywhere."

Warrick nodded his agreement. "We've been over it twice, Gris—there's nothing."

Grissom's eyes moved over the hallway, took in the spilled tomato sauce and the trail of water from the vase that had held the carnation. His eyes followed the trail of wet carpeting, his gaze finally settling on the door across the hall. "Can we get into that room?"

"Someone's in there," Brass said, pulling out a list from his pocket.

Careful where he placed his feet, Grissom moved into the opposite alcove and knocked on the door.

"Mr. and Mrs. Gary Curtis," Brass announced.

Grissom heard a shuffling of feet on the other side and the door slowly opened. He stood face to face with a fortyish man with a peppery goatee.

"Can I help you?" the man asked.

Looking down at the end of the trail of water in the corner of the doorjamb, Grissom saw the brass shell casing winking up at him. "You already have, Mr. Curtis, you already have."

Brass said to the guest, "We're conducting an investigation, Mr. Curtis."

"I know," Curtis said, mildly annoyed. "I was interviewed already. How much longer are my wife and I going to be confined to our room?"

Brass smiled meaninglessly. "Not long. Be a good citizen. Murder was committed on your doorstep."

Curtis frowned, shrugged.

Ignoring all this, Grissom had bent down to scoop the casing into a small plastic bag; now he was holding the bagged shell casing up to the light. "No such thing as a perfect crime."

Brass said, "That's all, Mr. Curtis," and the guest was shut back in his room.

Grissom pulled a keycard from his pocket. He glanced at Warrick and Sara. "Party in Mr. Smith's suite. Interested in going?"

Warrick asked, "Get that keycard from the manager?"

With a quick nod, Grissom said, "You bagged the victim's, right?"

"You know I did."

"Well, you can't use that one, 'cause it's evidence. But now you two can do the room."

Warrick accepted the keycard.

Sara asked her boss, "What about you?"

"I'll take the stairwell."

"We're on it," Warrick said, and they retreated across the hall.

The EMTs now loaded John Smith onto a gurney and wheeled him down the hall toward the elevator.

"You can let these people off this floor now," Grissom said to Brass. "Have them take all of their bags with them—the manager needs to get them new rooms."

"It's a busy time of year," Brass said. "Might not be rooms available. . . ."

"Then have 'em pitch tents in the lobby, I don't care. This is a crime scene, Jim."

"Yeah, I was just starting to gather that."

The sarcasm didn't register on Grissom. "Station some of your men in the hall, though, and keep them to this side." He pointed to his left. "We don't want them tromping through like a chorus line. Just get them on the elevator and get 'em out of here."

Brass nodded and got out his cell phone. Warrick and Sara disappeared into the victim's room while Brass and Grissom walked to the stairwell.

The first thing Grissom did was run a piece of duct tape across the door latch so they could get back into the fourth-floor corridor. The fire escape stairwell consisted of eight textured metal steps rising to a metal landing, then did a one-eighty down eight more stairs to the third floor. No point in working the textured stairs, but the landings made Grissom smile.

"Sit on these and you'll be okay," Grissom said, pointing to the flight up to the next floor.

"Swell," Brass said, and sat, and made his phone calls.

When the fourth-floor landing yielded nothing, Grissom moved down to the next one.

On his hands and knees, he used a rubber roller to flatten a Mylar sheet on the landing. Black on the downside and silver on the upside, the sheet would help him lift footprints out of the dust. With the sheet pressed flat, Grissom turned to the small gray box nearby. The box's front contained a switch, a red light, a voltmeter, and two electric leads, one ending in an alligator clip, the other ending in a stainless steel probe roughly a quarter-inch in diameter.

Brass, off the phone, asked, "How about footprints?"

"We'll know in a second."

Grissom fastened an alligator clip to one side of the Mylar sheet, then touched the probe to the other side of the sheet. When the meter on the front of the box spiked, he smiled and removed the probe. Turning off the box, he took off the alligator clip, then turned his attention to the Mylar sheet.

"Here we go," he said, rubbing his palms on his pants legs.

Carefully, he pulled back the Mylar sheet, revealing two distinct footprints, one going up, one going down.

"Wouldn't you know," Grissom said. "One of them stepped right on top of the killer's print."

"One of them?"

"Either your man Patterson or the manager. Judging from the print, probably the manager."

"What makes you think it's the killer's footprint?"

"Running shoe. Looks like the bloody one in the hall, but it might just be wishful thinking, and the manager is wearing something smooth with a rubber heel. Florsheim maybe."

Next, Grissom dusted the right-hand banister between the landing and the third floor. The railing on the same side between the fourth floor and the landing yielded dozens of prints. The odds of getting a useful one from the killer were maybe one in a thousand or so. Guests, hotel staff, both security and maintenance, fire marshals, and who knew who else had touched these railings since the last time they were cleaned.

Looking up through the railing at Brass, Grissom asked, "Can you find out who cleans this stairwell and how often?"

"No problem. Find anything?"

"Anything?" Grissom echoed, with a hollow laugh that made its own echo in the stairwell. "More like everything. It's a fingerprint convention."

Grissom spent the better part of an hour and a half, finishing in the stairwell. He gathered scores of prints, but had very little confidence that any would prove helpful. The downside of public places, even one as seldom used as this stairwell, was that crime scene investigators could get buried under the sheer volume of information, most of which had no bearing at all on their case.

The hotel room looked like any other one in Vegas, with only a few differences. The bedspread lay askew, puddling near the bottom of the bed. A champagne bottle sat on the dresser with two glasses next to it. Clothes hung in the small closet and the victim's shaving kit was laid out neatly in the bathroom. A briefcase, a pile of papers and a Palm Pilot lay arrayed on the round table in the corner.

"I'll take the table and the bathroom," Sara said to Warrick, "you get the dresser and the bed."

"I had the bed last time."

Shaking her head, she said, "It's all the same, Warrick."

He gave her a slow look. "Like hell it is."

She threw her hands up. "Okay, you take the bathroom. I'll take the bed."

Glad he didn't have to enter the DNA cesspool that he knew existed on those sheets, Warrick entered the bathroom. On the right, the sink was clean. Next to it, on the counter, the signs of an exceptionally neat man. A washcloth had been laid out, a razor, toothbrush, toothpaste, and a comb lay on top of it, each one approximately an inch apart. Behind them stood deodorant, shaving cream, mouthwash and aftershave, each with the label facing front, each item about one inch from its neighbor, soldiers at attention. Warrick took quick photos of the bathroom, then passed the camera to Sara, who did the other room.

Lifting the wastebasket onto the counter, Warrick peered inside, thinking how his job seemed at times two parts scientist, three parts janitor. All he found was the tamper-proof shrink wrap from the mouthwash bottle and some wadded-up tissues . . . but one of the tissues had a lipstick smear.

"He had a woman here," Sara called from the other room.

Warrick looked quizzically at the tissue, then into the mirror, finally out into the other room to make sure Sara wasn't just messing with him, but she was nowhere in sight. He said, "I've got a tissue with some lipstick in here, says the same thing."

"Lipstick on one of the glasses and a cigarette butt with a lipstick stain in the ashtray. I'm betting our victim didn't smoke Capris."

Exiting the bathroom, Warrick studied the skinny cigarette in the bag in Sara's hand. "Not exactly a macho cigarette, is it?"

"Unless John Smith wore lipstick, it's not his brand."

Warrick almost smiled, and Sara put the evidence bag inside her kit, then moved to another, smaller, black briefcase. Opening it, she pulled out what looked like a telephoto lens with a pistol grip on it.

"I see our friend RUVIS made the trip," Warrick said.

"Yep," Sara said, flipping the switch on the gadget—

Reflective Ultra-Violet Imaging System. "If John Smith and his lady friend had sexual congress in this bed, RUVIS will show us."

"You make it sound so political."

The machine had been on for less than ten seconds when Sara let out a long sigh.

Warrick asked, "What's wrong? Didn't you find anything?"

Sara rolled her eyes. "What didn't I find? These sheets are covered with stains."

She handed the RUVIS to Warrick. He turned toward the bed and looked through the lens. With only the UV illumination, the bed looked like a giant camouflage blanket as the stains shown up like large white flowers in half a dozen different spots. "Busy guy if those are all his."

"You think they are?"

"Nope. Remember when Mike Tyson got busted?"

"Sure," Sara said. "Indianapolis."

"Right. The criminalist who investigated spoke at a seminar I went to. He said the suite went for eight bills a night. And the hotel was less than a year old."

"Yeah?"

Warrick turned off the RUVIS and set it back in its case. "How many semen stains do you suppose he found?"

Sara shrugged.

"One hundred fifty-three."

Her eyes widened. "A hundred and fifty-three?"

"Yep . . . and none of them were Tyson's."

Making a face, Sara said, "I may never stay in a hotel again."

"I heard that," Warrick said, and went back to work in the bathroom. He pulled some hairs from the shower drain, but found nothing else. Within minutes, he rejoined Sara in the other room. While she continued to take samples from the bed, he bagged the Palm Pilot, the papers, the champagne bottle and glasses.

"You know," Warrick said, in the bathroom doorway, "Grissom never once mentioned anything to me, about, you know . . . me working an investigation in a casino."

Still hard at it, Sara said, "Well, that's Grissom."

"Yeah. I just wasn't sure he would ever trust me again."

Studying him now, Sara asked, "Warrick?"

"Yeah."

"Is it tough for you?"

"What?"

"Being around it. A casino, I mean."

He looked at her for a very long time. "No harder than a recovering alcoholic working a crime scene in a liquor store."

Her gaze met his. "That hard?"

A slow nod. "That hard."

Awkwardly, she said, "Look, uh . . . if I can help . . ."

"If anybody could help," he said, "we wouldn't be having this conversation."

They continued working the scene, silently.

4

THE LAS VEGAS CRIMINALISTICS DEPARTMENT—HOUSED IN A modern, rambling one-story building tucked between lush pine trees—was a rabbit warren of offices, conference rooms, and especially labs, with a lounge and locker room thrown in for the hell of it. This washed-out world of vertical blinds, fingerprint analysis, glass-and-wood walls and evidence lockers was strangely soothing to Catherine Willows—her home away from home.

Catherine had managed to pick up her daughter Lindsey from school, have a quality-time dinner, and even catch a couple hours of sleep before coming into work a little after nine in the evening.

Now, a few minutes after ten, her eyes already burned from the strain of studying the computer monitor. Buried in the minutiae of an unsolved missing persons case—this one a fifty-two-year-old white man named Frank Mayfield who had disappeared thirteen years ago—she sensed someone standing in the doorway to her left.

She turned to see Grissom there, briefcase in one hand, the other holding a stack of file folders and a precariously balanced cup of coffee. In a black short-sleeve sportshirt and gray slacks, he managed to look casual and professional at once. He held the door open with a foot.

"You're in early," he said.

"Trying to figure out who our mummy is."

His eyes tightened. "And you are . . . ?"

"Going through missing persons cases, back ten to twenty years ago. The preliminary report says Imhotep died about fifteen years ago."

He was at her side now, the coffee cup set down on the desk. "How many cases?"

"No more than grains of sand in the desert," Catherine said, stretching to release the tension in her spine. "You know, there's been over thirty-two-hundred missing persons calls in the last two years alone."

Grissom shook his head. "Any luck?"

"Not yet."

"Is this kind of fishing expedition productive?"

She smirked, shrugged. "I've got to do something. Can't use DNA or dental until we at least have some idea who our guy is."

He sat on the edge of the desk. "Got anything at all?"

"A ring with an 'F' in diamonds inlaid in it."

Grissom's eyebrows rose; he liked that. "First name or last name?"

Catherine shrugged again. "Your guess is as good as mine."

"Any other engraving? To so-and-so, from so-and-so? With love?"

"No. Just an effin' 'F.' "

Grissom raised an eyebrow. "Do we know how the victim died?"

"Shot in the head."

". . . Funny."

"Ha-ha?"

"The other kind—our hallway corpse was shot in the head."

Another smirk. "Well, nothing separating the corpses except maybe fifteen years."

Grissom pressed. "Have you fingerprinted him yet?"

"I was waiting for Nick to come in. Our mummy's in pretty bad shape. One foot already fell off when they were hauling him out from under the trailer."

"I hate when that happens."

"I figured it would be easier processing the prints with two of us."

Nodding, Grissom said, "Good call. But you're here now, and Nick isn't—how about I lend a hand?"

"Or a foot?" Her sigh turned into a yawn. "I appreciate the offer—I can use a change of scene. It's like searching for a needle in a hundred haystacks."

Grissom nodded, hefting the stack of files. "Let me put this stuff in my office and we'll get right on it."

Turning off the computer, she rose; he was already back to the door, but had left his coffee behind. Detail work on a crime scene was Grissom's strength; but in daily life he had a hint of the absent-minded professor.

Joining him at the doorway, she said, "Hey, thanks for the coffee, Grissom."

He frowned at her, as she seemed about to drink it. She handed him the cup. "I'm kidding. Come on."

In the hallway, between sips of coffee, Grissom said, "Sometimes I can be a little thoughtless."

"I wouldn't say that. Not just any guy would walk a girl to the morgue."

And soon that was where they stood, blue scrubs over their street clothes, John Doe #17 outstretched on a silver metal table in front of them, his hands still bagged at his sides.

"I can't believe we already have seventeen John Does this year," she said.

Putting on a pair of glasses, Grissom moved forward; he didn't seem to have heard her. Catherine stood back a little as he studied the corpse. She knew he loved this part of the job—he was much better with dead people than live ones. There was something almost innocent about Grissom, something pure in his love for investigation and the search for truth.

But even more, Grissom loved to learn. Each new body presented the opportunity for him to gain more knowledge to help not only this person, but other people in the future. Wherever his people skills lagged, the criminalist made up for it in a passion for serving the victims of crime, and compassion for the grieving survivors.

At first, he took in the whole body. Catherine got the impression that Grissom wasn't so much seeing the body as absorbing it. *Stay curious,* he always said. He circled the metal table, observing the mummy from every angle.

"Your killer did us a big favor hiding the body the way he did," Grissom said.

"You didn't crawl under a rotting trailer to get at him."

His eyes flicked to her. "You know if we lived anywhere but the desert, there wouldn't have been anything left but a few bones."

She nodded. "Your bugs got cheated out of their buffet."

He stepped in next to the body and pressed gingerly on the abdomen. "Feels like the organs might still be intact."

Grissom with a body reminded her of how Lindsey had been when Catherine had given her that glass tea set last Christmas, the little girl examining each item, careful not to damage or crack the tiny pieces as she inspected each one. The criminalist did the same thing with the mummy, poking here, prodding there, bringing the work light down to more closely examine a section of the chest.

"Okay," he said finally.

"You through?"

He looked at her sheepishly. "Sorry. This is your deal—where do you want to start?"

Before they could move, Dr. Robbins, the coroner, walked through the swinging doors, a set of X rays in one hand. "Oh, sorry—didn't know anybody was in here."

"Bad place to be startled, Doc," Catherine said with a half-smile.

Around sixty, bald with a neatly trimmed gray beard, the avuncular Robbins—like them, he was in scrubs—slid his arm out of the metal cuff of his crutch and leaned it against the wall.

"What have you got, Doc?" Grissom said.

"Cause of death." Robbins stuck the first X ray under a clip on the viewer and turned on the light. The fluorescent bulbs came to life, illuminating a side view of the skull of John Doe #17 with several dark spots readily apparent. The second X ray the coroner put up showed the back of the skull with only two dark spots. He pointed to that picture first. "These two dark spots are your entry wounds."

"Are you *sure?*" Grissom asked, eyes tight.

Robbins looked at Grissom the way a parent does a backward child. "Why wouldn't I be sure?"

"Have you got the right X rays?" Grissom was having a closer look—much closer. "Is this John Smith or John Doe #17?"

"The mummy, of course, John Doe #17," Robbins said, more confused than offended, now. "I don't even know who John Smith is."

"Victim from the Beachcomber," Grissom said. "Two entry wounds vertically placed almost precisely one inch apart. Just like this. . . ."

Catherine frowned, shook her head, arcs of reddish-blonde hair swinging. "The same pattern? You're kidding."

Grissom twitched half a frown back at her. "When do I kid?"

"Well," Robbins said, "there's no mistake, I haven't even seen the other corpse yet. Hell of a coincidence."

"I don't believe in coincidences," Catherine said. "There's always a way to explain them away."

Grissom shook his head slowly. "I don't deny the

existence of coincidence—particularly when our corpses are separated by so many years."

Mind whirling, Catherine said, "Do we have two cases, or one case?"

Grissom's eyes almost closed; his mouth pursed. Then he said, "We have two victims. We work them as two cases. If the evidence turns them into one case, so be it. Until then . . . we live with this coincidence."

"But we keep our eyes open."

Grissom's eyes popped wide. "Always a good practice."

Pointing to the other X ray, Robbins indicated a dark spot on the right side of the forehead. "Here's a good place to start looking—there's one of your bullets. Embedded itself in the skull."

Grissom asked, "And the second one?"

"EMTs found it on the gurney when they brought him in. Little devil just rolled out."

"Where's the slug now?" Catherine asked.

"With the other evidence," Robbins said, picking up his crutch again. "Now, if you'll excuse me, I think I better go make the acquaintance of Mr. John Smith."

After the coroner left, Catherine and Grissom got down to work. They carefully unbagged the hands.

Grissom said, "Killer took the fingertips. Thinks he stole the victim's prints."

"I love it when we're smarter than the bad guys."

He raised a lecturing finger. "Not smarter—better informed."

"You think we should rehydrate the fingers?"

Studying the desiccated fingers, he finally said, "It might help raise the prints."

Catherine set out two large beakers, each a little more than half full of Formalin; behind her, Grissom was rustling in a drawer. When she turned back, Grissom stood next to the body with a huge pair of pruning shears.

Taking a deep breath and letting it out slowly through her mouth, Catherine moved into position next to the mummy.

"You okay?" he asked.

"Yeah." No matter how many times they did this, she never learned to accept it easily. At least this would probably be better than the times he had made her wear the skin stripped from dead hands as gloves, to provide fingerprinting pressure.

She held the leathery right hand still as Grissom stepped in and lopped it off. Catherine flinched a little, the sound echoing in her ears like the snapping of a pencil. She took the hand, slipped it into one of the beakers and they moved to the other side of the body and repeated the process with the left hand.

Setting the shears aside, Grissom said, "I can't get over the similarity of those wounds."

Slowly, Catherine turned the mummy's head so Grissom could see the bullet holes.

He stared at the wound. "You know what Elizabeth Kubler-Ross said?"

"About what?"

"Coincidence."

"Why don't you tell me."

He gave her an unblinking gaze, as innocent as a

newborn babe, as wise as the ages. " 'There are no mistakes, no coincidences—all events are blessings given to us to learn from.' "

"I thought you didn't deny the existence of coincidence."

"I don't accept it, either."

"Identical wounds, over a decade apart. And from this we learn . . . ?"

He shook his head. "Just keep digging. It's two separate cases. We treat it as two separate cases."

Was he trying to convince her, she wondered, or himself?

Catherine examined the wounds. "It is funny."

Nodding, Grissom said, "But not ha-ha. Sooner you find out who this guy is, the sooner we can lay the coincidence issue to rest."

"Nick and I will be all over this."

Grissom granted her a tiny smile. "Keep me in the loop, Catherine."

She nodded and watched him leave. Something in his manner didn't seem right, but she couldn't quite put her finger on it; he seemed vaguely distracted, even for Grissom. She told herself to keep an eye on her boss.

In the meantime, she'd hunt up Nick and if he didn't have any ideas, she'd go back to digging in the computerized records. The hands would take about an hour to rehydrate.

Nick sat in the break room, sipping coffee, a forensics journal open in front of him.

"Hey," he said to her.

"Hey," she said.

She poured herself a cup of coffee and sat across the table from him. "Where have you been?"

He turned to the clock on the wall. "You mean since the shift started three minutes ago?"

Following his gaze, she looked at the clock. She grinned and shook her head. "Sorry. I came in early. Tired, I guess."

"I thought we were going to do the mummy's prints."

"Been there, done that. Grissom helped."

Nick frowned. "I wanted to lend a hand."

"So to speak." Catherine shrugged. "Grissom offered."

Nick was already over his disappointment. "Well, he's the best. Learn anything?"

"I've got the mummy's hands in the Formalin now—we can look at them later."

He grinned at her. "Isn't that an old movie?"

"What?"

"The Mummy's Hands?"

"His hands are only part of the show. We found one of the bullets in his skull. Popped up in the X ray."

"Just one?"

She nodded. "The other fell out on the gurney. We'll wait for Robbins to dig the one out of the skull, then take them both to the firearms examiner."

He sipped his coffee. "What do we do in the meantime?"

"Back to the computer for me. I've been going through missing persons cases that somehow involve the initial 'F.' "

"Seems worth doing. I think I'll go through the guy's effects—maybe I can find something."

They finished their coffee, sharing a little small talk, and exited the break room, moving off in opposite directions.

Nick went into the morgue to study John Doe #17's clothes more thoroughly. Though the suit had survived fairly well, it had now become part of the mummy, in essence, his second skin. Head wounds bleed a great deal, which was the reason for the dark stain on the back of the jacket.

The clothes gave the mummy a musty smell, not exactly the aroma Nick would have expected to find coming from a dead body. He took scrapings from the bottom of the mummy's shoes in hopes that Greg Sanders, their resident lab rat, could tell him something about where the man had been walking before his death. He picked lint out of the mummy's pockets and bagged that. Anything that might give them some kind of hint to who this long-dead murder victim was.

Next, he studied the two dollars and fifteen cents in change: six quarters, five dimes, two nickels and five pennies. The newest was a 1984 quarter, the oldest a 1957 nickel. The coins, except for the '57 nickel, were all pretty clean and Nick dusted them but lifted only two usable partials.

The ring yielded no prints, but did have a set of tiny initials carved into it—not an inscription. He knew enough about jewelry to recognize they probably belonged to the jeweler that crafted the piece and not the victim. Well, at least that gave him something to go on. It would still be a few hours before he'd be able to find any jewelers in their stores.

Finally, he looked at the bag with the cigarette filter remains. Not much left after fifteen years, but more than he would have expected. Filters never biodegraded—an environmentalist's nightmare, a CSI's dream. Taking the bag, he wandered back toward the lab to find Greg Sanders.

Nick found the skinny, spiky-haired guy, as usual, poring over his microscope. Though well into his twenties, Sanders always had the cheerfully gleeful expression of a kid with a new chemistry set.

"Studying the DNA of another prospective soulmate?" Nick asked.

Sanders looked up, eyes bright. "Dude—science can be used for better things than putting people in jail."

"Marriage and jail—I sense a connection there."

Sanders batted the air with a hand. "Some guys are boob men—some're leg men. Me, I'm an epithelial sort of guy."

Nick held out the bagged cigarette. "Swell—'cause I need DNA on this."

Picking it up, holding it to the light, Sanders said, "Ugh—grotty! How long has this baby been part of the ecosystem?"

With a shrug, Nick said, "I don't know. You tell me."

"Take a number. Got a backlog. Gonna be a while."

"What else isn't new?"

Sanders shot him a look. "Hey, I'm only one guy."

"I know, Greg, but who else is ready to loan you *Gran Turismo Three* on PlayStation Two?"

All business now, Sanders said, "You just hit the top of my list."

The files rolled by one after one, blurring into each other, the coffee growing more bitter with each cup, and still Catherine couldn't seem to find a lead.

Nick came through the door and plopped down on a plastic chair just inside her office. "Anything?"

"Well, I think I've eliminated about forty missing persons with either a first initial or a middle initial of 'F.' "

"And now?"

"Starting on the 'F' last names."

"How many are there?"

"From ten to twenty years ago, only another hundred or so that are still open."

"*If* our mummy's from Vegas."

A look came across Catherine's face. "Got a better idea?"

Nick checked his watch. "Time to try the prints."

Returning to the morgue, they lifted the hands out of the Formalin, and set them on an autopsy table to dry.

"Give them a while, then we'll print them," she said. "Let's get something to eat, then come back."

He nodded. "Sounds good."

She smirked, shook her head. "You think there's anything gross enough to spoil a CSI's appetite?"

"When something comes up," Nick said slyly, "I'll let you know."

Forty-five minutes later, after their deli sandwiches, they returned and printed both the palms and the second flange of the fingers below the amputations. They fed the prints into AFIS, got fifteen possible matches.

It took the rest of the shift to go through them and, when they finished, they still had nothing.

Catherine stretched her aching muscles, looked at her watch and said, "I've got to get home to get Lindsey off."

Nick nodded. "I'm going to catch some breakfast."

"Food again."

"Then I might log a little overtime, try to run down the jeweler's initials on the ring. You wanna join in, after you get Lindsey to school?"

She shook her head. "I need some sleep. I put my overtime in on the front end of my shift. . . . Call me later, tell me what you find."

"You got it," he said, picking up the evidence-bagged ring.

In the parking lot, Catherine headed left toward her car and the trip home to her daughter while Nick went right, climbed into his own ride and took off to find a bite to eat. When he had first moved from Dallas to Vegas, he frequently took advantage of the casinos' breakfast buffets. But now, after working off the pounds he had gained doing that, he was more careful about where and how much he ate.

He only knew one jeweler, personally, in the city—an older guy named Arnie Mattes, who a while back Nick had helped to prove innocent of robbing his own jewelry store in a suspected insurance scam. Mattes wouldn't be at his store for another hour at least; this gave Nick time for a leisurely breakfast at Jerry's Diner, and a chance to actually read the morning paper, instead of just glancing through it.

Though the *Las Vegas Sun* carried a front-page story

about the discovery of the mummy at the construction site, the murder at the Beachcomber found itself relegated to a small story on page two of the Metro section. The mummy story was unusual, just a hint of sensationalism for morning reading; but the dead man in the hallway might have alarmed tourists, so that was played down. The city fathers, Nick knew, were sensitive to any scandal that might ruin the wholesome, family environment they'd been working so hard to cultivate.

He moved on to the sports section. Nick was a dyed-in-the-wool baseball fan—the Las Vegas 51's had shutout the Nashville Sounds last night—but because of his work attended few games and was forced to follow the team's progress in the paper when he got the chance.

After finishing his meal, Nick drove the short distance from the small café to Mattes' jewelry store, just off Charleston Boulevard. The CLOSED sign still hung in the door when Nick pulled up, but he spotted Mattes placing a necklace in the window, and parked the car in front. Walking briskly to the door, Nick knocked.

Mattes recognized the young criminalist at once, waved, and moved to the door to unlock it. "Nick Stokes, as I live and breathe. Welcome, welcome—come in, get out of the heat."

Smiling, Nick entered. "How are you doing, Mr. Mattes?"

"Fine, Nick, fine, fine." Pushing seventy, the jeweler stood maybe five-six and seemed almost like a child playing dress up, his skinny arms practically swallowed up by the baggy short sleeves of his white shirt. Black-rimmed glasses slid halfway down his nose, with a small magnifying glass, looking like a little crystal flag, waving from the left corner of the frames. "What about you, son?"

"I'm good, but I've got a problem I thought you might be able to help me with."

"Anything."

Pulling the evidence bag from his pocket, Nick held it up so Mattes could see the ring inside. "Can you tell me who made this?"

Mattes took the bag from Nick, held it up to the light. "May I remove it from the bag?"

"Please."

Carefully, the jeweler set the plastic bag on the glass counter, separated the seal, and almost religiously lifted the ring out. "Kind of gaudy, for my taste. Of course, that's typical in this town."

A crooked smile played at the corners of Nick's mouth. "What else can you tell me?"

Pulling his magnifying glass down over the left lens of his glasses, Mattes studied the ring for a long moment, turning it this way and that. "These initials," he said, pointing inside the gold band.

"J-R-B."

"Yes. The manufacturer of this particular item. The initials of J.R. Bennett."

"You know him?"

Mattes nodded. "An acquaintance from many years in the business. He runs a shop in the mall attached to the Aladdin. . . . Oh, what is it called?"

"Desert Passage?"

"That's it, son, Desert Passage. His store is

called . . . something a little too precious . . . uh, yes. Omar's."

"Omar's?"

"Silly theme they have, there, desert bazaar. When you visit Mr. Bennett, give him my regards."

"I will, Mr. Mattes, and thanks."

"Stop by any time, Nick. Remember what I said—you find a girl, we'll find a ring for her."

Nick glanced to one side and grinned, then looking back at the jeweler said, "I'll keep that in mind, sir."

Supposedly fashioned on a Casablanca marketplace, the Desert Passage mall was the only place in Vegas that could be counted on for regular rainfall. Every quarter hour, in fact, the mall's indoor thunderstorm broke loose for five minutes; positioned over the lagoon, the manmade storm managed to rain a great deal and yet never get anything wet. The tourists seemed to love it, stopping to take pictures of the water gushing from hidden sprinklers in the ceiling, amazed by the white flashes of strobe lightning.

Nick had walked about a quarter of the way around the mall—thinking about his late girlfriend, Kristi, for whom he'd bought bath and body oil at a little kiosk, here—when he spotted Omar's.

The jewelry store was small, but Nick could tell the good stuff when he saw it—and this was the good stuff. Only one U-shaped glass counter showed the various wares of the store, designed for lucky winners with new money to burn; but for the most part, this wasn't the place to buy off the rack: this was where the wealthy had jewelry designed for them.

Behind the counter stood a fiftyish man who had to be six-seven, at least. The tall man had short hair thinning on top, an angular face that gave away very little, and large brown eyes that revealed even less. He gave Nick what might have been a smile. "May I help you, sir?"

Showing the man his credentials, Nick asked, "Are you J.R. Bennett?"

"Yes."

Nick withdrew the evidence bag from his pocket, showed the jeweler the gold ring with the diamond "F." "Have you seen this ring before?"

"Most certainly," Bennett said. "I designed and crafted it."

"Can you tell me for who?"

"Whom," Bennett corrected.

Sighing, Nick turned back to the jeweler and said, patiently, "Can you tell me for whom you made this ring?"

"Malachy Fortunato."

That was a mouthful.

Nick frowned. "You don't have to check your records or . . ."

"Malachy Fortunato. I designed and crafted this ring exactly eighteen years ago at the order of Mr. Fortunato himself."

"One glance, and—"

"Look at it yourself. The ring has no elegance, no style. I remember most of the pieces I have created fondly. Not this one—but it was what the customer wanted."

"So," Nick said, "you're sure about the ring—but the timing? Eighteen years ago . . . ?"

"Yes, three years before he disappeared."

"Disappeared?"

The jeweler sighed; this apparently was an imposition. "Yes, I don't recall the details. It did make the newspapers, though. Does this ring mean that you've found him?"

"I don't know, Mr. Bennett. But you've been a big help. Thanks for your time, sir."

"My pleasure," he said, though it clearly hadn't been.

Nick was barely out of the shop before he was punching Catherine's number into his cell phone. He had a strong suspicion she would want to log some overtime on this one, too.

5

In the chem lab, Warrick checked the instruction sheet on the counter for the fourth time, then slowly stirred the fluid in the beaker. Sara appeared in the doorway just as he was finishing up. Her jeans and dark blue blouse looked crisp enough, but Sara herself looked about as tired as he felt.

"What witch's brew is that?" she asked.

Tapping the beaker with his glass stirring rod, Warrick said, "Smith's Solution."

"Whose solution?"

"Smith's."

She drifted in, leaned against the counter. "New to me."

"New to everybody. Just got printed up in the journals, couple months ago. I found the recipe in *The Journal of Forensic Identification.*"

"Always a handy cookbook." Sara nodded toward the beaker. "What wonders does it work?"

"Fingerprints on shell casings come up nice and

clean. . . . Intern named Karie Smith, working in Bettendorf, Iowa, came up with it."

"God bless the heartland," she said, flashing her distinctive gap-toothed smile. Her interest was clearly piqued. "No kidding—no more smears?"

"Thing of the past—buggy whips and Celluloid collars." Using a forceps, Warrick picked up one of the hotel shell casings by the rim and dipped it into the solution. He left it there for only a few seconds, then pulled it out and ran some tap water over the casing. Holding it up to the light, he let out a slow chuckle. "Got it."

"Show me."

He turned the casing so Sara could eyeball the partial print near the base. Her smile turned wicked as she said, "Let's shoot this sucker, and get it into AFIS."

They both knew there was no way to successfully lift the print off the casing. All they could do was photograph it. But that would get the job done just fine. While Sara got the camera, Warrick set up the shot on the countertop. He placed the casing carefully on top of a black velvet pad, with the print facing up. She snapped off four quick shots.

"Where you been all night?" he asked.

"Running the prints from the room."

"Yeah? Come up with anything?"

She moved to a different angle and shot the shell casing four more times. "Not much—just the victim."

"Give!"

"A Chicago attorney—one Philip Dinglemann."

Warrick frowned at her. "Why do I know that name?"

"I don't know. Why do you?"

"Don't know . . . but I do. . . ." He sighed, frustrated at the rusty gears of his own thinking; long night. "What about the woman's prints?"

"A hooker."

"What a shock."

"Working girl's been busted three or four times in town, but mostly she works outside Clark County at the Stallion Ranch. You'll love this—her name's Connie Ho."

Warrick's sleepy expression woke up a little. "Ho?"

Sara lifted her hands palms up. "What're you going to do? She's from Hong Kong; is it her fault her name's a pun? Been in the States almost ten years. Became a citizen year before last."

"Long enough to know Ho is a bad idea for a hooker's last name."

"Maybe she considers it advertising."

Warrick smiled a little. "I can't wait for you to tell Grissom we need to go to the Stallion Ranch to interview a Connie Ho."

Sara gave him a wide smile; even Warrick had to admit that gap was cute. "We only work the evidence, remember? Isn't that what you always say?"

It was—but Warrick, like the rest of the CSIs, sometimes questioned suspects relative to evidence because, frankly, the detectives just didn't have the familiarity with crime scene findings to pull it off properly.

"Anyway," she was saying, "I already filled Grissom in. He called Brass and got him to go out to the ranch, so we could work the evidence."

"Great," Warrick said. "Much rather spend my time with prints and shell casings than go out to the Stallion Ranch."

Her grin turned mischievous. "I knew you wouldn't want to be bothered interviewing a bunch of silly half-naked women."

Actually, she was right, but he wouldn't give her the satisfaction.

"So," she said, their photography session completed, "what's next?"

"First, we put these prints into AFIS," he said, nodding to the camera, "then we go downstairs and see how Sadler did with that Palm Pilot. I asked him to rush it."

Before long they were in the minuscule basement cubicle of computer technician Terry Sadler. In his late twenties, with short brown hair and long narrow sideburns, Sadler had skin with the pale glow of someone who saw the sun far too infrequently.

"What's up, Terry," Warrick said. "Find anything on our Palm Pilot?"

Like a manic ferret on a double cappucino, Sadler sat hunkered over his work station with his fingers flying and his keyboard rattling. "Just the usual stuff," he said, his words as rapid as his actions. "A list of phone numbers, his schedule, couple of pieces of e-mail. I printed it all off for you."

"Where is it?"

Rooting around his desk with one hand, other hand hunt-and-pecking, Sadler finally held up a thin manila folder. "Here you go."

Sara was watching this with wide eyes.

"Thanks, Terry," Warrick said, as low-key as Sadler wasn't. "I owe you."

"That's right." The computer tech threw a glance at the criminalist. "The usual."

"Usual. . . . How's tomorrow night?"

"Just fine, Warrick. Just fine."

They headed back up the stairs, Warrick leafing through the papers in the file as they went.

"What's 'the usual'?" Sara asked.

"Once a week, I spring Chinese delivery for him and two of his cellmates down there."

"Jeez—that's gotta run fifty bucks."

He gave her a slow smile. "Sometimes the wheels of justice need a little grease."

Shaking her head, she asked, "So, what's in the file?"

Putting the e-mail file on top, he handed it to her.

Aloud, she read, " 'Phil, this is no time to get lost. Less than a week till showtime. We should be getting prepped. Where the fuck are you?' Touching missive—unsigned."

They moved into the break room; Sara sat while Warrick poured cups of coffee.

"We can trace the address of the sender, easy enough," Warrick said. "It's got to lead to somebody."

" 'Showtime,' " Sara said, re-reading the e-mail. "Was this guy an entertainment lawyer?"

Driving out to the Stallion Ranch was not how Homicide Detective Jim Brass really wanted to spend a July morning. The news radio voice had reported the temperature at 105° and he'd shut off the radio before any more good news could ruin his day further. The brothel was outside his jurisdiction, so Brass had taken the liberty of trading in his unmarked brown Ford Taurus for his personal vehicle, a blue Ford Taurus. Such small distinctions—brown car for blue—were the stuff of his life of late.

When he had been demoted to Homicide from heading up the Criminalistics Bureau, he'd been angry, then frustrated and of course bitter. But time—and not that much of it—had smoothed things out. Strangely, working as an equal with Gil Grissom and the quirky group that made up the crime lab unit was proving much easier—and more rewarding—than supervising them.

A desk was no place for Jim Brass. Now he was back in the field, doing what he did best—doggedly pursuing murderers, and the suspects, witnesses and evidence that bagged them.

When Grissom had called him toward the end of night shift, Brass had been only a little surprised to learn that his victim had been a lawyer and not at all surprised to find the woman was a prostitute. But the hooker's name—Connie Ho—just had to be a put on.

The Stallion Ranch sat all alone in the scrubby desert landscape, just south of Enterprise, on the other side of the county line. The only other sign of life out here was a truck stop half-mile down the road. The neon sign of a horse rearing was hard to miss even shut off in the morning sun. He swung into the short drive that led to the actual "ranch house," which was what they called it in the brochures, anyway. The structure looked more like a T-shaped concrete bunker with the top of the "T" facing the road. Only a few other cars, and two eighteen-wheelers parked off to one side, dotted the nearly deserted dirt parking lot.

A teasing breeze kicked up some dust around the car as he got out and ambled toward the building. On the trip out here, he had considered several ways to play this. Several scenarios had been rehearsed in the theater of his mind. Now, none seemed right, so he would play it straight.

Jim Brass always did.

He opened the door, the rush of cold air like a soothing slap. A tall, impressive redhead stepped forward to meet him in a reception room running to dark paneling, indoor-outdoor carpeting and gold-framed paintings of voluptuous nudes, none more voluptuous than the hostess approaching him. and her voice carried a soft southern lilt. "Hello, Handsome. I'm Madam Charlene—and how may we help you, today?"

She was probably fifty and looked forty—albeit a hard forty. She had been gorgeous once, and the memory lingered.

He flipped open the leather wallet and showed her his badge.

"Oh, shit," she said, the southern lilt absent now from a Jersey-tinged voice. "Now what the fuck?"

He said nothing, let her take another, closer look at the badge to see that he was from town.

She frowned. "You're not even in the right county, Sugar."

He twitched a nonsmile. "I'm looking for one of your girls."

Her hands went to her hips and her mood turned dark. "A lot of fellas are. For anything in particular?"

"For information. She was with a trick at the Beachcomber. That *is* my county."

The frown deepened, crinkling the makeup. "And you're going to bust her for that? What two adults do in the privacy of their own, uh, privacy?"

Brass shook his head. "This isn't a vice matter. The trick ended up dead—shot twice in the head."

Alarm widened the green eyes. "And you think one of my girls did it?"

He kept shaking his head. "I know she didn't. I just need to ask her a few questions. She was with the guy some time before he died—probably the last to see him alive, other than his killer."

She studied Brass. ". . . Just some questions and nothing more?"

"That's right. I don't want to be under foot any longer than necessary."

"Considerate of you. . . . Which girl?"

He gave her half a smile. "Uh, Connie Ho. That's not her real name, is it?"

Madam Charlene gave him the other half of the smile. "Sad, ain't it? I think she's come to wear that name as badge of honor."

"If you say so."

"Anyway, she's one of our best girls. Popular, personable. Trim little figure—but legal."

"Thanks for sharing."

"You can go on back." She pointed the way. "Room one twenty-four. Down the hall and to the right."

"Thank you, Charlene. We'll do our best not to make each other's lives miserable."

She gave him a smile that didn't seem at all professional. "For a cop, you have possibilities."

Brass made the turn, walked down more indoor-outdoor carpeting and finally came to room 124 almost near the bottom of the "T." He knocked, waited, knocked again.

"Coming," said a female voice through the door.

Very little accent, he noticed. "Ms. Ho?"

She opened the door. Connie Ho was Asian, yet very blonde—platinum, in fact. Maybe five-four and 110, she wore a tissue-thin lavender negligee and black pumps and nothing else.

"What can I do for you, Handsome?"

Brass had been called "Handsome" maybe four times in recent memory—two of them, this afternoon. He flashed the badge and her eyes and nostrils flared, as she tried to shut the door in his face. Wedging his foot inside, door-to-door-salesmen style, and bracing the door with both hands, he forced his way in.

She backed to the far wall and wrapped her arms around herself, as if she'd suddenly realized how nearly naked she was.

The room was small, just big enough for a double bed and a mirrored makeup table with a chair in front of it. The walls were pink brocade wallpaper, and the bedsheets were a matching pink, no blankets or spread. An overhead light made the room seem harsh, and the smell of cigarette smoke hung like a curtain.

"Who the hell do you think you are," she snarled, "barging into my room without a warrant!"

"The proprietor invited me in, Ms. Ho—I don't need a warrant."

"You know we work within the law out here. I'm a professional."

He held up a single hand of peace. "Ms. Ho, I just want to ask you a few questions."

"I've got nothing to say."

"How do you know, when I haven't raised a subject?"

"That was a Las Vegas badge. I don't have to talk to you."

"It's about the other night—at the Beachcomber?"

"Never heard of the place—never been there." She stalked over to the makeup table, where she plucked a cigarette out of a pack and lit it up. Suddenly she seemed much older.

"Maybe we got off on the wrong foot, Ms. Ho. Shall we make a fresh start?"

"Go to hell."

He just smiled at her. "I've got your fingerprints and lip prints on a wineglass, and I just bet if we check the stains on the bedspread, your DNA is going to turn up. And you're telling me you've never heard of the Beachcomber?"

"Never. I don't work Vegas. I work the ranch."

"Then it won't be much of an incentive to you, if I make it my life's work to bust you every time you come into the city to turn a trick?"

Her upper lip curling back over tiny white teeth, she gave him the finger. "Sit and spin."

Exasperated, he started for the door. Turning around, he said, "That john, at the hotel? Here's how serious this is: he got murdered, shortly after you left him."

Her face changed but she said nothing. She took a

few little drags on the cigarette, like she was trying to make it last.

Brass said, "Hey, I know you didn't kill him. I just want to ask you about the time you spent with him."

"I don't know anything."

He started to turn away again, but her voice stopped him.

"Listen—he was nice to me. Seemed like a nice enough guy."

Brass went over to her—not rushing. He got out a small notebook and a pen. "Did you know him? Was he a regular?"

She shook her shimmering blonde head and plopped onto the chair in front of the mirror. "Charlene sent me. I'd never seen the guy before."

"What can you tell me about him?"

She shrugged. "He was clean and that's about as nice as tricks get."

"Anything else? Did he talk about his business or anything?"

She shook her head.

"Did he seem nervous or overwrought?"

Another head shake.

"Walk me through the night."

She sighed, thought back. "I went up about eight. We had some champagne. I gave him a blowjob, he came real fast. He'd paid for a full evening, so I helped him get it up again and we did it again. You're not gonna find any DNA, though."

"Oh?"

"We used rubbers both times."

How little they knew. "Go on," he said.

"He showered, got dressed, and said he was going out. He said I could stay in the room for a while, order room service, take a shower or a nap. He didn't care. He just said that I had to be out before he got back and he said that would be around five in the morning."

Brass jotted notes, then asked, "Can you think of anything else?"

"That's it. I kind of liked him. It's too bad."

"Yeah."

"Well, I gave him a good time before he went."

"Twice," Brass said, nodded at her, thanked her, and went out into the hall.

He found Madam Charlene inside a small wood-paneled office off the lobby. She sat at a metal desk with a telephone and several small piles of what looked like bills; Post-it's were all over the place. A computer on the desk symbolized how far prostitution had come.

Knocking on the doorjamb, still being polite, Brass asked, "Charlene—could I talk to you? Won't take long."

She stopped in the middle of writing a check and looked up at him with large green eyes. "Anything else I can do for you, Sugar?" she asked, the southern lilt back in her voice.

He mimicked the drawl back at her. "Why didn't you tell me you set up Connie's date at the Beach-comber—Sugar?"

Again the Southern lilt wilted. "I provide rides out here, for guys who wanna get laid."

"You don't provide an . . . out-reach service?"

"I don't risk it—I leave that to the escort services in Vegas. Not my gig."

"So Ms. Ho is lying—she booked this client herself, against your wishes."

She sighed, leaned forward. "Look—I just didn't think it was important. You said you wanted to talk to her. Have I cooperated?"

He nodded. "Yeah—and I do appreciate it. Now I'm asking you to cooperate a little more—what about setting up that date? You did set it up?"

"I did, but . . ." Madam Charlene gave him an elaborate shrug. "It was just another date."

Shaking his head, he said, "I don't think so. If it was a normal date, you would have told the guy to come out here. Let him find his way, or send your limo service. So why'd you send Connie into the city? You said it yourself: it's a risk; not your gig."

She shrugged again.

"Look, Charlene, I don't want to sit at the county line and bust any of your girls that enter Clark County, but I will."

". . . Close the door."

He did.

"If I tell you what I know, you'll leave me and my girls outa this?"

"If I possibly can."

"You promise?"

"Boy Scout oath."

She sighed heavily, found a pack of Camels on her desk, and lit up a cigarette.

Everybody in this joint must smoke, Brass thought. For about the millionth time, he wished he hadn't quit.

She took a long drag, then blew it out. "You know who the guy is?"

"Lawyer named Philip Dingelmann."

Her forehead frowned; her mouth smiled. "And that doesn't mean anything to you?"

Brass shrugged. "Such as?"

"Dingelmann is the lawyer for, among other illustrious clients, a fine citizen name of Charlie Stark."

That hit Brass like a punch. "As in Charlie 'The Tuna' Stark?"

Stark was high up in the Chicago outfit—a mobster with a rap sheet going back to the days of Giancana and Accardo. Sinatra had sung at Stark's daughter's prom.

"Maybe it's some other Charlie Stark," she said dryly. "And maybe I did this favor for Dingelmann 'cause he represents little old ladies in whiplash cases."

"A mobbed-up lawyer," Brass said to himself.

"You will keep me out of it?"

"Do my best," Brass said, "do my best."

And he stumbled out of the brothel into the sunshine, at first shellshocked, and then a smile began to form.

He had said, from first whiff, that this was a mob hit; and Grissom had, typically, pooh-poohed it. Evidence was Grissom's religion; but Brass had known that his twenty-two years in the field, as an investigator, counted for something.

Jim Brass headed back to Vegas.

6

After three-and-a-half hours' sleep, a shower, and some fresh clothes, Catherine found herself back in the office again. She grabbed a cup of the coffee from the break room and forced herself to drink some of it. Not so bad—a little like motor oil laced with rat poison. She found Nick in her office, camped in front of the computer monitor.

"I don't get out of bed in the middle of the day for just any man," she told him.

"Glad to hear it." He cast one of those dazzling smiles her way, and pointed to the screen. "Check this one out."

Catherine peered over his shoulder. "Fortunato, Malachy? How 'fortunate' was Malachy?"

"Not very," Nick said, referring to the file on screen. "Disappeared from his home fifteen years ago, leaving a bloodstain in the carport, on the gravel driveway—no sign of Malachy since. The original investigators let the case drop—a bloodstain does not a crime scene make."

"True."

"Plus, the detectives were convinced the married Mr. Fortunato ran off with his girlfriend, and that the blood stain was a dodge to throw the mob off the track."

"The mob?"

"Gamblers, anyway. The variety that breaks limbs when markers go unpaid."

"If Malachy's the mummy, I'd say his dodge didn't work." Looking over Nick's shoulder, she slowly scanned the file. "Small-time casino worker, big gambling debts, suspected of embezzling at work. Ouch—that might have gotten a contract put out on him."

"He worked at the Sandmound," Nick said, referring to a long-since demolished casino, which had dated back to the days when Vegas had been a syndicate stronghold. "Two bullets in the back of the head, that's a fairly typical expression of mob displeasure."

"Okay," Catherine said. "I'm liking this . . . but why do you think Malachy's our mummy?"

Nick's tight smile reflected pride. "I traced the ring you found on the body. Jeweler who made the bauble recognized it. Bada-bing."

"Please. . . . Okay, you did good. Let's print out this report so we can look at it a little closer."

Nick printed the file.

"There's a sample of the bloodstain from that carport and a cigarette butt from the backyard in Evidence," Catherine said, sitting, reading the hard copy. "We can pull them, and try to get a DNA match, to make sure this is our guy."

Nick flinched. "Damn—that's gonna take forever."

"Good things come to those who wait . . . and while we're waiting . . ." Her voice trailed off as she noted Fortunato's address, and reached for a phone book. "Says he lived with his wife Annie." Thumbing the white pages, Catherine found the FOR's, ran a finger down the column, and said, "And she still lives there."

Neither was too surprised; the real residents of Vegas put down roots, like anyone anywhere else.

Nick squinted in thought. "Does that mean we have a fifteen-year-old crime scene?"

"It means I'm going to track O'Riley down, and run out there." She waved the printout. "I want to meet the little woman whose husband ran off with his girlfriend . . . and have a look at what may be a *really* not-fresh crime scene."

Nick bobbed his head. "I'll get on the DNA."

"Good." Glancing through the file one more time, she noticed a note that said the police had returned Mr. Fortunato's personal effects to his wife. "What the hell?"

She handed the note to Nick, who read it and shrugged. "So?"

Catherine's half-smile was wry and skeptical. "If Malachy the mummy was missing, what personal stuff did they have of his?"

"There's no inventory?"

She shuffled through the papers one more time. "Nope."

Nick shrugged. "Could be anything."

"Could be something." She rose, went to the door and turned back to him. "Nice work, Nick. Really nice."

He gave her another dazzler, pleased with himself. "I'm not as dumb as I look."

"No one could be," she said with affection, and he laughed as she waved and went out.

O'Riley met Catherine in front of the Fortunato house and she filled him in. She liked working with the massive, crew-cut detective because the man knew his limitations, and wasn't offended when she broke protocol and took the lead in questioning. She did wonder where he'd come up with that brown-and-green-plaid sportshirt; maybe the same garage sale as the who-shot-the-couch sportcoat.

The one-story stucco ranch had an orange tile roof and a front yard where the sparse grass was like the scalp of a guy whose transplant wasn't taking. Heat shimmered up off the sidewalk, and from the asphalt drive that had, in the intervening years, replaced the gravel driveway of the file photos. The carport, at least, remained.

The detective knocked on the door and almost immediately it opened to reveal a thin, haggard, but not unattractive woman in her fifties, with a cigarette dangling between her lips.

"Mrs. Fortunato?" O'Riley asked, flashing his badge. He identified himself and Catherine.

"I used to be Mrs. Fortunato. But that's kind of old news—why?"

Catherine said, "You're still listed under that name in the phone book, Mrs.—"

"I'm still Annie Fortunato, I just don't use the 'Mrs.' It's a long boring story." She looked from face to face. "What's this about, anyway?"

Catherine held the evidence bag containing the

ring out in front of her—the distinctive gold-and-diamond ring winked in the sunlight, the "F" staring at the woman, the woman staring back.

Taking the bag, a slight tremor in her hands, Mrs. Fortunato studied the gaudy ring. A tear trailed down her cheek and she wiped it absently. Another replaced it and another, and soon the woman shook violently and slipped down, puddling at O'Riley's feet even as he tried to catch her.

A burly man in a white T-shirt and black jeans bounded into the living room from the kitchen. "Hey, what the hell?" he yelled, moving forward toward the stricken woman.

O'Riley, surprised to see the guy, pulled his badge and tried to show it to the man who barreled toward them, his fist drawn back ready to punch O'Riley in the face. The badge slipped from O'Riley's grasp and his hand came back toward his hip.

In horror, Catherine realized the big cop, spooked and unnerved, was going for his gun. She grabbed O'Riley's gun hand, keeping him from drawing his pistol and, in the same fluid motion, stepped in front of the detective, ready to take the blow from the large man freight-training toward them.

Facing the oncoming potential attacker, she almost yelled, "It's all right, sir! We're with the police."

The punch looped toward her and Catherine flinched, but the blow never landed. Her words registered just in time, and the brute halted the punch just short of her face.

She gasped; but she would have done it again, because if she hadn't, O'Riley might well have been up before the shooting board for firing on an unarmed citizen. A lousy career move. And dead or wounded citizens were not helpful to an investigation.

"Police?" the big guy was asking, dumbfounded.

Behind her, on the stoop, O'Riley stumbled backward, regained his balance, and stood there staring at Catherine as the big guy helped Annie Fortunato to her feet. The apparent man of the house led the shaken woman inside, helping her to take a seat on the sofa. Finally, O'Riley followed.

"Who are you, sir?" Catherine asked, as she quickly took in the living room, an ode to the brass-and-glass movement of the eighties. After picking his badge up, O'Riley relegated himself to the background. The big detective was trembling, and embarrassed, and Catherine was only too happy to carry the ball.

Catherine repeated: "Sir, who are you, please?"

The T-shirted brute's attention was on the weeping woman, but he said, "Gerry Hoskins. I'm Annie's . . . uh . . . friend." Middle-aged, the powerfully built six-foot Hoskins wore his brown hair almost as short as O'Riley's; his oval face had a bulldog look, offset by deep blue eyes which Catherine supposed would look attractive when they weren't blazing with anger . . . as they were now.

"What did you do to her?" he demanded.

Fighting to regain control, Annie Fortunato handed Hoskins the evidence bag.

"They . . . they found Mal," the woman managed between sobs.

He looked at the initial on the ring. Then he stared at his agonized lady friend, and, finally, Hoskins seemed to get it. "Oh, God. You finally found him? You wouldn't be here, he wasn't dead, right?"

Catherine ignored this; and O'Riley was just another outmoded hunk of furniture. Crouching on her haunches so she could look the woman in the eye, Catherine said, "We think your husband is dead, Mrs. Fortunato . . . but we need to make sure. I know it's been many years . . . do you remember, did Malachy have a dentist he visited regularly?"

Not missing a beat, the woman said, "Dr. Roy McNeal."

"You're sure? It has been a long time—"

"He's still my dentist. And Mal was so busy, at work, I always made his appointments for him."

"Good. Good."

Clutching her boyfriend's hand, Mrs. Fortunato kept her eyes on Catherine. "You really think you've found Mal? I mean, after all these years?"

"A body discovered yesterday was wearing this ring—on the third finger of his right hand."

Annie Fortunato drew in a breath; then she nodded. "Yes, that's where he wore it. Where did you find him?"

"A vacant lot toward the end of the Strip."

Eyes tight, Mrs. Fortunato said, "I know that lot—the one with all the garbage?"

"Yes. A resort's going in. Romanov's."

"I read about that in the paper," Hoskins said, as he plucked a tissue from a box on an end table. He handed Mrs. Fortunato the tissue, and she managed a weak smile of thanks, dabbing at her eyes.

"A crew has started to clear the lot," Catherine said.

"They found the man we believe to be your husband under an old abandoned trailer."

The woman seemed to have another question that she couldn't quite get out. Catherine leaned in, touched Mrs. Fortunato's arm. "Yes? What is it, Mrs. Fortunato?"

Shakily taking a cigarette from a pack on the glass end table next to her, the woman lit it, took a deep drag, let it out in a blue cloud, and finally turned her attention back to Catherine. "Was she with him?"

"She?"

"His whore," she snarled. "Was *she* with him?"

Woah . . .

Catherine said, "He was alone. We searched the lot thoroughly—no other body was present."

Patting Mrs. Fortunato's knee, Hoskins—his manner very different now—said to Catherine, "There was this dancer that some people thought Mal was sleeping with. You know—a stripper."

"I know about strippers," Catherine said.

"Slut disappeared the same night Annie's husband did. Annie had some trouble with some . . . uh . . . people Mal owed money, bad debts, you know. They told Annie that Mal had probably just run off with this woman, and they wanted her to give them the money Mal owed."

Something like a growl escaped Mrs. Fortunato's throat. "Like *I* had a goddamn penny to my name, back then. It wasn't until we got Mal declared legally dead after seven years that I got any peace from anybody."

"These people," Catherine said, "were they organized crime?"

"Yeah," Hoskins said. He shook his head. "It was different, back then. Mal worked for one of the old-school casinos, Chicago or Cleveland guys owned it . . . they claimed he was skimming. Anyway, some characters who make me look like a fashion model come around a few times, right after Mal . . ."

Struck by how vivid this recapitulation was, Catherine interrupted. "Excuse me, Mr. Hoskins, were you here, then?"

He shook his head. "No—but I heard Annie talk about it so much, it's like—"

"Then I need to hear this from Mrs. Fortunato, okay?"

The big guy looked sheepish. "Oh. Yeah. Sorry."

Mrs. Fortunato picked up right where he had left off. "They came around right after Mal . . . disappeared. They made a lot of noise, made me show them my damn bank book. Tax statements, too, they made me show 'em. Wanted to know what safe deposit boxes I had, God. Finally they saw I didn't have the money, and left me alone."

Catherine nodded. "They wanted to make sure you weren't in with your husband on the embezzlement."

Defensively, the woman said, "It was never proven that Mal stole their money."

"Mrs. Fortunato, your husband's death is a murder, and it looks like a mob assassination." Catherine let it go at that; she preferred not to share any details with the woman, not this early in the investigation, anyway.

Mrs. Fortunato took this in blankly, eyes not teary anymore—red, glazed, but not teary.

Catherine said, "If you're up to it, I'd like to ask you a few more questions."

"I suppose we should get this over with," Mrs. Fortunato said, and sighed. "What do you think, Gerry?"

"Yeah. I'll make us some coffee, okay?"

A tired smile crossed the woman's face. "Thanks."

Awkwardly, Hoskins looked from Catherine to the totem pole that was O'Riley. "Would you people like anything? Coffee? I got diet root beer."

Catherine said, "No thank you," and O'Riley shook his bucket head.

Hoskins swallowed, stood, and went over to O'Riley in his corner. He extended his hand. "Sorry, man. I shouldn'ta swung on you. It's just that it looked like . . ."

"Forget about it," O'Riley said, taking the guy's hand.

"Am I gonna get charged with anything? Swinging on a cop like that?"

O'Riley waved it off. "Simple misunderstanding."

"Sure you don't want any coffee?"

"I could use some," O'Riley admitted.

Wanting to keep Hoskins busy, Catherine said, "Me, too. Thanks."

Hoskins went into the kitchen and O'Riley melted back into the corner.

"Gerry's been good to me," Mrs. Fortunato said, her eyes following Hoskins into the kitchen. "These last years, he helped me survive."

Catherine pressed forward. "Mrs. Fortunato, tell me about the day Malachy disappeared."

Again, not missing a beat, the woman knew: "January twenty-seventh, nineteen eighty-five."

"Yes. What do you remember?"

"Everything," Mrs. Fortunato said, stubbing out one cigarette in the ashtray on the end table and immediately lighting up another. "Mal had been nervous—trouble at work, I figured. He never really told me much about things like that. He always got up early, around five-thirty, and by six-thirty, he was on his way to work. He was dedicated to his job, despite what those people said. Anyway, on that morning, I didn't hear him get up."

"Go on."

"I worked late nights, in those days. I was a cashier over on Fremont Street. Mal worked at the Sandmound, in the office, accounting."

"Excuse me—wasn't your husband a gambler?"

"Oh yes."

"I thought the casinos didn't hire gamblers for jobs of that nature."

"No one knew he was gambling . . . except me. He was doing it from phone booths. Calling bookies out east. By the time anyone found out what was going on, him and that dancer had disappeared." She drew on the cigarette; her eyes glittered. "I hope the bastards killed her too. She was the one turned him from a guy who liked a friendly bet into a gambler."

"How do you mean?"

"Well, it's obvious. If he hadn't tried to keep us both happy, he wouldn't have stolen that money. He wouldn't have been betting on games trying to make enough money to support two women."

Catherine frowned. "So, he really was embezzling? Whether it was proven or not?"

Another shrug—a fatalistic one. "Why would they lie to me about it? What could they get out of me? They weren't so bad, anyway, for a bunch of goddamn mobsters. I worked in casinos for years, myself."

Catherine hit from another side. "Could it have been the bookies he bet with out east that put out a contract on him? Not his bosses at the casino?"

"Your guess is as good as mine." Mrs. Fortunato snuffed out her latest cigarette. "You know, in my head, I always hoped he ran off. Then at least, he'd be alive. But in my heart? I knew he was dead."

Steering her back, Catherine asked, "About that day?"

The woman stared into the past. "I got up about ten that morning. Got the paper off the stoop. It didn't always come before Mal left for work. If it did, he brought it in. But that morning it was on the stoop. I picked it up, looked toward the carport, and Mal's car was gone, just like it ought to be. So, I went about my business. I read the paper, had some breakfast, called my mom—she was still alive back then—you know, stuff and things."

Catherine nodded.

"About four-thirty, I decided to go to the grocery store, get something nice for dinner. I hadn't talked to Mal all day, but I expected him home around six or so. It was my day off and he usually came right home on my day off, so we could spend the evening together." A wistful smile flickered; her eyes grew moist again.

Catherine knew what it was like, loving a louse. "You must have loved him a great deal."

Tears overflowing again, she nodded.

Catherine moved up onto the couch and let the woman cry on her shoulder.

After several long moments, Mrs. Fortunato shuddered, then pulled away, mumbling her thanks. Then she spoke quickly: "I decided to go to the grocery, and went out the back door. We used the back door almost exclusively. I went out and saw this dark red blotch on the gravel of the carport. This was before we paved the driveway. Goddamn asphalt. It's for shit in this heat. But the contractor said it was cheap and I didn't know any better."

Catherine tried not to rush the woman, but she could see O'Riley getting antsy in the corner.

Hoskins returned, carrying a tray with four cups and sugar and cream.

The woman said to him, "I was just telling them about the asphalt."

"Contractor was a goddamn crook," he said and went back into the kitchen for the coffee.

"You saw the dark red blotch," Catherine prompted.

"Yeah, yeah, and I just knew. I looked at it close and I just knew it was drying blood. I came right back in the house and called the police."

Hoskins brought in the coffee. They each took a cup and he poured. Mrs. Fortunato used lots of sugar and some cream, Hoskins only the cream, while O'Riley and Catherine drank theirs black. Much better than the break-room swill.

Catherine thanked Hoskins, as did O'Riley—she

noticed a tiny tremor in the cop's big hand. She turned back to Mrs. Fortunato. "So, you called the police."

"Yes. They came, took a sample of the blood, and were never able to tell me anything. They never even found Mal's car."

"The report said that the police returned your husband's personal effects."

The woman nodded.

"There was no inventory in the report—I was curious what they had of his."

"Gerry, could you get the box? You know where it is."

Hoskins left the room again.

"When the cops brought back the box," the woman said, "I barely opened it. Mostly it was junk from Mal's desk at work." An edge was creeping into her voice. "One of the things they found, though, was a letter to him from his whore. That's what made them think he ran away with her."

Hoskins came back in carrying a plain brown cardboard box and handed it to Catherine.

"May I take this with me?" she asked.

The woman scowled. "Be my guest. And do me a favor—this time, don't bring it back. There's nothing in that box I ever want to see again. That was the property of a different man—not my Mal."

Accepting the box, Catherine asked, "By the way, did Malachy smoke?"

"No, not ever. He thought it was a filthy habit." She glanced at the cigarette in her hand. "Ironic, huh? I'd quit smoking 'cause of him . . . then when he disappeared, started in again. Nerves."

"I'm sorry, Mrs. Fortunato, but I have to ask you one more question."

"Yes?"

"Can you tell me the name of the dancer your husband was involved with?"

Mrs. Fortunato's jaw set, her lips whitened. She stabbed out the cigarette, repeatedly jabbing it into the ashtray, sending up a small shower of sparks.

Hoskins said, "Joy Starr."

"Why do you need her name?" Mrs. Fortunato asked.

"We'd like to talk to her," Catherine said. "But first we'll have to find out what became of her."

Hoskins offered, "Annie never knew if that was her real name, or just a stage name. . . . But she worked at a place called Swingers. It's still there—way down south on Paradise Road."

Catherine knew the place. "Okay, Mr. Hoskins—thanks." She turned to the woman. "Thank you, Mrs. Fortunato, for your time and patience. I know this has been difficult. We'll be looking into your husband's murder, now, so we may have more questions later."

Catherine held out her hand and the woman grasped it, warmth in her grip. The stoniness in Mrs. Fortunato's face seemed to melt away.

"Somehow," the woman said, "I feel . . . better. Thank you."

When the cop and the criminalist got outside into the July heat, O'Riley stopped Catherine, near her car.

"Thanks for doin' my job in there. And, uh . . . well, just thanks."

She gave him a look.

The crew-cut head shook, and he blew out wind. "I was ready to draw down on the S.O.B."

"Forget it, Sarge. Could have happened to anyone."

Catherine noticed a slight shudder in O'Riley's hands as the detective got into his car. After placing the box of Malachy Fortunato's effects in the backseat, she climbed into the Tahoe and phoned Nick.

"Nicky, Malachy's our mummy. Get the address of a dentist named Roy McNeal and get back to me. I want to pick up Fortunato's dental records before I come back to the office."

"Cool," Nick said. "Get right back to you."

She sat in the SUV and studied the house as she waited for Nick's call. So Malachy didn't smoke, and at the time of his disappearance, his wife wasn't a smoker, either. A cigarette butt in the backyard could mean somebody waited for Malachy Fortunato to leave the house, that morning fifteen years ago. . . .

He lit the cigarette, clicked the Zippo closed, and leaned against the house as he took a long drag. Dew still clung to the new sod. Grass probably wouldn't last long here, but they always seemed to make the effort when they put up one of these new homes. The house he stood behind had been built within the last six months and only inhabited for the last two. The mark inside, some guy named Fortunato, had pissed off the wrong people.

Houses on either side held families that still slept peacefully. Behind the house, where he now stood puffing away on his Marlboro, the backyard butted up against one from the next block. Those homes, however, had not been completed, and the construction crews hadn't yet arrived to begin the day's work. So he had the neighborhood to himself. . . .

Fortunato's schedule seemed etched in stone. For the week the hitter had been watching him, the mark had left the house within a two-minute window, every morning. The hitter loved a clockwork guy. Same time, same path, everyday, an invitation for someone to cap a poor, sad son of a bitch.

He took another drag, let the smoke settle in his lungs, then slowly blew it out through his nose. Glancing at his watch, he smiled. Plenty of time to enjoy this cigarette, no reason to rush. Finish the smoke, put on his gloves, then go to work.

Taking one last drag, the hitter held it in for a long time before blowing the smoke out and stubbing the butt into the yard with his foot. He pulled the gloves from his pocket and slipped them on. Rotating his head, he felt the bones in his neck crack as he loosened up; then he checked his watch one last time.

Time to punch the clock.

He withdrew his automatic from its holster, checked the clip, then screwed on the silencer. He shifted slightly so he could see around the corner. No target yet. Ducking back, he slowed his breathing, waited. . . .

The mark walked out of the door, closed it, then the screen, and turned to his car. The hitter came up behind Fortunato, squeezed the trigger and felt the small pistol buck in his hand. A tiny flower of red blossomed from the back of the mark's head. Didn't even have time to yell, simply folded in on himself and dropped.

Going down with him, the killer put another shot one inch above the first—an insurance policy and a signature. Then the killer pulled the car keys from the dead man's hand, peered over the fender of the car to make sure no one had seen the action. Satisfied the neighbors still slept, he jumped up, opened the trunk, picked up the body and dumped it in, slammed the lid, then got in the front, behind the wheel, and turned the key.

The engine turned over, rumbling to life and, not rushing, the hitter backed the car out of the driveway and eased down the street, just another middle-class joe on his way to work.

There was no one around when he arrived at the vacant lot off Russell Road. None of the passing motorists paid any attention to a guy driving into the lot to dump his trash, like so many others had before him. It took only a moment to find what he sought. To his left, shielded from the road, was the abandoned house trailer he'd spotted earlier. The hulk had already begun to rust, and he figured no one would be nosing around it for some time. Several sheets of its aluminum skin had slipped off. Some hung precariously from the side, others lay scattered like molted scales.

He pulled the body from the trunk, careful to avoid the bleeding skull, and dragged the meat by its feet to the trailer. He shoved the body onto a sheet of aluminum, then pushed the sled of metal underneath the trailer. As a parting gift, he unscrewed the silencer, which he dropped in a pocket; then removed the barrel from the automatic and tossed it under the trailer with the corpse. With more strips of trailer skin, some wood and rubble, he blocked the opening. Then, using his foot, he covered over the blood trail with dirt, wiping out most of the footprints (among so many footprints already), and casually drove off. He would ditch the car elsewhere.

The cell phone rang and shook Catherine from her reverie-cum-reconstruction.

"Write down this address," Nick said, and he gave it

to her, and she did. "Dr. McNeal's nurse'll have Malachy Fortunato's file waiting for you."

Within an hour an energized Catherine Willows was driving back to headquarters with the dental records in hand, certain she was about to establish the identity of their mummy.

Finding him had only been yesterday; today, with the victim identified, the search would shift to his killer.

7

AS IF HYPNOTIZED BY A FASCINATING WORK OF CINEMATIC art, Grissom watched the gray grainy picture crawling across the monitor; this was yet another Beachcomber video, one of scores he'd examined over the past twenty-four hours. Right now he was taking a second pass through the stack of tapes that represented the morning of the shooting. Occasionally he would remove his glasses and rub his eyes, and now and then he would stand and do stretching exercises, to relieve the low back pain all this sitting was engendering.

But mostly he sat and watched the grainy, often indistinct images. A normal person might have gone mad by now, viewing this cavalcade of monotony; but Grissom remained alert, interested. Each tape was, after all, a fresh piece of evidence, or at least potential evidence. Right now, in an angle on the casino, the time code read 5:40 A.M.

The ceiling-mounted camera's view—about halfway back one of the casino's main aisles, looking toward the front—included a blurry picture of the path from the lobby to the elevators. At this time of morning, casino play was relatively sparse. Notably apparent in frame were a man sitting at a video poker machine, on the end of a row near the front, and a woman standing at a slot two rows closer to the camera, this one facing it. For endless minutes, nothing happened—the handful of gamblers gambling, the occasional waitress wandering through with a drink tray; then Grissom noticed a figure in the distance—between the lobby and the elevator.

Sitting a little straighter, forcing his eyes to focus, Grissom felt reasonably certain the blurry figure in the background was their victim from upstairs. He hunched closer to the screen, eyes narrowed, watching—yes!—John Smith as he took a few steps, and then glanced casually in the direction of the man at the video poker machine. Almost as if Grissom had hit PAUSE, John Smith froze.

Smith was too far in the background for the security camera to accurately record his expression; but Grissom had no trouble making out Smith as he abruptly took off toward the elevator. Nor did Grissom have any trouble seeing the poker player start after him, get stopped by something attaching him to the machine, which he pulled out, and then followed Smith to the elevator.

As the man on the monitor screen moved away from the poker machine, Grissom was able to note the same clothes he'd seen on the fleeing killer on the videotape from upstairs, right down to the black running shoes.

Damn—how had he missed this first time around? Grissom shook his head—it had all happened quickly, in the time it might have taken him to rub his eyes from fatigue.

Grissom stopped the tape, replayed it, replayed it again. As with the hallway tape, the killer never looked at the camera. *Had he knowingly positioned himself with his back to the security camera? Was he a hitman stalking his prey?*

He watched the tape several more times, concentrating now on the hesitation in the killer's pursuit. Finally he noticed the flashing light on top of the machine. The killer had hit a winner just as he took off after the victim! Was that what had stopped him?

No. Something else.

Grissom halted the tape. He knew who could read this properly. He knew *just* the man. . . .

He stood in the doorway and called down the corridor: "Warrick!"

When this got no immediate response, Grissom moved down the hallway, a man with a mission, going room to room. He stuck his head inside the DNA lab, prompting the young lab tech to jump halfway out of his skin.

"I didn't do it, Grissom," Greg Sanders said. "It's not my fault!"

This stopped Grissom just long enough for him to twitch a tiny smile. "I'm sure you didn't do it, Greg—whatever it is. Have you seen Warrick?"

"Last I saw him, he and Sara were working on AFIS . . . but maybe that was yesterday. . . ."

At that, Grissom frowned. "Precision, Greg. Precision."

Back in the hallway, he moved on in his search,

and almost bumped into the lanky Warrick, stepping around the corner, typically loose-limbed in a brown untucked short-sleeved shirt and lighter chinos.

"You rang, Gris?"

Grissom was on the move again. "Come with me—I want to show you something."

Back in his office, Grissom played Warrick the tape—twice.

"Well?" Grissom asked.

There was never any rushing Warrick; his eyes were half-hooded as he played the tape for himself one more time.

Then Warrick said, "Looks to me like he's pulling a casino card from the machine."

Grissom smiled. "And we know what that does for us."

"Oh yeah. Casino can track the card. They can give us the *name* on the card." Warrick frowned in thought. "You don't suppose the killer's local?"

"I don't suppose anything," Grissom said. "But that possibility hasn't been ruled out. . . . What are you working on?"

Warrick jerked a thumb toward the door. "Sara and me, we were working on tracing the sender of a piece of e-mail on Dingelmann's Palm Pilot."

Grissom frowned. "Dingelmann?"

Warrick gave him a look. "That's the victim's name—Philip Dingelmann."

"Were you waiting for Christmas to give it to me?"

"Didn't you see Brass's report—it's on your desk."

Grissom nodded toward the monitor. "I've been in here a while."

"You were in here yesterday when shift ended. This is a *new* shift, Gris. You oughta get some sleep, maybe even consider eating a meal now and—"

"Dingelmann! Chicago. The mob lawyer?"

Warrick, now wearing his trademark humorless smirk, just nodded.

Grissom put a hand on Warrick's shoulder. "Okay, let Sara work the e-mail; she's the computer whiz—you're my resident gambling expert."

"Is that a compliment?"

"I don't care what it is—I want you back at that casino, now. Check that machine for prints, and find out whatever you can from the slot host."

"Should I page Brass, and call in a detective?"

"When the time comes."

Already moving, Warrick said, "I'm on it," as Grissom assured him, "I'll tell Sara what's up."

Grissom walked back down the hall to the office where Sara worked at a keyboard. "Any luck?" he asked.

"Sure—all lousy," she said. "This guy covered his tracks pretty well. This e-mail must have been laundered through every freakin' ISP in the world."

"Okay, relax." Grissom sat on the edge of the desk, smiled at her; he'd hand-picked the Harvard grad for his unit—she'd been a seminar student of his, and he valued her tech skills, dedication and tenacity. "There are other things to be done, right?"

"Always. Where's Warrick?"

"I sent him back to the Beachcomber."

Her brow tightened. "Without me?"

"Yes."

"Think that's a good idea? Sending him to a casino all by his lonesome?"

Grissom shrugged a little. "I trust him."

A sigh, a smirk. "You're the boss."

"Nice of you to notice," Grissom said. "Anyway, I need you."

She looked at him, eyebrows up, not quite sure how to take that.

"We have a date in the morgue."

They both wore blue scrubs and latex gloves, and stood between the two autopsy tables. In front of them lay Philip Dinglemann, behind them Catherine and Nick's mummy.

"So, what are we doing here?" Sara asked.

"Read this," he said, handing her the autopsy report for John Doe #17.

She scanned it quickly, stopped, read part of it more slowly. "What's this, a screw-up? Robbins got the bodies backward?"

Grissom shook his head. "The pattern's the same, to within an eighth of an inch."

"That can't be right. . . ."

"The evidence says it's right, it's right. But you and I are going to measure them again just to be sure."

"It's a heck of a coincidence."

"Is it?"

"Grissom, why didn't you tell Warrick and me about this?"

"Keeping the cases separate. No assumptions that we have one case, here, until or unless the evidence tells us so."

Nodding, she said, "Which one first?"

"Age before beauty," Grissom said, turning to the mummy.

Warrick parked in the vast lot behind the Beachcomber, entering through the casino, a smaller version of his field kit in hand, including fingerprinting gear. He knew (as Grissom surely did) that this was probably a pointless exercise, all this time after the killer had left the machine behind; but you never knew.

Grissom had sent him here alone, even making the questionable call of not inviting a detective along for any questioning that might come up. Either Grissom finally trusted him completely, Warrick figured, or this was a test. The whirrings of slots, the calling out of dealers, the dinging, the ringing, made for a seductive madhouse through which he walked, somehow staying focused on the job at hand.

Soon he found himself standing under the camera that had captured the videotape images Grissom had shared with him. He ignored the bells and whistles, the smoke-filled air, the expressions on faces—defeat, joy, frustration, boredom—and just did his job. He strode to the video poker machine where, less than twenty-four hours ago, the killer had sat.

The patron sitting there now, bald, bespectacled, in his mid-thirties, wore a navy Polo shirt, tan Dockers, and sandals with socks. Warrick watched as the man kept a pair of tens, drew a wild deuce and two nothing cards. Three of a kind broke even, returning a quarter for the quarter bet. Big spender, Warrick thought, as the man kept a four, six, seven and eight, a mix of clubs and diamonds.

Sucker bet, Warrick thought; trying to fill an inside straight, what a joke. The guy drew an eight of spades—another loser. Mr. Sandals-with-socks quickly lost four more hands before he turned to Warrick, standing peering over his shoulder.

Irritation edged the guy's voice. "Something?"

Warrick flashed his badge. "I'm with the Las Vegas Criminalistics Bureau. Need to dust this machine for fingerprints."

The gambler flared with indignation. "I been sitting here since Jesus was a baby! I'm not giving up this machine."

Nodding, Warrick bent down closer. "A killer sat at this very machine yesterday morning."

The man didn't move; but he also didn't return his attention to the poker machine.

Warrick gestured with his head. "You see that camera over my shoulder?"

Looking up at the black bulb sticking out of the ceiling, the guy nodded.

"From a videotape shot by that camera," Warrick said calmly, "I viewed the killer sitting right here. Now, I'm going to call over someone from the staff and we're going to dust this machine, so I can find out who that guy was."

"What about me? What about my rights?"

"Do you want to cash out now, or you wanna wait in the bar till I'm done? That way you can get your machine back . . . protect your investment."

The guy gave him a sour look. "I'll be in the bar. Send a waitress over when you're finished."

"Thank you," Warrick said. "Be advised I may decide to print you, as well, sir—so I can eliminate your prints."

Grumbling about his right to privacy, the guy hauled away his plastic bucket (with several unopened rolls of quarters in it) and walked toward the bar, padding away in his socks and sandals. Right then a casino security officer came gliding up to Warrick.

"May I help you, sir?" he asked, his voice mingling solicitude and suspicion.

The guard was black and Warrick's height, more or less, but carried an extra forty pounds—apparently of muscle—on a broad-shouldered frame. That much was evident even through the guy's snug-fitting green sports coat with its BEACHCOMBER patch stitched over the pocket. The walkie-talkie he carried in a big hand looked like a candy bar.

Again, Warrick flashed his badge and explained the situation. "I need to see the slot host."

"I'll have to call my supervisor," the guard said.

"Okay."

The guard spoke into the walkie-talkie and, in less than two minutes, Warrick found himself surrounded by half a dozen of the crisply jacketed security guards, a green sea that parted for a California-ish guy in a double-breasted navy blue suit. Though he was the youngest of them, this one seemed to be the boss—six-one, blond, good-looking.

"I'm Todd Oswalt, the slot host," he said, extending his hand. He smiled, displaying the straight white teeth and practiced sincerity of a TV evangelist.

"Warrick Brown," the criminalist said, shaking with the guy, "crime lab following up on the murder, yesterday."

Oswalt's smile disappeared, his eyes darting around to see if any of the customers had heard Warrick. "Mr. Brown, we'll be happy to help you if you'll please, please just keep your voice down."

Now Warrick smiled. "Gladly, Mr. Oswalt. There was a man sitting here around five-thirty yesterday morning. I need to know everything about him that you can tell me."

"Based on what? We have a lot of patrons at the Beachcomber, Mr. Brown."

"This one used a slot card on this machine at 5:42 A.M yesterday."

Oswalt's eyes were wide; he nodded. "I'll get right on that."

"And while you're doing that," Warrick said, easily, "I'll need to fingerprint this machine."

Oswalt frowned, glanced around again. "Right now?"

"I could do it after business hours."

"We never close."

"Neither do we—so is there a better time than right now? Since I gotta be here anyway, while you're checking out that slot card?"

"Uh . . . your point is well taken. Go right ahead, Mr. Brown."

The slot host instructed two guards to stay nearby, then he and the other of his green-jacketed merry men disappeared. Warrick spent about an hour on the machine, at the end of which time he had dozens of prints and doubted that any of them would be of any use. There was just no telling how many people had tried this machine since the killer left.

Gesturing that burly guard over, Warrick said, "You can tell your boss I'm done."

The guard pulled out a walkie-talkie and talked into it. He listened, then turned back to Warrick. "We're supposed to escort you to the security office."

"Fine. And I need to have this machine held for a guy in the bar—can you send a cocktail waitress after him?"

"Sure thing. How will I know him?"

"He'll be the only bald guy with glasses wearing socks and sandals."

"All right. Man, you're certainly thoughtful."

"Hey, gamblers got it hard enough already."

The other guard was called over to escort Warrick, and the blond Oswalt was waiting for them at the security-office door. "We've got your information, Mr. Brown. The man's name is Peter Randall."

Warrick got out his notepad and pencil. "Address?"

"P.O. Box L-57, 1365 East Horizon in Henderson."

Warrick felt a sinking feeling in his gut. He jotted the address down, knowing it would wind up being one of those damn rent-a-mailbox places. "Anything else, Mr. Oswalt?"

"Not really."

Warrick put the notepad away. "We're going to need to go back a few days, maybe a few weeks, to look for this guy some more—the tapes we have so far don't give us a look at his face."

"He could be a regular customer," Oswalt admitted.

"Right. How long to round up those tapes?"

"I'm short staff, and those tapes are stored—"

"How long, sir?"

Oswalt thought about it. "Tomorrow morning?"

"Can I look at them here?"

"We'd prefer it if you did."

Warrick nodded. "Thanks. I'll be back."

From the car, Warrick called Grissom and told him the name and address. Again Grissom approved him going alone—a killer was on the loose, and trails could go quickly cold.

The drive to Henderson—a community of stucco-laden homes aligned like green *Monopoly* houses, many of them behind walls and/or gates—took twenty minutes on the expressway. Just as he thought, the address belonged to a strip mall rent-a-box storefront.

The mailboxes ran down one wall, a long counter along the opposite one. The girl behind the counter might have been eighteen, her blue smock covering a slipknot T-shirt and faded jeans. Her hair was dishwater blonde and she had a silver stud through her left nostril.

"Can I help you?" she asked with no enthusiasm.

"Is the manager here?"

"No."

"Will he be back soon?"

"She," the girl corrected. "She just went to lunch."

"Do you know where?"

"Yeah, the Dairy Queen around the corner."

"Thanks," Warrick said. "Can you tell me her name?"

"Laurie."

This was like pulling teeth. "Last name?"

The girl thought for a moment. It seemed to cause her pain. "I dunno."

"You don't know?"

"Never came up."

"Yeah. Well. Thanks again." Meaning it, he said, "You've been a big help."

With the pep of a zombie, she said, "Come back any time."

Warrick walked to the Dairy Queen around the corner, spotted the woman who must be Laurie, sitting at a table alone, picking at an order of chicken strips and fries. She wore the same blue smock as the girl back at the store; her brown hair, cut at shoulder length, matched her brown eyes in a narrow, pretty face, and she appeared to be about six months pregnant. He went straight to her. "Laurie?"

She looked up and, guardedly, asked, "Do I know you?"

"No, ma'am. My name is Warrick Brown. I'm with the Las Vegas Criminalistics Bureau." He showed her his badge. "May I sit and talk to you for a moment?"

"Well . . ."

"It'll just take a few moments."

"I suppose. Can you tell me what this is about?"

Pulling out one of the plastic-and-metal chairs, Warrick joined her at the small square table. "I need to talk to you about one of your clients."

Laurie shook her head. "You know I can't talk to you about my clients without a warrant. Their privacy is at stake."

"This man is a killer and we can't waste time."

That impressed her, but still she shook her head again. "I'm sorry. I just can't . . ."

Warrick interrupted her. "His name is Peter Randall."

Her eyes tightened.

"What is it, Laurie?"

"Funny you should ask about Mr. Randall. He closed out his account just yesterday."

"Can you talk to me, off-the-record, while we're waiting for a warrant to arrive?"

Again she looked as if she didn't know what to do.

Warrick pulled out his phone, called Grissom, and explained the situation.

"Sara will be there with a warrant within the hour," Grissom said. "And I'll alert Brass."

While they waited, Laurie finished her lunch and they returned to the storefront. The nose-stud girl seemed as bored as ever, paying little attention to them as they came to the counter, Warrick staying on the customer side, Laurie going behind it. The woman had decided to cooperate—she asked him several times, "He's a murderer, right?"—and she pulled Randall's record right away.

"His home address?" Warrick asked.

Laurie looked at the file. "Forty-six fifteen Johnson, here in Henderson."

Warrick made a quick call on his cell to dispatch, for directions.

Moments later, he said, "Damn."

"What's the matter?"

"No Johnson Street or avenue or anything like it in Henderson. That's a fake address."

"Oh. I mean, we don't check these kind of things. We take our customers at their word."

Warrick went to Box L-57. "I know you can't open this for me, until the warrant arrives. But can you say whether or not Mr. Randall has cleared it out?"

"I'm afraid he has," Laurie said. "There's nothing in it—Mr. Randall emptied it when he closed his account.

"Shit."

"I'm sorry," Laurie said.

"You're just doing what I'm doing."

"Huh?"

He smiled at her. "Our jobs."

She smiled back, and the nose-stud girl rolled her eyes.

Five minutes later, Sara—accompanied by Detective Erin Conroy—turned up with the warrant; he filled them both in on the situation.

Sara smirked and shook her head. "So, there's nothing?"

Warrick shrugged. "We can print the mailbox door, but that's about it. Looks like a dead end."

Conroy said, "I'll question her . . . what's her name?"

"Laurie," Warrick said.

"Last name?"

Embarrassed, he shrugged again. "Never came up."

Conroy just looked at him; then she went over to question the woman and put on the record the things that had been told to Warrick, off.

Sara sighed and said, "I gave up running prints for this?"

"You were tired of doing that, anyway."

She tried not to smile, but finally it broke through. "Yeah, I was."

"Well, you're gonna love it when I give you the dozens of prints I got off that slot machine."

"More prints. You find anything good?"

"Yeah." He leaned in conspiratorially, as Conroy's questioning echoed in the hollow storefront. "A Dairy Queen, around the corner. Lunch. You buy."

She clearly liked the sound of that; but as they were exiting, Sara nudged him in the ribs, saying, "Buy your own damn lunch."

Two hours later, back in the office, Warrick had already struck out with "Peter Randall"—an alias, of course—and Sara had run the prints from the casino, which had also proved worthless. And the guy's mailbox door had failed to yield a single usable print.

Laurie Miller, the manager, had waited on "Randall" both times he'd been in the store, and her description of him to Detective Conroy was painfully generic: dark glasses, dark baseball cap was all that got added to what the hotel tapes had already told them. A witness sketch would be worked up, but not much hope was held for it.

Backing up, Warrick decided to see what they could get on the footprints from the hallway.

Sara used a database that identified the running-shoe design as the probable product of a company called Racers; the match was not exact, due to the imperfect nature of the crime-scene footprint. So Warrick went online and found the number for the corporate office in Oregon.

"Racers Shoes and Athletic Apparel," said a perky female voice. "How may I direct your call?"

"My name is Warrick Brown. I'm with the Las Vegas Criminalistics Bureau. I need to talk to someone about sales of different product lines of your shoes."

There was a silence at the other end.

Finally, Warrick said, "Hello?"

"I'm sorry, sir," the voice said. "I had to ask my supervisor how to route your call. I'm going to transfer you to Ms. Kotsay in sales."

"Thank you."

He heard a phone ring twice, then another female voice—somewhat older, more professional—said, "Sondra Kotsay—how may I help you?"

Warrick explained the situation.

"This is a most unusual request, Mr. Brown. We manufacture many lines of shoes."

"I know. And we have a tentative match from a database, already. But I could really use your expert confirmation."

"Am I going to have to testify?"

He smiled to himself. "Probably not. I'd just like to fax you a footprint."

"Oh," she said, "well, that would be fine," and gave him the number.

He chose not to send her the bloody print he'd highlighted with the Leuco Crystal Violet and instead sent her one from the landing that Grissom had obtained with the electrostatic print lifter.

A few minutes later, he was asking the woman, "Did you get that?"

There was a moment of silence on the line, then

Sondra came back on the phone. "Came through fine," she announced. "Give me a little time. I'll call you back when I've got something."

How tired he was just dawning on him, Warrick wandered down to the break room and got himself some pineapple juice out of the fridge. He went to see Sara, at her computer, but she wasn't there. He tracked her down—in all places, at the morgue, standing over Dinglemann's corpse.

"You okay?" he asked.

"Yes," she said. "No . . . I don't know."

"What?"

"Why are we working so hard to find out who killed this guy? Why am I busting my butt to find his killer?" She pointed at the body. "I mean, mob lawyer, getting the scum of the earth off, scot free . . ."

"Better not let Gris hear you talking like that."

She threw her gaze at him, and it was almost a glare. "I'm not talking to Grissom. I'm talking to you."

"You know it's not for us to decide." Warrick moved a little closer, so that Dinglemann lay between them. "This guy, he's past all that now. Good, evil—doesn't matter. He's been murdered. That puts him in the next world, if there is one—but his body's in our world."

She thought about that, then she shrugged. "Maybe it is that simple. I don't know. It's just . . . hard for me."

"Well, if you can't divorce yourself from the good and bad, think of the guy who did this. Somebody who takes money to take lives. That bad enough for you?"

She smiled, just a little. "Yeah. Yeah, that'll do it."

His cell phone rang and they both jumped. He almost dropped it in his haste to answer. "Warrick Brown."

"Sondra Kotsay, Mr. Brown. I think I can help you."

Waving at Sara that he had to take this call, Warrick went back down the hall to his office, grabbed a pad and plopped into his chair.

The professional voice said, "The print that you faxed us is for our X-15 running shoe."

"Okay."

"It's a line that, I'm sorry to say, has not done very well for us."

Warrick knew that the smaller the production run, the better his chances. "How many have been produced?"

"Before production stopped, just under one million pair."

His heart dropping to his stomach, his head drooping, he said, "A million?"

"I know that sounds daunting, Mr. Brown. But it's not that bad—at least not for you."

"Uh huh."

"Over half were never sold."

That helped—sort of. As she gave him her report, he scribbled the information on the pad.

"And of the remaining half-million," she said, "only about one hundred pair were sold in the greater Las Vegas area."

He was liking the sound of this more and more.

"The particular size that you gave us, men's size eleven, sold less than two dozen pair in the Vegas area."

The smile split his face nearly in half. "Thank you, Ms. Kotsay. Great work."

"Would you like the names and addresses of the retailers that sold them?"

Would you like to marry me? he thought. "Thank you, Ms. Kotsay—that would be incredibly helpful."

She faxed him the list.

And then Warrick Brown went looking for Grissom.

8

As Catherine looked on, Dr. Robbins matched Malachy Fortunato's dental records against the teeth of the mummy. Both criminalist and coroner were in scrubs, but underneath his, Robbins was in a pin-striped shirt and diagonally striped tie with charcoal slacks; he'd had a court appearance today.

It was a little before seven P.M.—Catherine in early again, shift not officially beginning till eleven.

The coroner would study the dental X ray, then bend over the mummy, then straighten to check the X ray, a dance Robbins repeated half a dozen times before waving her over. "Catherine Willows, meet Malachy Fortunato."

She smiled. "At long last?"

Nodding, he said, "At long last—trust me, this is indeed the elusive Mr. Fortunato. We have a textbook dentalwork match."

"Well, well," she said, looking down at the mummy, her hands pressed together as if she were contemplating a fine meal. "Mr. Fortunato, it's nice to finally meet you. . . . Now that we know who you are, we'll see if we can't find your murderer."

The leathery mummy had no reply.

"Nice work, Doc," she said, and waved at Robbins on her way through the door.

"That's what I do," he said to the swinging door.

Out of her scrubs, Catherine ran into Nick, coming out of the lab.

"Hey," she said. "You're in early, too, I see."

"Hey," he said. But he looked a little glum. "DNA's going to take another week—they're completely backed up in there."

"Doesn't matter," she said with a grin. "Dr. Robbins just matched the dental records to our mummy—Malachy Fortunato."

"All right!"

"You did good with that ring, Nick."

"Thanks."

They headed into the break room for coffee. Nick poured, asking, "When was the last time this office solved a mob hit?"

"A week ago never. Surprisingly little of that in Vegas."

"Like they say, you don't defecate where you dine."

"I always try not to." She sipped her coffee, feeling almost giddy. "We're on a roll, Nick. Let's get this guy."

"Sure—what's fifteen years between friends?"

She half-frowned, half-smiled. "You tryin' to rain on my parade?"

"No way. No statute of limitations on murder. What do you need from me?"

She headed out of the break room, coffee cup in

hand. "We'll get to that. First, let's go tell Grissom what we've got."

After Warrick explained what they'd turned up at the casino and at the storefront in Henderson, Grissom said, "This still doesn't prove he's local."

Grissom was behind his desk, jumbles of papers, a pile of binders seemingly about to topple, and an unfinished glass of iced tea cluttering the desk, as well as assorted displayed insect specimens, dead and alive. Warrick sat in one of the two chairs opposite his boss, and Sara leaned against a file cabinet in the corner.

Sara said, "But the maildrop—"

Grissom shook his head. "Our man could just be using the maildrop. And who knows how many slot cards he has in how many names, and in how many casinos . . . in how many towns."

"What about the shoe?" Warrick asked.

Grissom said, "That will help, particularly in ascertaining whether he's local. But half a million pair were sold nationally, you said."

Warrick nodded, unhappily.

Grissom continued: "For that shoe to be of any real benefit, we've got to find the foot that goes in it."

Sara smirked. "The guy attached to the foot would also be nice."

Warrick sighed and said, "Tomorrow morning, I can start watching the older tapes at the casino. If our man is local, that's a good place to look."

"It is," Grissom said, nodding. "No luck with the prints? Anything on 'Peter Randall'?"

"No and no," Sara said.

Warrick shook his head. "Gris, you really think we're going to track this guy down? I mean a mob hit . . ." He shrugged helplessly.

"You're thinking of that guy at the Sphere," Grissom said, "aren't you?"

Not so long ago, Warrick had worked the murder, still unsolved, of a bad debtor who had been shot to death in a glass elevator at the Sphere Hotel—that M.O., though different, also reeked mob.

"Maybe," Warrick said. "What makes this different?"

"Among other things," Grissom said, "the evidence."

Before Grissom could amplify, Brass came into his office from one direction, quickly followed by Catherine and Nick from the other. Brass, a stack of files tucked under an arm, gave Grissom a quick nod.

"We've got a positive ID from the dental records," Nick said, dropping into the chair next to Warrick. "Our mummy is Malachy Fortunato, a local who disappeared fifteen years ago, owing the mobbed-up casino bosses a whole lot of money. The mummy's a mob hit."

Warrick—who'd been kept in the dark about the similarity of the wounds on the two murder victims—sat forward, alert.

"The mummy seems to be," Grissom said. "I'm still not sure about Philip Dingelmann. But I do believe they were both shot by the same man."

With the exception of the blank-faced Brass, mouths dropped open all around the room.

The homicide detective stepped up and tossed the stack of files on Grissom's desk. "We're pretty sure both crimes are the work of an assassin the FBI has monikered, of course, 'The Deuce.' He is apparently responsible for at least forty contract killings across the length and breadth of our fine country, over a period approaching twenty years."

Perched in the doorway, Catherine asked, "How do you know?"

"By the signature," said Brass. "Two vertically placed small caliber wounds approximately an inch apart."

" 'Deuce,' " Warrick said dryly.

"But we're going to need more than just the signature," Grissom said, "to prove we're right that these murders share a murderer."

A brief discussion ensued, as those who knew about the similarities between the corpses skirmished with those who hadn't been in the know.

Finally Grissom notched up his voice. "We may have a legitimate coincidence in the discovery of these bodies," he said.

"The timing, you mean," Catherine said.

"Yes—Dingelmann was killed prior to the discovery of Fortunato's remains, but basically they were simultaneous, unconnected events . . . a murder going down just about the same time as a long-dead victim of the same killer is unearthed. And nothing here indicates the two murders have anything to do with each other. Nothing yet, anyway."

Nodding, Catherine said, "But the signature suggests the victims share a killer."

"Now that's a coincidence I *can't* accept," Grissom said. "That two different murderers, connected to two different mob-related murders, would have the same M.O."

Warrick said, "Two bullets in the back of the head,

Gris, that's a sign of mob displeasure that goes *way* back."

"This is more specific—vertically placed shots in this exact same location, an inch apart. That struck me from the start, not as a coincidence, but as the signature we now know it is."

"*How* do we know?" Nick asked.

Grissom sat forward. "After I examined your mummy, Nick . . . Catherine . . . I told Jim my theory, and he got his people digging in the national computers."

Brass tapped the stack of files on Grissom's desk—twice. "This guy is not tied to any one organized crime family, in any one part of the country. He is apparently a freelancer with a shared client base—no one knows what he looks like and, as far as we can ascertain, no one's ever seen him in action . . . and lived to tell."

"We already knew we had a contract assassin who did mob hits," Sara pointed out. "We now believe two murders, fifteen years apart, were the work of the same assassin. Other than that . . . how does this help us?"

"It's more than we had," Grissom said. "We have context, now—we have direction."

"Swell," Catherine said. "What do we do different?"

"Nothing." His gaze met hers, then swept around the room including them all. "We still operate as if it's two separate cases . . . but now we keep everybody informed about what we learn. Catherine, you and Nick keep working on the mummy. Like Brass says, we need corroborating evidence. Find it."

"You want us to prove this is the same hitter," Nick said.

Catherine, an eyebrow arched, stared at Grissom.

He looked back at her for a second. "No," he said to Nick, but holding her gaze. "Follow the evidence—it's still possible we might have two murderers."

Catherine smiled.

"What about the farm team?" Sara asked.

Grissom turned to Warrick. "Watch those hotel tapes till your eyes bleed. . . . Sara, I want you to find out everything that's known about this killer. Study the files, but dig deeper. Look for linkages. Maybe other investigators missed something."

She nodded.

"Nicky," Grissom said, "get the bullets from both cases to the firearms examiners for ballistics tests."

"Sure thing," Nick said. "But, uh . . ."

"But what?"

Nick shrugged. "We already know the riflings on the bullets match the gun barrel found half-buried next to Mr. Fortunato."

Grissom nodded. "The killer ditched the barrel, yes, but maybe he didn't ditch the gun. We've still got bullets with a matching caliber on these two murders. We've got to cover all the bases."

Warrick had been studying his boss, and his voice conveyed confusion as he said, "I don't get it, Gris. Why do you think Dingelmann may not have been a mob hit?"

"Just staying objective."

"I'm the subjective asshole," Brass said, pointing a thumb to himself. "Philip Dingelmann was getting ready to represent Charlie 'The Tuna' Stark in the biggest mob trial since Gotti—why kill him? He's a golden mouthpiece, who'd already gotten Frischotti off, and Vinci, and the two Cleveland guys, Tucker and Myers."

"What was he doing in Vegas?" Warrick wondered aloud.

Brass shrugged. "This was probably his last chance to blow off steam, 'fore going into the tunnel of the trial."

Nodding, Warrick said, "Yeah, yeah . . . but why kill him?"

No one had an answer for that.

"Let Jim here worry about motive," Grissom told his unit. "Concentrate on the only witnesses who never lie: the evidence."

Nods and smiles, all around—they'd heard it before.

Brass said, "We've done a lot over the years to get the mob influence out of this city. We need to catch this son of a bitch to remind these scumbags this is not their turf anymore—it's never going to be like the old days again."

The homicide detective told Grissom the files were copies for the unit, reminded the others to stay in touch, and slipped out.

"Personally," Grissom said, now that Brass was gone, "I think we owe less to the city fathers, and more to our two victims. Time doesn't lessen the injustice done to Malachy Fortunato—and an unsavory client list doesn't justify what was done to Philip Dingelmann."

Warrick and Sara exchanged glances.

"So," Grissom said, cheerfully. "Let's go to work."

Outside the office, Catherine stopped Nick with a hand on his elbow. "After you get those bullets dropped off, can you check something for me?"

"Sure—what?"

"Mrs. Fortunato mentioned a dancer her husband was involved with at the time of his disappearance. She said the dancer . . . a stripper . . . disappeared the same day as her husband."

"Do we have a name?" Nick asked.

"Joy Starr. It may be a stage name. . . ."

"You think?"

"Either way, Nicky, we need to find her if she's out there somewhere. Preferably, alive."

"You mean she could be another corpse, hidden away someplace?"

"Definite possibility."

Nick sighed. "Know anything else about her?"

"Not much. She worked at Swingers—that dive out on Paradise Road. When she was dancing, it would have been a little nicer than now."

"And?"

"And what?"

"She worked in a strip club before disappearing fifteen years ago? That's it?"

"That's it. Maybe you can round up one of Brass's people and go out there—though this many years later . . . Check the newspaper websites first. Check missing-persons records—she apparently dropped out of sight when Fortunato did."

He shot her one of his dazzlers. "Hey, if you want me to hang out at a strip club, I guess I can make the sacrifice."

"First, check the records. That club, at this late date, is a real long shot."

"Okay. What about you?"

Catherine was on the move already. "I'm going back to the house. Back when Malachy wasn't a mummy yet, this was a missing persons case. Now it's the scene of a murder."

"A crime scene," Nick said, understanding.

Catherine wheeled the Tahoe out of the lot and pointed it toward the Fortunato home. She was considering calling in O'Riley, but decided against it. This was an evidential fishing expedition, and didn't involve interrogation; not a lot of point in him wasting time, too.

On her way, on her cell phone, she called the Fortunato home, got Gerry Hoskins, and asked if it would be all right to come around at this time of evening.

When she arrived, Catherine told Mr. Hoskins what she would be doing and got his okay. Annie was lying down, he said, and he wanted her to try and rest, after the stress of today's news.

Understandable.

While Catherine prepared, Hoskins moved their two cars out of the driveway and onto the street. The scene had been done once, fifteen years ago, and now she hoped to turn up something those guys had missed. Although massive changes had occurred in the science of investigation since then, sometimes you just had to fall back on the old stuff.

Hauling the metal detector from the back of the Tahoe, Catherine pulled the headphones on, cranked the machine up, and started at the end of the driveway nearest the street. Moving slowly back and forth, Catherine combed the driveway. In the original Fortunato file, there had been nothing about shell casings; of course, blood on the gravel drive or not, the detectives hadn't known they were searching a murder scene.

And the file said nothing about the discovery of shell casings.

Even though the sun had long since started its descent, the fiery orange ball seemed in no hurry to drop behind the mountains, the heat still hunkered down on the city, settling in for the long haul. If she weren't at a crime scene, she wouldn't have minded one of those refeshing if rare summer rains, though that would bring the danger of flash flooding.

She made it all the way to the far end of the carport and nothing had registered on the metal detector. Her shoulders ached, her eyes burned, and she seemed to be sweating from every pore in her body. She'd been working crazy hours, even for her. Taking the headphones off, she ran a hand through her matted hair and pulled a paper towel out of her pocket to mop her forehead.

"Brutal, huh?"

Mildly startled, Catherine turned to see Annie Fortunato standing there, holding two large glasses of lemonade, a smoke draped from her lip. The woman of the house handed one of the moisture-beaded glasses to Catherine.

"Why, thank you, Mrs. Fortunato."

"Would you stop that? Call me Annie."

"Sure. Thanks, Annie." Catherine took a long gulp from the icy glass. "You're saving my life."

The woman shrugged. "It's just powdered . . . but this hot, even that junk'll hit the spot."

Smiling, Catherine nodded and pressed the cool glass against her forehead.

Mrs. Fortunato removed her cigarette long enough to gesture with it toward the metal detector. "What're you lookin' for out here, with that thing?"

"Frankly," Catherine said, seeing no reason to withhold the information, "I was hoping to find the shell casings from the bullets that killed your husband."

She frowned in alarm. "You think he was shot . . . *here?*"

"Blood was found."

"Yes, but . . . I didn't hear any shots, and I was a light sleeper. Hell, I still am."

"The killer could have used a noise suppresser—a silencer. . . . Are you okay with me being so blunt?"

"Hell yes. I had my cry. Go on."

"Anyway, the gun barrel we found with your husband's body belonged to an automatic. That means shell casings, which had to go somewhere."

Mrs. Fortunato nodded, apparently seeing the logic of that. "Well—you havin' any luck?"

Catherine sighed. "No, not really—and it would have been a lucky break if we had." She took another big drink of the lemonade. "I'm going over it one more time, before I hang it up."

Mrs. Fortunato was studying Catherine. "You know, I want to thank you for what you've done."

Catherine didn't know how to react. "You're welcome, Mrs. Fortunato . . . but I haven't really done anything yet."

The woman sipped at her lemonade, then puffed on her ever-present cigarette, and a tear trickled down her cheek. "Yes, you did. I know Malachy wasn't perfect, but he was . . ." The tears overtook her. She stubbed out the cigarette on the ground.

Catherine put her arm around the woman.

"Shit, I had my cry."

"It's all right," Catherine said, "it's all right."

"Don't get me wrong—I love Gerry!"

"I know. It shows."

Something wistful, even youthful touched the woman's well-grooved face. "But, Mal, he was the love of my life. You only have one—and sometimes they're even sonuvabitches . . . you know what I mean?"

Catherine smiled a little. "I'm afraid so."

"When you brought me his ring out here today, well, I finally knew what happened to him. No more wondering, weaving possibilities in the middle of the night . . . that's why I say, 'thank you.' "

Squeezing the woman to her, Catherine said, "In that case, Annie, you're very welcome."

Catherine walked her over to the stoop and they sat on the cement, where they finished their lemonade in silence, the sun finally touching the horizon, the sky turning shades of violet and orange and red.

Finally Mrs. Fortunato said, "I better get back inside. I need a cigarette. You want to join me?"

"No, thanks." Catherine rose. "I better get going, if I'm going to get this done before it's too dark to see."

"I'll turn on the outside lights." Picking up the empty glasses, the woman said, "If you want some more lemonade, holler."

"I will," Catherine answered, and returned to the

metal detector as Mrs. Fortunato disappeared back into the house. Again Catherine slipped on the headphones.

"High tech," she said to herself wryly.

Starting at the back end of the carport, Catherine swept back and forth holding the three-foot handle, the disk-shaped detector barely two inches off the black asphalt. The machine always made her back hurt from the slightly stooped posture she assumed working it. Halfway back through the carport, on the side nearest the house, she got a tiny hit.

It was so small, at first she thought her ears were playing tricks on her. Over and back, over and back, the same spot, each time—the small sound echoing in her head.

Might be a shell casing, might be a screw, could be anything. One thing for sure, though: it was definitely something, something metallic. She pulled out her cell phone and punched Grissom's number on speed dial.

"Grissom."

"I think I've got something here," Catherine said.

"What?"

She explained the situation. "Any ideas?"

"Maybe. Give me half an hour. How's your relationship with the homeowners?"

"They love me."

"Good. Get permission to dig a hole."

". . . In their asphalt driveway?"

"Not in their flower bed."

"Oh-kay, Gil, I'll be waiting." She pressed END,

slipped the phone away as she walked to the front door, where she knocked.

Gerry Hoskins, still in T-shirt and jeans, opened the screen.

"I think I may have found something," Catherine said.

Mrs. Fortunato had apparently filled him in already, as he did not hesitate. "I'll get Annie."

By the time Grissom showed up, the three of them stood in the yard, waiting. Catherine met Grissom at the Tahoe. "Are you going to do what I think you're going to do?"

"No—*we* are. And it's going to be slow and it's probably going to be messy."

He and Catherine put on coveralls and carried the equipment to the spot she'd marked on the asphalt. She handed him the headphones so he could hear the faint tone.

"All right," he said. "Let's get started."

Catherine watched as he picked up a small propane torch and lit it. She asked him, "Is this going to work?"

"It's the only way I could think of that would give us a decent chance of preserving the evidence. If that's what it is."

The torch glowed orange-blue in the darkness.

"I hope so," she said, worried. "This is a lot of trouble to go through if I just located some kid's lunch money."

Grissom smiled. "Then we'll turn the treasure over to these good citizens, with our thanks."

On their hands and knees, with only the porch light

to aid them, they hovered over the area as Grissom held the torch to the spot she had marked. As the asphalt softened from the heat, Catherine carefully dug the material out with a garden trowel. The closer they got to the bottom, the slower they went. Grissom held the torch further away, heating smaller and smaller sections of the carport at a more measured pace. Catherine now used a table spoon to scrape away the heated asphalt, and a miniflash to light the area as she scoured it for the bit of metal that had pinged her detector.

Finally, after nearly two hours of this tedious labor, her knees killing her from kneeling, and with bits of the old gravel visible at the bottom of their short trench, Catherine saw something that looked out of place.

"Hold it," she said.

Grissom pulled back even further. "You see something?"

She said, "I think so," and moved forward, shining the light down at the hole. Setting the spoon aside, she pulled on a pair of latex gloves and carefully picked at the edge of the hole. Her gloves were no match for the hot asphalt and she had to be careful. She poked and prodded at the spot until finally the thing popped loose.

Grissom turned off the torch and took her flashlight, so she could use both hands.

Scooping up the small dark object, she juggled it from palm to palm, blowing on it as it cooled. He shone the light on the thing in her hand. Small, about the size of a fingertip and about a third the diameter, the object was obviously metal but covered with the sticky black mess.

"When we get back to the lab and clean all this goop off," she said, holding the object up to the light, "I think we'll find we have a twenty-five-caliber shell casing."

Grissom said nothing, but his eyes were as bright as the torch, right before he shut it off.

9

For nearly two hours Sara immersed herself in the files Brass had provided, learning several significant facts the rumpled homicide detective had failed to mention.

While the killer's career covered nearly twenty years, only a handful of thumb prints from shell casings linked a single suspect to any of the murders. The two vertical bullet holes approximately one inch apart, his signature, had shown up in forty-two murders (prior to this week's discoveries) in twenty-one states. Interestingly, the signature seemed to have dropped off the planet just under five years ago. Their very new murder—the dead mob attorney in the Beachcomber hallway—was the only known exception.

Nick popped in. "Any luck?"

"Predicatably, Brass missed a few things," Sara said.

File folder in hand, he took a seat beside her.

She filled him in quickly, concluding, "I'm not sure any of this is stop-the-presses stuff. How about you?"

"Tests are going to take a while," Nick said.

Her chin rested in her palm, elbow propped against the desk. "There is one other little item Brass overlooked."

"Yeah?"

"None of the investigators seem to have made it an issue, but . . ."

"Give."

"The bodies of victims are found . . . although who knows how many other vics, like your mummy, remain hidden away . . . but their cars? Never."

"I'm not sure I'm following you."

"Okay, I'll give you the large print version. Take Malachy Fortunato—did the police ever find his car? Both he and his wheels were missing from that driveway, remember."

Nick, thinking that over, said, "I'd have to check the file for sure, but you know . . . I think you're right."

"Of course I'm right." She leaned toward him. "Hey, trust me—nobody's seen that car since it pulled outa the driveway that morning . . . with Mr. Fortunato most likely riding in the trunk."

"And a pretty darn docile passenger, I'd bet," Nick said. "But what about Dingelmann?"

"That, I grant you, doesn't fit the pattern," she said. "But then, Dingelmann didn't have a car. Took the shuttle from the airport."

"No rental?"

"No rental. Doorman saw Dingelmann taking cabs a couple of times."

Nick was interested. "All the victims' cars disappeared?"

"If they had cars, yeah. Also, victims tended to disappear from home, from work, or some other familiar haunt—and the bodies turned up elsewhere."

Nick was nodding. "Dumped, here and there."

"That would seem a reasonable assumption . . . of course you know how Grissom feels about assumptions."

Nick gestured to the stack of file folders. "Anything else in there we can use?"

"Well," she said, shrugging, "there is one thing I can't quite get a handle on."

"Which is?"

Sara went back into full analytical mode. "For some reason this prolific, professional assassin disappears almost five years ago. Why does he show up now? Especially if Grissom's on to something, and Dingelmann wasn't a mob hit . . . in which case, what the hell is this guy doing in Vegas, getting proactive again, all of a sudden?"

With a shrug, Nick said, "Maybe he was hired by somebody else."

"Like who?"

"Dingelmann's ex-wife, a disgruntled business partner, who knows? Just because no bodies have turned up with that distinctive 'Deuce' signature doesn't mean our man hasn't been active."

"Yeah, yeah, possible, possible—and we know at least one instance when he hid a body. So what do you think?"

Nick threw his hands palms up.

"You suppose Grissom wants to hear . . ." She mimicked his gesture.

"Okay," he said, rising, throwing a grin off to the sidelines, "I get it—more digging."

Sara gave him a mock sweet smile. "Well, don't go away mad—what have you dug up, thus far? I showed you mine, you show me yours."

His smile in return was almost embarrassed, and he laughed, and leaned against the doorjamb and said, "I went to the website for the *Las Vegas Sun*, and plowed through all the old newspaper coverage on Fortunato and his disappearance, him and this dancer he was involved with . . . as well as going over the original file for the dancer's disappearance. She was also officially a missing person, it turns out."

Sara frowned in interest. "Dancer?"

"Exotic type. A stripper. Innocent child like you wouldn't know about such things."

"Catherine would."

Nick grinned. "Yeah—that's where I heard about 'Joy Starr'—stripper having an affair with casino employee Fortunato . . . a stripper who disappeared on the same *day* as casino employee Fortunato."

Sara was grinning; she made a yummy sound. "This is getting good."

"Seems 'Joy Starr' was a stage name for a Monica Petty. I'm going to turn the name over to Brass, see what he can do with it."

"But you might just ride along to the strip club with him."

"I might. . . . She was a doll, in her day."

"Joy whatever?"

"Starr." Nick pulled a photo from the file folder,

handed it to Sara. "Next on the bill, ladies and germs—the exotic dance stylings of Joy Starr."

"Cue the ZZ Top," Sara said, looking at an 8-inch by 10-inch head shot of a pretty, dark-eyed, dark-haired woman of maybe twenty-one, with that overteased '80s-style hair. "That's some mall hair."

"What?"

She laughed a little. "That's what we used to call it, my girlfriends and me—mall hair."

"You ever have hair like that?" he asked, puckishly. "Middle school maybe?"

"I was a heartbreaker then," she said, "and I'm a heartbreaker now. Run before you get hurt, Nicky."

"Ouch," he said, glanced again at the photo, then tucked it back in the folder, and went back to his work.

Once she and Grissom had returned, Catherine went directly into the lab and spent the next hour painstakingly cleaning the asphalt off the casing, dabbing it with acetone, doing everything within her power to make sure she did not damage it. Preserving fingerprints was a hopeless cause, but the casing itself could have other tales to tell.

She found the firearms examiner, a friendly twenty-eight-year veteran named Bill Harper, already examining the bullets that Nick had brought in earlier.

Harper's longish curly gray hair looked typically uncombed and he apparently hadn't missed a meal at least since the Nixon administration; but Catherine knew there was no better firearms examiner in the state.

"Anything?" she asked him.

"Not much," he replied.

"Nothing?"

"Something, but . . ." He shrugged and stepped away from the microscope, gesturing for her to look. She stepped up and looked down at two different shells. Obviously they had not come from the same barrel.

"Rifling's completely different," he said. "Of the four shells, each pair matches, but the two pairs don't match. The pair from the mummy matches the barrel found with the body. These other two slugs are strangers. The only commonality between pairs is they're all the same caliber."

Nodding, Catherine pulled back from the microscope and held up three evidence bags. "You want to take a crack at the shell casings?"

Harper's brow creased in interest. "What have you got?"

"Number one is from our mummy, two and three here are from the shooting at the Beachcomber."

"Sure," Harper said. "Understand, this could take a while."

"I'll wait," she said, sitting down at Harper's desk in the corner, allowing herself to lean back.

Watching him work, she counted the hours since she had last slept. Somewhere around twenty-four, she nodded off.

Greg Sanders found Nick at a computer, and presented him with the DNA match for Malachy Fortunato.

"Thanks, Greg. Matched the dental already though."

"*Gran Turismo* is still a deal, right?"

"I don't renege on a man who controls so much of my destiny."

"Smart move." Sanders shrugged. "Not much off the guy's shoes, either. He'd been on some sort of loose rock. Driveway maybe. That make any sense to you?"

"Yes it does," Nick said. "What about the cigarette filter?"

Sanders smirked. "That piece of crud was about fifteen years old—barely anything left."

"Way it goes."

Now Sanders grinned; the demented gleam in his eyes meant he was proud of himself. "Got some DNA off it though."

Nick sat up. "You're kidding."

"Not workable, though."

This guy was a walking good news/bad news joke. "Thanks, dude," Nick said wearily. "I'll bring that game in tomorrow."

"Yes!" Eyes dancing with joy-stick mania, Sanders departed.

Nick Stokes spent two hours trying to find Brass and had no luck; the detective was not answering his page, so finally Nick decided he'd make the first run out to Swingers himself. At least the change of pace might help him stay awake. Figuring he'd be a nice guy about it, he went hunting for Warrick, to give his fellow CSI a chance to tag along.

He found Warrick in a darkened lab, his head on a counter, snoring. With the hours they'd all been working, this made a whole lot of sense to Nick; and, instead of waking his co-worker, Nick retreated and closed the door.

Grissom's door, usually open, was shut now, lights off. The boss had kept pretty much to himself since returning with Catherine, and Nick wondered whether to bother him. On the other hand, if he didn't check with him, Grissom might be pissed—and Nick hated that.

He knocked on the door.

"Yeah," came the tired voice from the other side.

Nick opened the door and stuck his head into the darkened office. "Boss—hey, I don't mean to disturb you."

"Get the switch, will you?"

Nick did, bathing the room in fluorescent light.

Grissom, catching a nap on the couch, sat up; his graying hair was mussed, black clothes rumpled.

"You look like hell."

"Thanks," Grissom said, getting to his feet, stretching, "you too." Grissom met Nick at the doorway. "What?"

"Did Catherine tell you about the dancer that disappeared, same night as Fortunato?"

Little nod. "Yeah."

"Well, she used to work at this place called Swingers."

"On Paradise Road," Grissom said. He rubbed his eyes, yawned a little. "Sorry."

"Even you get to be human."

"No I don't. And don't let me catch you at it, either."

Nick couldn't tell if Grissom was joking or not; drove him crazy.

"That place still open?" Grissom asked, meaning Swingers.

"Should be," Nick said, with a thumb-over-his-shoulder gesture. "I thought I'd go out there, see if anybody remembered her."

"That's Brass's responsibility."

Nick shrugged. "Can't find him."

"O'Riley?"

Nick shook his head. "Off duty."

"Conroy?"

"The same."

Grissom considered the possibilities. "Take Warrick with you."

"He's snoring in a lab," Nick said. "I don't think he's slept in, I dunno, twenty-four hours."

"Okay," Grissom said casually, "then let's go."

Nick reacted as if a glass of cold water had been thrown in his face. "What—you and me?"

Cocking his head, Grissom gave Nick a look. "Something wrong with that?"

Hurriedly, Nick said, "No, no, it's fine. You want to drive?"

"That's okay. You drive . . . but this isn't official, understand. We're just taking a break."

"Right."

"Give me a second to brush my teeth."

"Sure, boss."

"And, uh—brush yours, too. There'll be ladies present."

Shaking his head, Nick went to quickly freshen up. Every conversation with Grissom was always a new experience.

The clapboard barn-looking building housing Swingers squatted on Paradise Road, a couple of miles southeast of McCarren Airport. Fifty years ago, before the tide of the city rolled out here to engulf it, the place had been a particularly prosperous brothel. Now, with the paint peeling and the gutters sagging, the structure looked like a hooker who'd stayed a little too long in the trade.

Even though Vegas was a twenty-four-hour town, the strip joint closed at three A.M., though the red neon SWINGERS sign remained on, with its pulsing electric outline of a dancing woman. Nick eased the Tahoe into a parking place with only about five minutes to spare. Perhaps half a dozen cars dotted the parking lot, with only a battered Honda parked near the Tahoe and the front door.

"Slow night," Nick said.

"Experience?" Grissom asked.

"I mean, looks like," Nick said. "Looks like a slow night. I wouldn't really know."

Skepticism touched Grissom's smile.

A shaved-bald, short-goateed bouncer met them at the door; he wore a bursting black muscle T-shirt and black jeans. "We're closing," he growled. Maybe six-four, the guy had no discernible neck, cold dark eyes, and a rottweiler snarl.

Nick said, "We're . . ."

"*We're* closed," the bouncer repeated. "We look forward to fillin' your entertainment needs some other night."

Nick keep trying. "We're from the Las Vegas . . ."

The bouncer's eyes bulged, his upper lip formed half a sneer. "Are you deaf, dipshit?"

Grissom stepped between the two men, showed the bouncer his badge. "Las Vegas Criminalistics Bureau."

The bouncer didn't move. "So?"

"We'd just like to speak with the owner."

"About what?"

Giving the big man a friendly smile, Grissom said, "Well, that would be between us and him."

The bouncer's eyebrows lifted; he remained unimpressed. "Well, then, you girls must have a warrant."

Nick's patience snapped. "Just to talk, we don't need a warrant!"

The bouncer glared and took one ominous step forward.

"Forgive my co-worker's youthful enthusiasm," Grissom said, moving between them again, getting in close to the guy, keeping his voice low.

The soft-sell caught the bodyguard off-balance—Grissom had the guy's attention.

With an angelic smile, Grissom said, "You'd like us to get a warrant? Fine, I'll make a call and we'll do just that. I can have it here in ten minutes. . . . Of course, in the meantime no one leaves the premises, and when it gets here we'll come in and find every gram, every ounce, every grain of any illegal drug here. Of course we'll do background checks on all the girls working here, to make sure they're of legal age. After that comes the fire marshal and the building inspector." He flipped his phone open. "I'm ready if you are."

Suddenly smiling, the bouncer patted the air in front of him. "Whoa, whoa. The owner? I think he's back in the office. Just a minute. You can wait at the bar." He pointed inside. "Anything you want, on the house."

They strolled into the smoky room, where southern

rock music blared, neon beer signs burning through the haze, the walls rough, gray barnwood that never met primer let alone paint. A dozen men were present. The bouncer was disappearing toward the back.

"Nice work," Nick said.

Not surprisingly, the bar smelled of stale beer, cigarettes, urine and testosterone—not the most attractive joint in town, but low maintenance. Green-and-white plastic tables and chairs—lawn furniture—were scattered around the room. They faced a stage that ran most of the length of the far wall, chairs lining it for the front-row patrons; the only show-biz accouterments were cheap colored lights and two fireman's poles, one at either end of the stage.

A skinny blonde was sliding down one of the poles, half a dozen customers watching. Wadded-up dollars were scattered about the hardwood floor of the stage like so much green refuse.

To the left edge of the stage a doorway said DANCERS ONLY—this was where the bouncer had gone, and was clearly the pathway to the dressing room and the owner's office. Nick and Grissom stood at the right end of a U-shaped oak bar. Behind it, a tired-looking blonde woman of at least forty, wearing only a skimpy bikini, gave Nick the eye as she washed glasses in one sink and rinsed them in the next one.

"We just had last call, fellas," she said over the blare of southern rock, the flirtation heavy in her voice. "But if you want somethin', who knows? I been known to make exceptions."

She might be too old to strip, but she remained attractive enough to hustle.

"We're fine," Grissom said.

Frowning now, but still eyeing Nick, the woman resumed washing glasses, pumping them up and down on the brushes. The action was not lost on Nick and he turned away before allowing himself a little chuckle. Grissom either didn't notice, or was pretending as much.

The bouncer came out of the DANCERS ONLY door, holding it open for a thin young man who looked like a high school kid in his low-slung jeans and UNLV T-shirt; neither one, Nick knew, was a "dancer" he would pay to see perform. The young guy had curly blond hair, a scruffy goatee and a gun metal gray barbell stud through his left eyebrow.

"Wanna talk to me?" he asked, in a voice not far removed from puberty.

Nick couldn't help himself. "You're the owner?"

"I'm the manager." The kid looked from Grissom to Nick. "You boys got a problem with that?"

Both criminalists shook their heads.

The kid gestured. "You mind if we step outside? I don't want to bother the customers—few we got left, tonight."

They moved into the parking lot, where a desert breeze stirred weeds surrounding the driveway. The flush of red neon bathed them as their conversation ensued, during which an occasional customer or two would exit to their cars.

Forehead tensed, Grissom asked, "How old are you?"

Neon buzzed, shorting out, like a bug zapper.

"Twenty-three," the kid said. "I'm workin' on my MBA at UNLV. This place is paying for it. My uncle owns it. Hey, I'm a business major—works out swell for both us."

"What's your name?"

"John Pressley."

"Like Elvis?" Grissom asked.

"Like Elvis but with two *s*'s."

Nick had his notepad out, and was jotting that down, as he asked, "How long has your uncle owned this business?"

"Not very—couple years. It was an investment property."

"I see. Can you tell us anything about the previous owner?"

Pressley gave him a dubious look. "Why?"

"We're trying to find a woman who danced here fifteen years ago. Way before your time."

Pulling a crumpled pack of cigarettes from his jeans pocket, Pressley lit up; he looked at Nick, then at Grissom, as if taking their measure.

"Marge," he finally said. "Great old broad. She owned this dump forever."

That piece of information was a nice break, Nick thought, and asked, "What was her last name, do you remember?"

"Sure. Kostichek. Marge Kostichek." He spelled it for Nick, who wrote the name down.

"Address?"

The kid puffed on the cigarette. "I got no idea—you're gonna have to work harder than that, guys."

Grissom smiled the angelic smile again. "How hard, Mr. Pressley?"

"Oh, she's still around. You could probably find

her in the phone book. Let your fingers do the walkin'."

"Thanks," Nick said.

The kid raised his studded eyebrow. "You gonna hassle us anymore?"

Grissom stepped forward. "Is Marge Kostichek the straight skinny, or are you blowing smoke?"

Keeping his eyes on Grissom, Pressley snorted a laugh and said, "She's so real I can't believe you never heard of her. She's a legend in this business, man."

"She pans out," Grissom said, "no hassles."

"Yeah . . . for how long?"

"Till next time," Grissom said, pleasantly, and led the way as they walked toward the Tahoe.

Outside, Grissom said, "Let's go back to the office. We'll find an address for Marge Kostichek, and you can round up Conroy or Brass to go with you."

"Yeah," Nick said. "Uh, Grissom."

"Yeah?"

" 'Straight skinny'?"

Grissom just smiled, and Nick laughed.

They climbed back into the Tahoe and Nick started the engine. They were passing the airport when Grissom finally spoke again. "I guess you've picked up on my being hesitant to let you out on your own."

Nick said nothing.

"You don't like that much, do you?"

Turning, Nick met Grissom's eyes, but he said nothing.

"You know why that is, don't you?"

Nick shrugged. "You don't think I'm ready." A traffic light turned red and Nick braked to a stop.

"I *know* you're not ready."

Nick turned to his boss and even he could hear the earnestness in his voice. "You're wrong, Grissom. I'm ready. I'm so ready."

Grissom shook his head.

The light turned green and Nick fought the urge to stomp on the gas. He slid ahead slowly.

"That bouncer," Grissom.

Embarrassed, Nick said, "Yeah, yeah . . ."

"If I hadn't stepped in, you'd have wound up in a fight with a citizen. Which would have led to suspension for you, and a black eye for our unit."

"I just . . ." Nick stopped. He knew Grissom was right and somehow that made him even angrier. He looked down at the steering wheel, his knuckles white.

"You forgot why you were there," Grissom said, "and let it turn into some kind of . . . macho foolishness. The case is the thing, Nick. It's the only thing."

Nick hung his head. "You're right. I know."

"Don't beat yourself up—fix it."

"Yeah, I will. Thanks, Grissom."

"Anyway, this is a good example of why we let Brass and his guys handle the people. We're better at evidence."

"Hey," Nick said, pulling into the Criminalistics parking lot, "we didn't do so bad, end of the day, did we?"

"Not so bad," Grissom admitted.

"Of course I'm not so sure we needed to brush our teeth."

In the firearms lab, Bill Harper laid a hand on Catherine's shoulder and she jumped.

"Sorry," he said, jumping back himself.

"No! No, I'm sorry. I must have . . ."

"Slept for hours?" he offered.

"Oh, no, I couldn't have. . . ."

He pointed at the clock on the lab wall.

"Oh, my God," she said, flushed with embarrassment. "I'm really sorry, Bill."

His smile told her it was okay. "Hey, it was all right—you seemed to need it. You really looked bushed."

"Do I look any better?"

"Catherine, few look any better, at their worst. . . . Go wash up, and then we'll talk."

With a reluctant smile, she took his advice.

Ten minutes later she returned from the locker room to the lab, face washed, hair combed. She hated to admit her own human frailty, but she felt worlds better after the nap. "Okay, Bill, what have you got?"

"Have a look at the monitor."

She looked at the computer screen on Harper's work table and saw the butt ends of two casings next to each other.

"What do you see, Catherine?"

Studying the two images, she said, "Twenty-five caliber, one Remington, one Winchester."

He pointed to the primers.

"They've both been struck," she added.

"They've both been struck—*identically.*" Reaching over, he clicked the mouse and the two primers suddenly filled the screen. He pointed out three different bumps. They were correspondingly placed on each primer.

She could feel her whole face light up as she smiled. "The same firing pin?"

He nodded. "Helluva thing, ain't it? Fifteen years apart—two different crimes . . . same firing pin."

Catherine took a step back.

Harper clicked again and the picture zoomed back out to show the ends of the casings. "And look here," he said, pointing to tiny barely visible indentations at four points on the end of the cartridge, "this is where each one hit the breech wall."

She felt almost giddy. "You're going to tell me they're identical, too, aren't you?"

"Yes, ma'am—and that ain't all. . . . The scratches from the extractor, when the shell was ejected?"

She nodded her understanding.

Harper grinned. "They match too."

Catherine let out a long breath, shaking her head, amazed and delighted at the findings. "He's using the same gun . . . and thinks he's fooling ballistics, changing out the barrels. Grissom was right—Malachy Fortunato and Philip Dingelmann were killed by the same gun, presumably the same killer, fifteen years apart."

Harper said, "That's what the evidence says."

"And that's what Grissom likes to hear," Catherine said, on her way out. "Thanks, Harper—I needed this as much as that nap. More!"

Grissom sat behind his desk, munching a turkey-and-Swiss sandwich. He sipped his glass of iced tea, and looked up to see a figure pause in his open door-way—a man maybe six-one in a well-tailored light blue suit, muscularly trim, with blond hair combed slickly back from a high forehead, and a strong, sharp nose, narrow blue eyes . . . and a smile of cobra warmth.

"Special Agent Rick Culpepper," Grissom said, setting his iced tea carefully back on his desk. "Up late, or early?"

"How do you stand these hours?" The FBI agent smiled his oily smile. "With all the people you encounter, I'm complimented you remember me."

"How could I forget?" Grissom gave the agent a smile that had little to do with the usual reasons for smiling. "You're the man who tried to get one of my CSIs killed, using her as bait."

Strolling uninvited into the office, Culpepper said, "My God, you're still upset about that? Sara Sidle volunteered, and everything came out fine—let it go, Grissom. Get past it."

"I have trouble getting past you using . . . misusing . . . my people, Culpepper. We're busy here. What do you want?"

"You're takin' a lunch break," Culpepper said, nodding to the half-eaten sandwich Grissom had put down. "I won't eat up any of your precious crime-solving time. . . . Relax, buddy. Ever think I might be here to help?"

Bullshit, Grissom thought; but he said nothing. He would let the FBI agent do all the work.

Sitting, Culpepper said, "Your people ran a print from a shell casing through AFIS."

"We do that a lot."

"Yes, and your federal government is glad to be of service."

"Do you have a specific print in mind?"

Culpepper nodded. "Related to a recent shooting at a resort hotel—the Beachcomber."

"We got no match from that."

"That's right. That's because a little flag went up—AFIS wasn't allowed to make that match—classified information."

"Is that the federal cooperation you mentioned?"

"The man who belongs to that print is a contract assassin. No one knows what he looks like, or who he is . . . but we've been looking for him ourselves, for a long, long time. And that's why I'm here—to share information."

"Well thank you," Grissom said. "Let me think—when was the last time the FBI shared anything? Blame excluded."

Leaning forward, wearing a disingenuous grin, Culpepper said, "I know we've had our differences in the past, Grissom—but this is a crucial matter. It relates to a plethora of organized crime matters. Consider this a heads up, if nothing else—this guy is bad people."

Grissom remained cautious, skeptical. "Which is why you're going to help us catch him?"

"Yes, oh yes—he needs to be stopped . . . and your unit, and Detective Brass and his fine contingent of investigators, seem to have the best shot at finally doing it."

". . . Right."

"In fact," Culpepper said, "I've already forwarded our files to Detective Brass—everything we have on the Deuce."

"That *is* cooperative," Grissom said. He didn't tell Culpepper that he and Brass were already on the trail.

Culpepper beamed. "Now, you want to tell me what you have?"

"Anything to cooperate," Grissom said.

He didn't want to give up anything, but Gil Grissom knew how to play the game. He gave Culpepper the basics of the Beachcomber shooting—information he was pretty sure the FBI agent already had. He left out, among other things, the videotape evidence; and said nothing about the mummy at all. When he finally finished, he looked at Culpepper's insincere grin and said, "Now what?"

"Nothing in particular," Culpepper said, rising. "Just nice to know we can work together like this."

And he gave Grissom his hand, which Grissom accepted—the agent's flesh cool, clammy—and when Culpepper had gone, Grissom sat there for a while, looking at his own palm, as if thinking of running it through the lab.

10

THESE LINKED MURDER INVESTIGATIONS REPRESENTED JUST the sort of case Jim Brass needed—not that he'd ever admit it to anyone, himself included.

Since his unceremonious return trip to Homicide, after the Holly Gribbs debacle, many of his colleagues avoided him as if he were a terminal case. Sheriff Brian Mobley spoke to Brass only when necessary. In recent months, Brass had, whenever possible, avoided Mobley, and would have ducked out fifteen minutes ago if the sheriff hadn't ordered him to come in and provide an update.

With no enthusiasm, Brass knocked on the wooden door with Mobley's name and rank inscribed in raised white letters. After losing command of the Criminalistics Bureau, Brass had been reduced to a plastic nameplate on an anonymous metal desk in the bullpen.

"Come in," came the muffled response.

Bright sunshine from the huge window behind Mobley's desk infused the office with a white light that Brass supposed was meant to give the sheriff the aura of God. Unfortunately, it seemed to be working.

Despite a well-tailored brown suit and crisp yellow tie, attire worthy of the chairman of the board of a small company, the redheaded, freckle-faced Mobley looked not so much youthful as adolescent, a boy playing cops and robbers . . . and the top law enforcement officer of a city of over one million souls.

"Have a seat, Jim."

The politeness made Brass even more uneasy, but he did as instructed. The wall next to the office door was lined with shelves of law books; on the left wall, a twenty-one-inch television—tuned to CNN, at the moment, sound low—perched atop a credenza. A computer sat on a smaller table on the sheriff's left, while his desk—smaller than the Luxor—appeared, as always, neat and clutter-free. The detective in Brass wondered if the sheriff ever worked.

Brass had been under Mobley, some years before, when the latter had been captain of Homicide. In truth, the man was probably as conscientious and hardworking as anyone; but Mobley's job was more about politics, these days, than actual law enforcement.

In 1973, the Clark County Sheriff's Department and the Las Vegas Police Department merged into one entity, putting the Las Vegas Metropolitan Police Department under the command of the sheriff. Now, the office more closely resembled that of a corporate CEO. Mobley was the fourth man to hold the position since the unification; rumor had it Mobley had his sights on the mayoral office.

The sheriff used a remote to switch off the television. "Well, at least CNN hasn't picked up Dingelmann's murder yet."

Brass nodded. "Local press has stayed off it—mob stuff's bad for tourism."

"You got that right—but the national press will pick up on this, and soon. Dingelmann's too high-profile for some national stringer not to connect the dots."

"I know."

"It's bad enough that the newspapers and the local TV picked up on this 'mummy' business. Now that's everywhere. Is it true it was our CSIs who dubbed the corpse that way?"

"I don't know."

"Well, the press sure loved that baloney." Sighing, the Sheriff loosened his tie. "Tell me where we're at, Jim."

The detective filled him in.

Mobley closed his eyes, bowed his head, and pinched the bridge of his nose between two fingers. "Do we really think the same asshole killed two people, fifteen years apart?"

"The CSIs are working to prove it now."

"And?"

"Who knows?"

Mobley shook his head, scowled. "Stay on top of this, Jim. There's a lot riding on it."

"Sir?"

"We can look like champs if we catch this killer, or chumps if this guy gets away—bottom line'll be, *we* can't protect our city."

"Yes, sir," Brass said.

"And let's *handle* the FBI."

"Sir?"

A tiny sneer curled the baby upper lip. "Take all the help they want to give . . . but if the FBI makes the arrest, they get all the glory. Now, if we make the arrest before them . . ."

"Yes, sir."

"Okay, go get him."

Brass left the office, searching the halls for Grissom, wanting to tell him about Mobley's challenge, in particular the avoidance of the FBI, which put him in rare agreement with the sheriff. Instead Brass met Warrick Brown coming down the hall in the opposite direction.

"What are you still doing here?" Brass asked.

Warrick looked at his watch and laughed once and grinned. "Overtime, I guess. I was working on stuff, lost track. I've got something I need you to do."

Skeptical, Brass asked, "What?"

The CSI explained about the running shoes and the different retailers.

"All right, I'll look into it. You going home?"

Shaking his head, Warrick said, "No. I'm going to the Beachcomber to look at some more tapes."

"Cheaper than Blockbuster. Grissom still here?"

Warrick nodded back down the hall. "Yeah, we're all still here. Somethin' about these cases, you know, intertwined like they are—it's like a bug we all caught. Can't shake it."

Warrick disappeared one way down the hall, Brass continued the other. He finally caught up with Grissom in the break room. They sat on opposite sides of the table.

Grissom took off his glasses, rubbed his eyes and

looked at Brass. "So—tell me about our friend Brian."

Brass gave him the whole story, concluding, "The sheriff's hot to trot to close this case—these cases. Show the tourists we're on top of it. Show the citizens he's a great man."

Grissom's half-smirk was humorless. "We'd like to solve it too, Jim. We're all working double shifts, what more—"

"Whoa, whoa," Brass interrupted, holding up a palm. "Remember me? I'm on your side."

Shaking his head, Grissom said, "Sorry. Stress. We're all feeling the pressure on this one."

"Warrick said it was like a sickness."

"The flu you can get over," Grissom said. "Search for the truth has no cure."

"Who said that?"

Grissom blinked. "Me."

Looking surprisingly fresh in a blue silk blouse and black slacks, Catherine strolled in, a devious smile making her lovely face even lovelier.

"I was wondering who committed the crime," Grissom said.

"What crime?" she asked.

"So you're the one that ate the canary."

Her smile widened, eyes sparkled.

Brass looked at her, then Grissom, then back at Catherine. "What?"

"She knows something," Grissom said, his own smile forming.

Pouring herself a cup of coffee, she said, "I know a lot of things."

"For instance?"

"For instance . . . I know that the same gun killed both Philip Dingelmann and Malachy Fortunato."

Brass said, "I don't know whether to laugh or cry. The same killer responsible for two murders, fifteen years apart?"

Grissom remained skeptical. "We can't say that yet, can we?"

"No," Catherine said, sitting down with them. "Not quite yet. But I can prove that both men were shot with the same gun."

Astonished, Brass said, "I thought you found a discarded gun barrel with the mummy."

She said, "We did. Riflings matched the bullets we found in Mr. Fortunato's head, too."

Brass struggled to follow. "But the bullets didn't match Dingelmann, right?"

"No match, that's right."

"So," the detective asked, "how can you say they were shot with the same gun?"

Grissom—arms folded, sitting back—just watched her work.

"Wait," Brass said, thinking back, "I've got it. This is just like Brad Kendall, the coffee shop guy."

"Not quite," Catherine said. "Even though Kendall had changed out the barrel, we proved he used bullets from a box in his possession, matching the manufacturer's imprint. We can't do that here—these bullets not only didn't come from the same box, they didn't come from the same manufacturer. Doubtful our man would be using bullets from the same box of ammo, fifteen years later, anyway, right?"

"Right, right, of course," Brass said, bewildered.

Grissom just smiled.

Catherine continued, "When a bullet is fired from an automatic what happens?"

Brass sighed. "The firing pin strikes the primer, the bullet fires through the barrel, the casing gets ejected."

"Bravo," Grissom said.

"Shut up," Brass said.

"There are," Catherine said, "three distinct marks on any shell casing fired from an automatic. Like you said, the firing pin strikes the primer. The extractor scratches the casing as it grabs it, and the casing gets slammed into the breech wall before it's sent sailing out of the pistol. Each of those strikes leaves its own individual mark that, like fingerprints, is different for every weapon."

Eyes narrowed, Brass said, "And you're saying . . ."

"The shell casings from the Beachcomber and the casing we pulled from Mr. Fortunato's driveway are from the same weapon."

Brass allowed a smile to form. "Can we use that in court?"

"There's no way of arguing against it," Grissom said.

"But couldn't they say this evidence is tainted, because one of the casings was buried under asphalt for years?"

Catherine said, "The defense can *say* that, but saying it's tainted won't make it so, and the argument won't fly."

"Why?"

"You familiar with these guys that collect guns from the Old West?"

Brass shrugged. "What about them?"

"Lately they've been using these same marks to verify the authenticity of pistols from Little Big Horn."

"Matching firing pins to shell casings?"

"Yeah," she said. "They've dug up shell casings from the battlefield and matched them to firing pins from pistols used by Custer's men. Those casings have been in the ground for over a hundred years. Our casing was protected from the environment between the gravel and the asphalt, and for only fifteen years."

"Science and history meeting," Grissom said, loving it.

Brass could only ask, "And this will work?"

"Yeah," Grissom said. "It will work fine."

"But we don't have the gun?"

"Not yet," Catherine said. "But now we do know we're only looking for one gun, and the chances are if this guy hasn't gotten rid of it in the last fifteen years, he won't get rid of it now."

Now Brass had something to offer: "It is amazing how some of these guys have a sentimental attachment to a damn weapon. It's put a bunch of them away."

Sara joined the group. Grabbing a soda out of the fridge, she plopped into the chair next to Brass. She looked at Catherine, but her question was for all of them. "Why would a hitman . . . gee, somehow that's fun to say . . . why would a hitman *this* successful have a five-year hole in his career? Then, suddenly, resurface now?"

"A hole?" Grissom asked.

"Yeah," Sara said, nodding, sipping her soda, "no one's reported anything on this guy for just over five years. It's like he fell off the edge of the world."

"Or went to jail for something else," Brass offered.

Grissom shook his head. "No, there would have been a set of prints to match, then."

Brass said, "Yeah, right. Didn't think."

"Maybe he was sick," Catherine tried.

"For five years?" Sara asked.

"Or retired," Grissom said.

They all paused to look at him.

"Anything's possible," he said. "No more guessing—keep digging."

"Well, fine," Sara said, "but where do you look on the Internet for retired hit men?" And she rose and headed back to work, her soda in her hand.

Brass blew air out and said, "I better get going, too. I've got to hit the retailers that sold those running shoes." He got up, looked at Grissom and shrugged. "I guess we do what the man says."

Grissom nodded. "The part about keeping the FBI at bay, I got no problem with."

The detective departed leaving Catherine staring at Grissom. "And what was that about?"

He tried to shrug it off, but she was having none of it.

"C'mon, tell me."

"Politics. Mobley wants to let Culpepper 'help' us, then he wants us to make the bust and cut the FBI out of it."

"Kind of a dodgy game."

"Yes, it is."

She smiled. "But then, Culpepper is a real son of a bitch."

Grissom managed to keep a straight face. "Yes, he is."

In a nicely padded desk-type chair, Warrick sat next to a security guard in front of the wall of Beachcomber monitors. The guard, a short Hispanic guy in his early twenties, had just loaded the tape that Warrick brought in, showing Peter Randall's back at the poker machine, and Philip Dingelmann's reaction to seeing Randall. Then Dingelmann disappeared around the corner, Randall got dragged back to the machine, pulled his card, then followed, disappearing around the corner as well.

They reran the tape and Warrick pointed at Randall. "I want to see anything else you might have with this guy in it."

The guard nodded. "He's here nearly every Monday and Wednesday."

Warrick's pulse skipped. "What was your name again?"

"Ricky."

"Hey, Ricky. I'm Warrick."

Pleased, the guard said, "Hey, Warrick."

"Tell me more about this guy, this regular."

"Well, he didn't come this Wednesday, but he's a guy who likes the kind of off-times. Even a big place like this, you get to spot the regulars—particularly when studying these monitors for hours and hours."

Dingelmann had been murdered Monday morning; and "Peter Randall" had missed his usual Wednesday round of poker-machine playing.

"This guy, Peter Randall, he's a regular?"

"I mean, I don't know the guy's name, but he's been around a lot—but just Mondays and Wednesday, early hours, like I said, off-times, slow times. Some people don't like a crowded casino."

Warrick had never had a preference, as long as the dice were rolling. "Ricky, can you show me some more tapes of Mondays and Wednesdays?"

"Warrick, don't get too excited. I don't wanna get your hopes up, man. You're not going to see his face on camera any other day either."

"Why not?"

Nodding again, the guard said, "I noticed him, all right? But he's pretty careful."

"If you never saw his face, how do you recognize him?"

"I don't know, man—watch these monitors long enough, you get a feel for it. I mean, the back of him always looks the same, right?"

"Oh-kay," Warrick said.

"I mean his height, shape of his head, haircut, even the style of clothes . . . you just start to read people. Know 'em."

"Ricky, you ever get tired of this job, come see me where I work. I may have somethin' for you."

Warrick and his new best friend looked at a tape from the previous Wednesday, about the same time. Again, Randall sat at the poker machine, his back to the camera, obviously wearing a different sports coat. He never turned toward the camera and when they tried other cameras in the casino, he managed to avoid those too.

"How does a man come in here every day and never get his face on a camera?"

Ricky shrugged. "Beats me."

Warrick rolled his eyes. The guard had been right though, Randall came in every Monday and Wednesday; and his hair, frame, style of dress, made it easy enough to spot him, when you knew what you were looking for. They watched tapes for the Monday before the murder, and of the week before that, loading multiple tape decks of multiple angles on the casino, and Randall always showed up.

He didn't always play the same poker machine, but he never went to the tables where he would have to interact with a live dealer. In fact, he usually stuck to the row of poker machines closer to the back door. Monday, Wednesday, week after week, he came. He played for about two hours, then he left. Sometimes he won, sometimes he lost. Either way, the next Wednesday, the next Monday, there he was again. And never once did the son of a bitch show his face on any camera.

Todd Oswalt, the slot manager, stuck his head in once to ask how it was going.

"We're still working," Warrick said. "Still looking. Ricky's a big help—Ricky's the man."

Ricky beamed, and Oswalt said, "Glad to hear it—was that address a help?"

"Everything's a help, sir. But the maildrop he already abandoned. And the address he gave those people was for a street that doesn't exist."

Blond Oswalt in his navy blue suit shook his head and tsk-tsked. "Well, best of luck, Detective Brown."

Warrick didn't correct him. "I'm about due for some luck, sir."

Oswalt ducked back out.

They were five weeks back in the tapes now and Warrick wondered how many of these he should watch before he gave up. In truth, he wondered how many more of these he could take. It was like watching this bastard's boring life in reverse. On Wednesday of that week, Randall got up from his machine and disappeared off the screen. Warrick looked at the camera pointing up the main aisle—no Randall.

"Whoa, whoa! Where'd he go?"

Ricky shook his head as if he had been daydreaming. He swiftly scanned all the screens, finally spotting their man in the frame in the lower right hand corner.

"He's over there," Ricky said, pointing. "Just using the ATM, is all."

"Stop the tape," Warrick said quietly.

The guard was back in his own world and didn't hear.

Warrick said it again, louder. "Stop the tape, Ricky. Run it back."

Ricky did as told.

"That's it. We got him. Run it back."

Sitting up a little straighter, the guard again ran the tape back. Then, in slow-motion, ran it forward. They watched as Randall—back to the camera—used the ATM again.

"Yeah," Warrick said. "Yeah! What bank owns that ATM?"

Ricky shrugged. "I don't use the ATM here. I'm sure Mr. Oswalt would know."

"Get him. Please."

It took the slot host almost ten minutes to return to the security room, but Warrick didn't care—he had a clue.

Finally, Oswalt trudged in. "Yes, Detective Brown, what is it?"

"What bank owns this ATM?" Warrick asked, pointing at the frame.

"Uh, Wells Fargo. Why?"

"Mr. Oswalt, thanks." Warrick patted the guard on the shoulder. "Ricky, *muchas gracias* for your help, man. And you can take that to the bank."

"Hey, I remember that show," Ricky said, with a grin.

But Warrick was already gone.

11

NICK LEANED OVER TO OPEN THE DOOR FOR SERGEANT O'Riley, who hopped into the Tahoe for the ride to Marge Kostichek's. As they rolled across town, O'Riley made a point of studying the features of the SUV. "Nice ride," he said at last.

Nick nodded.

O'Riley shifted his beefy frame in the seat. "Lot better than those for-shit Tauruses they make us drive."

Stokes refused to rise to the bait. Though the crime lab unit had helped Homicide solve numerous cases, O'Riley and many of his brethren referred to the CSIs as "the nerd squad" behind their backs. Harboring a feeling that down deep O'Riley longed for the good old days when a detective's best friend was a length of rubber hose, Nick asked, businesslike, "What was that address again?"

Pointing up ahead, O'Riley said, "Two more houses—there on the left."

Pulling up in front of a tiny bungalow with peeling pale yellow paint and two brown dead bushes that needed removing, Nick parked the Tahoe facing the wrong way. The whole neighborhood looked as though it could use a coat of paint and some TLC. The scraggly grass was almost as brown as the bushes, and as they got closer Nick could make out where the stoop had started to draw away from the house, as if making a break for it. With O'Riley in the lead, they walked up the cracked-and-broken sidewalk and the two crumbly concrete stairs, the detective ringing the bell, then knocking on the door.

They waited—no answer.

O'Riley rang again, knocked again, with the same lack of success. O'Riley turned to Nick, shrugged elaborately, and just as they were turning away, a voice blared from behind them.

"Well, you don't *look* like Mormons!"

They turned, Nick saw a squat woman in a hot pink bathrobe and curlers.

"We're with the police, ma'am," O'Riley said, holding up his badge in its leather wallet. "We'd like to talk to you."

Waving an arm she announced, as if to the whole neighborhood, "Better get your asses in here then, 'cause I'm not staying outside in this goddamn heat!"

With arched eyebrows, Nick looked at O'Riley and O'Riley looked at Nick; whatever unspoken animosity might been between the cop and the CSI melted in the blast-furnace of this woman's abrasive personality. Nick followed O'Riley back up to the house and through the front door, glad to let the cop take the lead.

Little eyes squinted at them; her curlers formed a grotesque Medusa. "Don't just stand there! Close the damn door. Do I look like I can afford to air-condition the whole goddamn city?"

"No, ma'am," O'Riley said, the idea of a rhetorical question apparently lost on him.

Closing the door, Nick moved into the pint-sized living room next to the king-sized detective. Looking around, he couldn't help but feel he had just stepped into an antique mart—and a cluttered one at that. A maroon velvet chaise longue stood under the lace-curtained front window. Next to it, a fern stretched toward the ceiling, threatening to outgrow its pot. The room also contained two tall cherry end tables with doilies on them, a nineteen-inch TV on a metal stand, and the oversized Barcalounger tucked in a corner. In the opposite corner was a writing desk, and everywhere were stacks of things—*TV Guide*s, women's magazines, antiquing newsletters, newspapers, mail.

O'Riley, rocking on his feet, said, "Are you Marge Kostichek?"

"That's the name on the mailbox, isn't it? Aren't you a detective?"

"I'm Detective O'Riley," he said, either ignoring or not recognizing the sarcasm, "and this is CSI Nick Stokes."

"Cee ess what?"

Nick amplified: "Crime Scene Investigator."

"Why, is it a crime to be a goddamn slob, all of a sudden?"

"No, ma'am," O'Riley said, flummoxed. "What I mean is, ma'am—"

"Let me see that goddamn badge again. You can't be a real detective."

Flustered, O'Riley was reaching for the badge when the woman grabbed his arm.

"I'm just pulling your pud, pardner." She laughed and various chins wiggled. "A big dumb boy like you couldn't be anything *but* a cop."

Nick had to grin. In spite of himself, he was starting to like this cranky old woman, at least when she wasn't on his ass.

"We'd like to ask you some questions," O'Riley said.

"I didn't figure you stopped by to read the meter."

Listening, Nick began to prowl the room—just looking around, stopping at this pile of magazines and mail and that, snooping. It was his job.

O'Riley was saying, "We'd like to ask you about Swingers."

"Oh, Jesus Christ on roller skates," she said, plopping into the Barcalounger. "I've been outa the skin racket for years now. I figured this was about that damned dog, two doors down! Goddamned thing won't shut the hell up. Bark, bark, bark, all the time, yapp, yapp, yapp. Isn't there a law against that crap?"

"Well . . ." O'Riley said.

"Actually," Nick said, back by the writing desk, "we're here about a girl who used to dance at your club."

"Just make yourself at home, good-looking. You gotta pee or something?"

"No, ma'am."

"Are you nervous? Why don't you light in one place?"

"Yes, ma'am. About that girl, at Swingers . . ."

She waved a small pudgy hand. "Been a lot of them

over the years. Hundreds. Hell, maybe thousands. They don't keep their looks long, y'know—small window, for them to work."

From the file folded in half in his sport-coat pocket, O'Riley pulled out the photo of Joy Starr and handed it to the woman.

Nick noticed her lip twitch, but she gave no other outward sign that she might recognized the girl.

"Joy Starr," O'Riley prompted.

Ms. Kostichek shook her head. "Don't remember this one."

Interesting, Nick thought: suddenly no wise-ass remark.

O'Riley pressed. "About sixteen years ago."

She shook her head some more.

"Her real name was Monica Petty. She disappeared . . ."

Marge Kostichek cut him off. "A lot of them disappeared. Here one night, gone the next. Met some guy, did some drug, had a baby, overdosed, here a sad story, there a happy ending, they all had one or the other. So many little girls with nothing but a body and face to get 'em somewhere, hell—how could I remember 'em all?"

Nick, still poised at the writing stand, said, "But you do remember this girl."

The old woman looked at Nick and suddenly her face froze, the dark eyes like buttons. "Why don't you come closer, Handsome? Where I can hear you better?"

The better to see you with?

Something about this "granny" struck Nick funny—and something told him he was standing right where he needed to be. . . .

"I'm okay here, ma'am," Nick said. "The detective asks the questions."

The eyes tightened; something was different in that face now. "I musta been dreamin', then, babycakes, when you asked me that shit?"

O'Riley said, "Please take another look at the picture, Ms. Kostichek."

Giving it only a cursory glance, she said, "Don't know her, I said. Said I didn't, and I don't—if she worked for me fifteen, sixteen years ago, why the hell are you askin' about her now?"

Nick, without turning, glanced down at the writing desk. Numerous piles of opened letters, back in their envelopes, were stacked here and there, overlapping, haphazard. Private correspondence, bills, even junk mail . . .

The woman thrust the photo out for O'Riley to take; he did. "Why are you digging up ancient history, anyway?" she asked. Almost demanded.

Nick didn't handle a thing—but his eyes touched the envelopes on the desk.

O'Riley said, "Her name has come up in the investigation of another case."

A cloud crossed the old woman's features and disappeared. But if she wondered what that case was, she didn't ask.

O'Riley cleared his throat. "Well, thank you for your time, Ms. Kostichek."

On the far side of the desk, barely within his eyes' reach, he saw it: a letter postmarked in Los Angeles, the name on the return address . . .

. . . *Joy Petty.*

Nick froze, only for an instant, then turned back to the frumpy, feisty woman. "Yes, thank you, ma'am."

"Don't let the door hit you on the ass on the way out, fellas," she said.

He followed O'Riley, as they let themselves out, O'Riley pulling the door shut behind them. Inside the Tahoe, Nick put the key in the ignition, but made no move to start the vehicle.

"Something on your mind, Nick?"

He turned to the detective. "She's lying."

With a shrug, O'Riley smirked, said, "You think? That old broad wouldn't give a straight answer to a *Jeopardy!* question."

"I don't *think,* Sarge—I know."

The creased face under the trim crew cut tightened with interest. "How?"

"Her mail. You see all those piles here and there and everywhere?"

"She's a pack rat—so what?"

"So back on that writing table, on top of one of those piles, was a letter from a 'Joy Petty.' What do you suppose the odds are that she knows a Joy Petty who isn't also the Joy Starr whose real name is Monica Petty?"

O'Riley's eyebrows had climbed. "I think the odds are we're goin' right back up there, right now."

"Can we do that?"

"Was the letter out in plain sight?"

"Oh yeah."

"Then watch and learn, bucko."

O'Riley was out of the SUV and going back up the sidewalk before Nick could pull the keys from the ignition. The CSI trotted to catch up, the pissed-off detective already ringing the bell, then throwing open the screen door and knocking on the inside door before Nick even got to his side. Just then, Marge Kostichek jerked the door open.

"What now?" she bellowed. "We already gave!"

"That's what you think, lady." Getting right in her face, O'Riley bellowed back, "Why the hell did you lie to us?"

She backed up, inadvertently making room for both men to re-enter the house.

O'Riley glared at her, saying to Nick. "Show me."

Pulling on a latex glove even as he moved, Nick went to the writing desk and picked up the top letter on the stack of mail.

"Hey," she shouted, "you can't do that! That's private property! Where's your warrant?"

"Evidence in plain sight, ma'am," O'Riley said. "We don't need a warrant."

Nick came over to the hair-curled harridan and held up the letter from Joy Petty for her to see. "You want to explain this to us?"

The old woman took a step back, then stumbled over to her Barcalounger and sat heavily down, with an inadvertant whoopee-cushion effect. It might have been funny if she hadn't been crying.

Sara Sidle and ponytailed Detective Erin Conroy caught up with Warrick in the lobby of the Wells Fargo branch on South Nellis Boulevard. The air conditioning seemed to be set just below freezing; even though it was July in the desert, the tellers all wore sweaters.

"I've got another shot at getting our guy," Warrick said.

Professional in a white pants suit, Conroy lifted an eyebrow. "Is this going to be like the mailbox place?"

He looked for evidence of sarcasm in her voice and didn't find any. "I hope not, but who knows."

"Nice piece of work, Warrick," Sara said, meaning the ATM machine.

"Thanks. I haven't been this lucky in a casino in a long time."

A plumpish woman of forty sat behind the receptionist's desk talking on the phone. When they approached, she held up a finger: she'd be with them momentarily. . . . At least that's what Sara hoped she meant. In her lightweight short-sleeve top, Sara felt like she was standing in a meat locker.

Finally, the receptionist hung up the phone and turned to Warrick as if the two women weren't even there.

But it was Erin Conroy who held up her badge, and said, "We need to speak to whoever is in charge of ATM transactions."

The woman checked a list on the pullout shelf of her desk. "That would be Ms. Washington." She picked up the phone, pressed four numbers and said, "Ms. Washington, there are three police officers here to speak to you." She listened for a moment, hung up, and said to Warrick, "She'll be right with you."

Sara was seething but she didn't bother to correct the receptionist's description of all three of them as police officers.

They'd waited less than a minute before Sara heard

the staccato rhythm of high heels on the tile floor to her right and behind her. Turning, she saw a woman in a conservative black suit approaching—with expertly coifed black hair, jade eyes, and a narrow, porcelain face. The woman held out her hand to Conroy and offered all three a wide smile. "Good morning—I'm Carrie Washington. May I help you, Officers?"

Conroy showed her credentials and shook the woman's hand. "I'm from Homicide, and Warrick Brown and Sara Sidle, here, are from the Las Vegas Criminalistics Bureau. We need to talk to you about one of your ATM customers."

"Fine. Quite a crowd of you, for one customer."

"Overlapping interests in our investigation," Conroy said.

Ms. Washington clearly didn't understand a word of that—Sara barely did herself—but the woman, crisply cooperative, said, "Won't you follow me to my office?"

In the smallish suite at the far end of a wide hallway off the lobby, Carrie Washington offered them seats in the three chairs that faced her large oak desk. A computer sat on the credenza next to it, a potted plant perched in the corner, and two picture frames were placed at the edge of her neat desk, facing away from them.

"Now," she said, steepling her fingers. "How may I help you?"

Conroy nodded to Warrick to take the lead. He did: "We need to know the name of one of your ATM customers."

Ms. Washington's expression conveyed her discomfort. "I'm afraid that would be—"

"It's quite legal," the homicide detective said, and withdrew the document from her shoulder-slung purse, and tossed the warrant onto the desk. "Judge Galvin has already authorized the action."

The woman put on a pair of half-glasses, read the warrant. "Tell me what you need."

"The ATM at the Beachcomber," Warrick said, "that's yours?"

Ms. Washington frowned thoughtfully. "I can find out—but I assume you already know as much, or you wouldn't be here in such an impressive array."

"It is your ATM," Conroy said.

"Five weeks ago," Warrick said, reading her the date from his notes, "your machine was accessed at five thirty-nine A.M. Can you tell me who did that?"

Typing the information into her computer, Ms. Washington said, "You're quite sure about the time?"

Warrick nodded. "Yes, ma'am."

"This is going to take a few minutes."

Conroy said, "That's fine. We'll wait."

O'Riley sat across from Marge Kostichek at the plain wooden table in the center of the interrogation room. She was no longer a sarcastic handful, rather a morose, monosyllabic interrogation subject.

Also in the cubicle were two other chairs, one on each side of the table, a digital video camera trained on the woman and an audio tape for backup on the table. A large wall mirror—nobody was kidding anybody—was really a window with one-way glass, on the other side of which were Grissom, Catherine, and Nick, who had already filled his boss and co-worker in on why he and O'Riley thought it best to bring the former bar owner in for more questioning.

The room they were in was small with no furniture. They stood there watching the interview in the other room.

"He's not getting anywhere with her," Grissom said.

"Maybe there's nowhere to get to," Catherine offered.

"No way," Nick said. "She knows something. That letter can't be a coincidence."

"Please," Grissom said. "Not the 'c' word."

Catherine seemed lost in thought; then she asked Nick, "Where's that letter now?"

"On top of my desk—why?"

She arched an eyebrow toward Nick, and Grissom noted it as well, as she said, "Remember the box of her husband's personal effects Mrs. Fortunato turned over to us?"

"Of course," Nick said.

Grissom was smiling.

Catherine said, "One of the things in that box is a letter to her husband . . . from Joy Starr."

Pleased, Grissom said, "This was the letter that made the police assume Fortunato and Joy Starr ran off together?"

"Yes," Nick said. "Am I missing something?"

"It'll come to you," Catherine said, mildly amused, her eyes alive with a fresh lead. "Get me your letter, I'll get mine, and meet me in the parking lot."

Nick was lost. "The parking lot?"

A slight grin tugged at a corner of Grissom's mouth. "I see where you're going, Catherine . . . nice thinking. But even if you're right, that won't completely settle the issue. Nick, where did you say that letter was postmarked?"

"L.A. Within the past month."

"I'll contact the California DMV," Grissom said. "Let's see what we can find out about Joy Petty. Then I'll call Jenny Northam and tell her you're on your way."

"Jenny who?" Nick asked. "On our way where?"

"Jenny's a forensic document examiner," Grissom said. "A fine one—she'll tell us whether or not 'Joy Petty' wrote both letters."

"And if she didn't?" Nick asked.

"Then," Catherine said, "the fun begins—let's get going."

The bank air conditioner continued to work overtime and even the unflappable Warrick looked chilly after twenty minutes of waiting in Carrie Washington's office. The small talk had evaporated and the four of them sat in awkward silence.

At last, the phone rang. Everyone jumped a little, the shrill sound serving as a release for the tension that had filled the room. Now, with the second ring, anticipation elbowed its way into the office.

Carrie Washington picked up the phone. "Yes?" She listened, and scribbled notes. "Address? . . . Employment?" One last scribbled note, and she hung up.

"Do you have something?" Conroy asked.

"Yes. The customer in question is Barry Thomas

Hyde. He lives in Henderson, at fifty-three Fresh Pond Court. Owns and manages a video rental store—A-to-Z Video—in the Pecos Legacy Center. That's a strip mall at twenty-five sixty-two Wigwam Parkway."

Conroy wrote quick notes on the addresses; Warrick had them memorized already. He said, "Thank you, Ms. Washington."

"Will there be anything else?"

Conroy rose, and then so did Sara and Warrick. The homicide detective said, "I think we've got what we need."

"We do what we can," Ms. Washington said, and something that had clearly been working on the woman finally emerged: "You said you were with homicide, Officer Conroy?"

"That's right."

"So this is a murder case."

"It is."

This seemed to impress the professional woman, and Warrick said, "That's why your help is so important. This involves a dangerous individual, still at large."

"Anything to help," the banker said. "Anything."

Anything with a warrant.

Sara fought the urge to sprint from this building, to stand in the sun and, with luck, regain some of the feeling in her feet.

"Holy shit," she said, once they were outside, "am I freezing."

Conroy laughed lightly. "Then it wasn't just me—my teeth were chattering!"

"That name and those addresses didn't warm you ladies up?" Warrick asked.

"If it's not another dead end," Sara said, "I'll be warm and toasty."

Warrick shrugged. "Let's go see."

As they walked to the Tahoe, which was parked nearby, Sara said, "I'll bring Grissom up to speed," pulling out her cell phone with gunfighter aplomb.

She got him at once, informed him they had a possible ID on the Deuce, filled him in on the details.

"We'll try the house first," Grissom said. "Meet me there ASAP—I'll have Brass with me."

"We already have Detective Conroy with us."

"Good. If this is our man, he's a dangerous suspect."

Sara said 'bye, hit END, and filled Warrick and Conroy in.

"Anybody know Henderson very well?" Conroy asked, looking at the address.

"Not really," Sara said.

"Can't say I do," Warrick admitted. "We've worked a few crime scenes there. . . ."

"Well, I don't really know where this address is," Conroy admitted, gesturing with her notepad.

The absurdity of it hit them, and they laughed: three investigators and none of them knew how to find an address.

Sara, giggling, said, "Maybe we better get some help from dispatch."

"Just don't tell anybody," Conroy said.

" 'Specially not Grissom," Warrick said.

12

Jenny Northam shook her head, her long dark hair bouncing gently, then she looked through the microscope one last time.

"Well?" Catherine asked.

"No fuckin' way," Jenny said, her voice deeper than would be expected for a woman her size—barely over five feet, weighing in at maybe a hundred pounds. "Shit, guys, this isn't even close."

Jenny's office nestled in the corner of the second floor of one of the oldest downtown buildings just off Fremont Street. Tiny and slightly seedy, the office boasted apparent secondhand office furniture and carpeting dating to when the Rat Pack ruled the Strip. The back room, where Catherine and Nick had an audience with the sweet-looking, salty-speaking handwriting expert, was exactly the opposite.

Cutting-edge equipment lined three walls with file cabinets and a drafting table butted against the other wall. Two huge tables topped with UV, fluorescent and incandescent lights stood in the middle of the room.

Nick and Catherine sat on stools near the walls while Jenny Northam rode a wheeled stool, rolling from station to station around the room, like she was piloting a NASCAR stock car.

"You're sure," Catherine said.

"Is a bear Catholic? Does the Pope shit in the woods? Whoever wrote this letter . . ." She held up Joy Starr's vintage note to Malachy Fortunato. ". . . wasn't worried about being discovered. This can only loosely be termed a forgery—it's just some dumb shit signing this Joy Starr's name *to* the letter."

Catherine frowned. "That's the only possibility?"

"No—this letter . . ." The handwriting expert pointed to the letter taken at Marge Kostichek's house. ". . . could be the forgery. But any way you look at it, they weren't written by the same person."

The two CSIs watched as Jenny dipped the letter into a series of chemical baths, then set it to one side to dry. She did the same thing with the original note to Fortunato.

"While we're waiting," Jenny said, "let's compare the handwriting, using the two photocopies we made earlier."

Catherine sat on one side of the handwriting expert, and Nick on the other, as Jenny read slowly aloud the letter to Fortunato:

"My loving Mal,

Im so happy that were finally going to getaway just the 2 of us.

It will be great to be together forever. You are everything Ive always dreamed of. See you tonight.

Love you for ever

Joy"

The new letter from Joy Petty read:

"Dear Marge,

Thanks for the great birthday card. I don't know why you keep sending me money, you know I make plenty. But you're sweet to do it. I hope you've been thinking about our invitation to come over and stay with us for a few weeks. The guy I been living with, Doug, could even drive over and pick you up so you don't have to take the bus. It would be great fun. Please come.

Love, Joy"

"She's older now," Nick said, "her handwriting may have changed."

"Not this much," Jenny said. "Just not possible. Over the years our handwriting changes, granted. To varying degrees. But somebody's signature? That's something that people do not drastically change."

Jenny displayed the two letters side by side on the table. "Look at the capital 'J' in 'Joy.' "

They moved closer.

"This new one, the Joy Petty letter, the 'J' is extremely cursive. She started at the line and made this huge fuckin' loop that goes over the top line, then the smaller bottom loop that's equally full of itself. See how it goes down, almost all the way to the next line? This is somebody who craves attention—wants to stand out in the crowd."

Catherine gestured to the older document. "Tell us about the person behind this other signature."

Jenny pointed. "This is a scrawl. Almost looks like a kid did it. Very straight, more like printing than script. No way this is the same person. I don't give a shit how many years you put between 'em."

She went on to point out the capital "M" in "Marge," which was round and smooth, "Demonstrating the same pressure all the way through." The "M" in "Mal," however, was pointed, extra pressure at the joints of the lines.

Jenny shook her head. "Definitely two different writers."

Catherine smiled at Nick; Nick smiled at Catherine.

"The documents should be dry now," Jenny said, heading back over to the original documents. "Let's have a look." The expert positioned herself on one side of the table, Nick on the other. Catherine studied the photocopies a few more seconds, then followed, joining Nick on his side of the table.

"You dipped this in Ninhydrin?" Nick asked pointing at the note.

Shaking her head, Jenny said, "Nope—that's the old mojo."

Catherine said, "I remember reading in the Fortunato file that the lab tried that, back in '85, when they first found the note . . . but came up empty."

"Yes," Jenny said. "Though it was good in its day, even then Ninhydrin wasn't always successful. It worked well on amino acids, left on paper by people who touched it. But this new stuff, physical developer, it's the shit—works on *salts* left behind."

Nick was nodding, remembering something from a forensics journal article he'd read a while back. "This is the stuff the British came up with, right?"

"Right," Jenny said.

"Oh yeah," Catherine said, "finds way more prints than Ninhydrin."

"We've got something," Jenny said. "Look here."

The expert held up the original note: a black print, the side of the author's palm presumably, and several fingerprints in various places, dotted the page.

Jenny grinned. "Looks like the writer tried to wipe the paper clean of prints. These shit-for-brains never seem to grasp fingerprints are ninety-nine-and-a-half percent water. They're *in* the document, not on it."

Fewer fingerprints showed up on the new letter, but there were some to play with.

"Your fingerprint tech'll tell you these two prints don't match," Jenny predicted. "The letters were written by different people, and the fingerprints will prove it, as well as the handwriting differences. Additionally, the writing style—the amount of schooling indicated—also suggests two authors; but that's a more subjective call."

Catherine looked at Nick. "So, now what are you thinking?"

"We already knew that Fortunato didn't run off with the stripper."

"Right."

"We also believe that she's still alive and well and living in L.A. as Joy Petty."

Nodding, Catherine said, "Yes, and we should know more about that when we get back and talk to Grissom."

Nick got up, pacing slowly. "So we have a forged note from Joy to our victim, right around the time of his murder . . . but why? Why was such a note written?"

"Whoever hired the killing planted it, obviously," Catherine said. "And it worked—Fortunato's disappearance was dismissed as just another guy with a seven-year itch that got scratched by running off with a younger woman."

Nick stopped pacing, spread his hands. "So—mob guys hire the killing, and plant the note . . . or have it planted."

Catherine shook her head. "Doesn't make any sense."

"Why not?"

"Okay, look at it from the mob end of the telescope. You don't want anybody to know you killed this guy—you don't even want it officially known the welsher is dead. You instruct your hired assassin to hide the body where it won't be found for years, if at all, then you write this letter to make it appear Fortunato left town with his girlfriend."

"Yeah, right," Nick said. "That all hangs together."

Catherine smiled. "Does it? If you do all that, why do you allow your assassin to sign the body? Give it the old trademark double tap?"

"Why not?"

"Because if the body is found, you know damn well it's going to look like a mob hit to the cops. What did it look like to us?"

"But the Deuce, he's a mob hitter . . ."

"No, Nicky," Catherine said. "He's a freelancer. His best customers are organized crime types; but they're not necessarily his only customers."

Nick was seeing it now, shaking his head, disappointed in himself. "Grissom always says, 'assume nothing,' and what did we do? Assumed it was the mob."

"If it wasn't," Catherine said, "it was a perfect set-up for anybody who wanted Fortunato dead, for personal reasons or business or any motive. Already owing bookies out east, Fortunato was a sure bet to have a contract put out on him, if the mobbed-up casino owners knew he was embezzling from the casino. Instant blame."

"If somebody else hired the Deuce—who was it?"

"Ever notice every time we answer one question on this case," Catherine said, "we end up asking ourselves another, brand-new one?" She turned to the document examiner. "Jenny, how much writing would you need to find a match on these two letters?"

Jenny's answer was automatic. "When you get a suspect, don't take a handwriting sample—that's for shit. Get me a sample they've already written, grocery list, anything."

"And if we can't?"

"Then, what the hell—get a new sample." The petite woman shrugged. "There are some things you can't disguise."

"How big a sample?" Catherine asked.

"Couple of sentences, at least. More is better."

"Usually is," Nick said.

"Thanks, Jenny," Catherine said. "You're the best."

"Not hardly," she said. "My father was."

Catherine nodded. "We'll be back when we've got something."

Jenny returned to some waiting work. "I'll be here till five, and you can page me after that—long as you don't need me tonight."

"What happened to your fabled 'twenty-four-hour service'?" Catherine kidded her.

"Don't break my balls," Jenny said. "I got choir practice."

Catherine guided the wide-eyed Nick out of the office, and, as they drove back down the Strip, Nicky behind the wheel, Catherine punched a speed-dial number on her cell phone. It only rang once.

"O'Riley," came the gruff voice.

"Is Marge Kostichek still with you?"

"Yep."

"No change in her story?"

"Nope."

"You gonna cut her loose?"

"Yep."

"She's in the room with you right now, isn't she?"

"Yep."

". . . Okay, we're going to get you a court order for nontestimonial identification."

"Say what?"

"A writing sample and fingerprints."

"Oh! All right."

Catherine heard Marge Kostichek's voice in the background. "Aren't you the gabby one?"

Catherine said, "I'll call Grissom—you should have the paper you need in less than an hour."

"I like the sound of this." He disconnected.

So did she; then she called Grissom, who said he'd take care of the court order and get it to O'Riley.

"Have either of you slept?" he asked.

"Earlier this year," she said, with a sigh. "Haven't eaten in recent memory, either."

"Well, stop and eat, at least. We're going to get sloppy if we don't watch ourselves. . . . I'll handle things here for a while."

"Thanks. We'll be back soon."

She hit END, leaned back in the seat; she wished Grissom hadn't reminded her how tired she was.

"What did he say?" Nick asked.

"That we should eat."

"Good. I haven't eaten since I got a bear claw out of the vending machine about twelve hours ago."

The Harley-Davidson Cafe looked like a cross between a fifties style diner, a pub, and a high-end heavy metal club. Though she'd been past it many times, Catherine had never eaten here before—she seldom stopped at tourist places like this. She made a decent living, but not enough to regularly afford eight-dollar hamburgers, and still raise a daughter.

An American flag made out of three-inch anchor chain filled one wall, all the way up to the thirty-foot ceiling, well above the open second-floor gameroom. A conveyer running through the restaurant, the bar, the gift shop out front and up to the second floor, carried twenty antique Harleys in a constant parade.

While waiting for Nick's lemonade and Catherine's iced tea, they talked the case.

"All right," Catherine said, "if the mob didn't kill Fortunato, who did?"

He thought about that. "How about the wife? Always the first place to look. And he was fooling around on her, after all."

"I don't know," Catherine said. "She seems pretty genuinely distraught, finally finding out he's dead . . . but her anger for Joy sure hasn't ebbed, over the passage of time."

"What about her boyfriend?"

The waitress set their drinks in front of them, took their order, and Catherine suffered through the requisite flirting ("Aikake" was a "beautiful name," according to Nick, and "Hawaiian," according to the waitress).

"You ready now?" Catherine asked as the waitress hip-swayed away.

"Sorry. The boyfriend?"

"Gerry Hoskins. Annie Fortunato claims he wasn't even in the picture when Malachy disappeared, but no one's checked the story."

"Someone should."

"That's why God made the likes of Jim Brass."

"I was wondering. Any other ideas?"

"How about Marge Kostichek?"

He shrugged. "She lied about knowing Joy, yeah—but what the hell motive could she have?"

Catherine sighed. "I don't know. How's that for an answer?"

Nick talked up over Steppenwolf. "What about Joy

herself? She disappeared the same day—and until we found that letter we had no idea she was alive."

"But the letter from fifteen years ago probably isn't from Joy—why hire somebody killed, and then plant a forged letter that would've been more convincing had you written it yourself?"

"My head is starting to hurt."

Catherine was thinking. "I wonder if Grissom had any luck with the California DMV."

"Later," Nick said, gazing up hungrily.

Their food had arrived—whether it was the waitress or the cheeseburger that put that look on his face, Catherine didn't really care to know.

In less than a day they had gone from identifying the killer back to square-one as they tried to figure out who paid for the Deuce to whack Malachy Fortunato. Perhaps, Nick did have the right idea. For now, maybe she should just eat her chicken sandwich and try to forget about the sudden multitude of suspects they had.

After lunch, Catherine dropped Nick off at HQ, so he could begin going through the evidence again. Such a reappraisal was always a necessary aspect of scientific criminal investigation, because new information and perspectives continually put the evidence in a different light. But if they were going to catch the person who hired the killer, that would likely depend upon matching the fingerprints on the documents, and Jenny Northam matching the handwriting.

Catherine wasn't far from Annie Fortunato's residence when her cell phone rang.

"Hey, it's Nick. Grissom had Joy Petty's driver's license photo waiting for me here when I got back."

"And?"

"It's her, all right. Older, not so cute, but it's her—Monica Petty or Joy Starr or Joy Petty or—"

"A rose by any name." Catherine's hand tightened on the wheel of the Tahoe. "Tell O'Riley or Brass—maybe one of them can go out to L.A. and interview her."

"Speaking of O'Riley," Nick said, "he got the fingerprints and writing sample from Marge Kostichek."

"Good—just pulling up in front of the Fortunato house," she said. "Be back in an hour."

"Later," he said, and disconnected.

Catherine parked the car and walked up to the door, the smaller version of her field kit in one hand. A single dim light shone through the living room curtains. Catherine knocked on the door.

After a moment, Annie Fortunato opened the door slowly. Though she was completely dressed, in a blue T-shirt and darker blue shorts, she looked a little disheveled; as usual, a glowing cigarette was affixed to thin white lips. "Hi, Miz Willows—come on in, come on in."

Catherine stepped inside.

Smiling, Mrs. Fortunato asked, "What can I do for you?"

A smell Catherine instantly recognized—Kraft macaroni and cheese—wafted through from the front room; it wasn't long after lunch.

"I apologize for not calling first . . ."

"Hey, no problem." She took a drag off the cigarette. "I know you're trying to help."

"I'm glad you understand that. I need to get a set of fingerprints from you."

Her eyes wide, Mrs. Fortunato said, "Pardon?"

"I need a set of your prints—I need them from Gerry, too."

"Why?" The warmth was gone from the woman's voice now.

"We found fingerprints on the Joy Starr note. In your husband's effects?"

"Why on earth . . ."

Hoskins's voice floated in from the back of the house. "What is it, Annie?"

Mrs. Fortunato turned and, in a loud hard voice, called, "Catherine Willows is here—she needs our *fingerprints!*" Then she turned back to Catherine and rage tightened the haggard features. "You think one of us did it? . . . hell, I didn't even know Gerry then. He didn't even live in this town."

The awkwardness of it lay heavy on the shoulders of the already-tired Catherine. "It's just a formality really, to make it easier . . . you know, to eliminate you from the others."

But the more Mrs. Fortunato thought about it, the more worked up she got. "You think I killed my own husband? I thought you were my friend."

"Mrs. Fortunato . . ."

Smoky spittle flew. "You bitch! How dare you come around here?"

Catherine held up her hands, tried to explain. "Honestly, Mrs. Fortunato, I'm not even considering the possibility that you killed your husband," she lied. At this point, she only knew she didn't want to leave without those prints. "But when we catch who did this terrible thing, their lawyer is going to be looking for any way to get his client off—including implicating either you or Gerry in the murder."

Mrs. Fortunato stood there frozen; she had been listening, at least. Catherine, with relief, watched as the woman's anger evaporated.

Hoskins came in from the bedroom, still pulling on a shirt, as he tried to zip his jeans with one hand. "You all right?" he asked.

Catherine wondered if she'd interrupted something—dessert, after the macaroni and cheese, maybe.

"She wants to take our fingerprints, yours and mine, she says."

"What shit is—"

"So that if they catch whoever killed Mal, their lawyer won't be able to implicate us."

They both looked at Catherine now—suspicion in their eyes.

Wearily, she leveled with them. "Look—it's my job to find out who murdered Malachy. And you're both going to be considered suspects, now that his body has finally been found."

"So you are just a bitch," the woman said.

"Listen to me—please."

Hoskins wrapped a protective arm around Mrs. Fortunato. "How in hell you could ever think . . ."

"I'm not your friend," Catherine snapped. "And I don't have an opinion one way or the other. I follow the evidence—that's my job. That's why I was digging in your driveway last night—that wasn't for fun. The more evidence I have, whether it convicts or exonerates, gets me closer to finding out who murdered Malachy Fortunato, and bringing that person or persons to justice. Not just the hired killer, but the person—or persons—who hired him . . . whether it was the mob, you, or someone else altogether."

Stunned, the pair just stared at her. Hoskins kept his arm around Mrs. Fortunato, but said, finally, "How can we help?"

Sighing, relieved but weary, she started over: "I need fingerprints from both of you."

The man nodded. "Can you do it here, or do we have to go to the station?"

From her field kit, Catherine removed a portable fingerprint kit. "We can do it here." She wanted to kick herself for botching this so badly. It shouldn't have gone like this; thank God Grissom wasn't around.

Mrs. Fortunato seemed embarrassed. "I'm sorry for calling you . . . for what I said."

Managing to summon up a gentle smile, Catherine said, "I'm sorry if I misled you in any way. I know this isn't how you thought things would go . . . but I have to investigate everything, every aspect—good or bad, comfortable or uncomfortable."

"I know, I know. It's just all been so . . . emotional. Gerry and I are both on edge. I'm sure you folks are too."

Every day, Grissom would remind them, *we meet people on the worst day of their lives.*

Catherine printed them quickly, now in a rush to get the hell out of there. She had just opened new wounds in this old affair, and she wanted to slip away as swiftly as possible.

As she finished and handed Hoskins a paper towel, to wipe off the ink, he said, "Thank you," and Catherine said, "No, thank you, Mr. Hoskins."

He walked her to the door. "Ms. Willows."

"Yes?"

"One favor?"

"Try."

He swallowed. "Catch the son of a bitch."

Her eyes met his and held. "Oh, Mr. Hoskins. I will. I will."

13

In Henderson, Warrick—with Conroy riding in front, Sara in back—guided the Tahoe down Fresh Pond Court, looking at street numbers; this was a walled (not gated) housing development, designed for, if not the rich, definitely the well-off. When the SUV pulled up at the house in question, Brass's Taurus was already parked in front, Grissom in the passenger seat. The two CSIs and the homicide detective got out and jogged up to the unmarked vehicle, Warrick taking the lead.

The stucco ranch was the color the local real estate agents called "desert cream," and sported the obligatory tile roof, with a two-car attached garage and a well-manicured lawn. Not many houses in the area could boast so richly green a lawn, or even grass for that matter; most front yards were either dirt or rock. This one rivaled a golf-course green, but instead of a flagged hole, a single sapling rose right in the middle. The rambling house had a quiet dignity that said "money"—no, Warrick thought, it whispered the word.

"Somebody made the American dream pay off," Warrick, leaning against the roof of the Taurus, said to his boss. "You been up to the door yet?"

His expression blank, Grissom still had his eyes on the place. He said, "When we got here. Nobody home. Where have you been?"

A sheepish half-grin tugged a corner of Warrick's mouth. "We kinda got lost."

"How many CSIs does it take to screw in a light bulb?" Brass asked, sitting behind the wheel.

"Two and a homicide detective, apparently," Sara said. "Conroy's with us."

"Hey, it's a new neighborhood," Warrick said. "Last time I was out this way, it was scrub brush and prairie dogs."

"Skip it," Grissom said. "Nobody home anyway."

Conroy had gone around the other side of the vehicle, to talk to Brass; she was asking him, "You want me to check around back?"

"We don't have a warrant," Brass said. "We're gonna step carefully on this—case like this, you don't want to risk a technicality."

"Almost looks deserted," Sara, sidling up next to Warrick, asked her seated boss. "Nobody home, or does maybe nobody live here?"

A dry wind rustled the leaves of the front yard sapling.

"Furniture visible through the front windows," Grissom said, "and the power company, water company, and county clerk all agree—this is the residence of one Barry Hyde."

"You don't let any grass grow," Warrick said.

"Except for occasionally getting lost, neither do you."

Warrick took that as the compliment it was.

"In fact, I think we've earned a break," Grissom said.

"Huh?" Sara said.

"I think we should go check out the new video rentals," Grissom said.

Warrick, pushing off from the roof of the Taurus, said, "Might be some interesting new releases, at that."

Conroy stayed with the Taurus, at the residence, while Brass piled into the Tahoe, in back with Sara, with Warrick and Grissom in front.

From the backseat Brass said, "If you'd like me to drive, I do know the way."

"I came up with this address," Warrick said, trying to keep the edge out of his voice. "I'll do the honors."

Barry Hyde's video store was close to his house, just a few turns away and onto Wigwam Parkway. Glad he had his sunglasses on, Warrick turned into the Pecos Legacy Center parking lot, where glass storefronts reflected bright afternoon sunlight. A-to-Z Video—a typical non-chain store of its kind with a neon sign in the window and movie poster after poster taped there—sat at the far end of the strip mall, a discount cigarette store its next-door neighbor.

Brass led the way into the video store, Grissom hanging back, in observer mode. To Warrick, it looked like every other non-chain video store he had ever been in—new releases around the outside wall, older movies in the middle. DVD rentals filled the section of the wall to the right of the cash register island, which was centered between the two IN and OUT doors. At the rear of the store was a door that presumably led to the storage area and the manager's office.

Behind the counter, in the cashier's island, stood the only person in the store, a petite American Indian woman of about twenty, a blue imitation Blockbuster uniform over slacks and T-shirt, her straight black hair worn short. Her name tag said SUE.

Fairly perky, and perhaps a trifle surprised to have customers, she asked, "Hi—welcome to A-to-Z Video. Are you looking for a particular title?"

"Sue, I'm looking for Barry Hyde," Brass said. He didn't get out his badge—this seemed to be a toe in the water.

The cashier smiled. "Mr. Hyde is out for the day. May I be of assistance?"

"When do you expect him back?"

"I'm sorry. He's not going to be available until after the weekend."

Now Brass displayed his badge in its leather wallet. "Could you tell me why he's not available?"

Seeing that badge, the cashier's cheerfulness turned to mild apprehension. "Oh, well—I'd like to help you, but I'm just . . . uh, maybe you should talk to Patrick."

Brass's melancholy face twitched a sort of smile. "And who is Patrick?"

"The assistant manager. He's in charge until Mr. Hyde gets back."

"I'd like to talk to Patrick. Is he around?"

"In the back," she said. She pressed an intercom button and said, "Patrick, someone to see you?"

The intercom said, "Who?"

"I think it's the police. . . . I mean, it *is* the police."

Patrick said, "Uh . . . uh, just a minute, uh . . . I'll be . . . uh . . . right . . . uh . . . out."

Four minutes later, more or less, Grissom was prowling the store like each video was potential evidence; but the others—Warrick included—were getting impatient.

Warrick realized that mid-afternoon wasn't a busy time for any video rental store; but this place seemed particularly dead. He noted the posted rental rates—they weren't bargains.

Brass leaned against the counter. "Sue—would you rattle Patrick's cage for me again?"

The cashier was about to touch the intercom button when the door in the back opened and ambling out came a zit-faced kid who seemed younger than the cashier. Bleached blond with a dark goatee and black mid-calf shorts, he had a sharp, short nose, small lips and green eyes with pupils the size of pinheads; but for the blue polo shirt with A-to-Z stitched over the breast pocket, he looked like a guitar player in a metal band.

As the kid stepped by him, Warrick noticed Patrick (as his name tag confirmed) smelled like a combination of Tic Tacs and weed. Which explained their four-minute wait.

The assistant manager said, "Can I . . . uh . . . like, help you?"

Brass seemed to be repressing a laugh; they'd sent for a manager and got back Maynard G. Krebs. "Are you Patrick?"

He thought about it. Then, without having to refer to his name tag, he said, "Yeah. McKee. Is my last name."

"Patrick, we'd like to talk to you about your boss—Barry Hyde."

The kid's sense of relief was palpable in the room and Warrick turned away to keep from laughing out loud. He pretended to study the new DVD release wall so he could still listen to the conversation.

Patrick asked, "What about Mr. Hyde?"

"He's out of town?"

Nodding, Patrick said, "Until Monday."

"Is Mr. Hyde out of town a lot?"

The kid had to think about this question for a while, too. Finally, he managed, "Some."

"For how long? How often?"

"He's been doing it since I've been here." Shrug. "Uh . . . eight months."

Brass shook his head. "That's not what I meant, Patrick. I mean, how long a period of time is he generally away?"

"Sometimes a couple of days, sometimes a week."

Warrick pulled a DVD box off the shelf and pretended to read the back—*Real Time: Siege at Lucas Street Market*. He knew Hyde couldn't be gone for long stretches, because the man had rarely missed his regular Monday and Wednesday visits to the Beachcomber.

Patience thinning, Brass was asking, "Do you know where Mr. Hyde is now?"

Patrick thought about that one for a long time too. "No. I don't think he said."

"What if there's an emergency?"

The kid's face went blank. "Emergency?"

"Yeah, emergency. He's the boss. Don't you have a number to call if you get robbed or a customer has a heart attack in the store? Or maybe a valuable employee, like you, has a family crisis?"

"Oh, sure," Patrick said.

"Could you give us that number?"

"Yeah—nine-one-one."

Brass just looked at the kid. Then he blew out some air, and called back to Grissom, at the rear of the little group."You want to take a crack at this?"

Grissom put his hands up in surrender.

Warrick put the DVD box back—*100% Multi-angle!!!*—turned, and stepped forward. "Why don't you guys wait outside. I'll talk to Patrick."

Sara's eyes met Warrick's—they were on the same wavelength. She said, "Yeah, guys—I'll stay with Warrick."

Grissom, sensing something from his CSIs, turned to look at Brass, shrugging. "Any objection, Jim?"

"All right," Brass said. He said to Grissom, "Why don't you run me over to the house."

His car and Detective Conroy were there, after all.

"Sure," Grissom said. Then to Warrick and Sara: "Pick you up in fifteen."

Once the homicide cop and Grissom had left, Warrick turned to the assistant manager. "Okay, Patrick, truth or dare—just how stoned are you?"

The eyes widened; however, the pupils remained pinpoints. "No way!"

Sara said, "Cut the crap, Patrick. Dragnet has left the building—this is the Mod Squad you're talking to. . . . We know there's stoned, and there's stoned."

Patrick seemed to have lost the ability to form words. He stood there with his mouth hanging open.

"Why don't the three of us," Warrick said, slipping

his arm around the skinny kid, "go into the back office, and just chill a little."

"Not the back room. I mean . . . uh . . . it's . . . uh . . . private."

"That's why we're going to use it," Sara said. "Because it's private—customer comes in, we won't be in the way."

The beleaguered Patrick looked to the cashier for help, but she turned her back, suddenly very interested in sorting returned videos. "Uh . . . I guess so . . ."

"Cool," Warrick said. He led the way to the back and was the first one through the door. The cubicle reeked of weed, even though the kid had lit three sticks of incense before he'd come out front. The "office" consisted of a shabby metal desk, a cheap swivel chair, some two-by-four-and-plywood shelves piled with screener tapes, and walls decorated with video promo posters, mostly for XXX-rated tapes.

"Sorry," Patrick said, coming through the door next. "It's kind of . . . uh . . . grungy back here."

"And," Sara said, just behind him, "it smells like Cheech and Chong's van."

"On a Friday night," Warrick added.

Unable not to, the kid grinned at that.

She wide-eyed the porno posters. "You actually carry this trash?"

Patrick's silly grin disappeared and professionalism kicked in: he was the assistant manager of A-to-Z Video, after all. He said "*American Booty* and *The Boner Collector* are our top two adult rental titles. You have to reserve them a couple weeks in advance."

"I'll pass," Sara said.

"So, then," Warrick said, sitting on the edge of the desk, "store does a pretty brisk business, huh?"

Patrick snorted. "Yeah, right, whatever."

Sara asked, "Is it always like this—tumbleweed blowing through the place?"

"Lot of the time," Patrick admitted. "We do pretty good on the weekends sometimes, but there's a Blockbuster on the next block, and the supermarket, at the other end of the mall? They rent tapes, too."

"Does Mr. Hyde seem concerned about business?"

"What do you mean?"

"I mean, if it's slow, do you have meetings—pep talks, try to figure out strategy, lower your prices. . . ."

"No, not really. Barry's pretty cool for a boss. He's got a wicked sense of humor—really dark, man, I mean brutal."

I'll bet, Warrick thought.

Patrick was saying, "He doesn't give us a lot of shit . . ." He glanced at Sara. ". . . trouble about stuff."

"Does Hyde come in every day? When he's in town, I mean?"

"Yeah, yeah, he does. He doesn't stay very long, most days. He comes in, maybe orders some tapes, checks the books, goes and makes the deposit from the night before. Oh, and sometimes he brings in munchies like doughnuts and stuff."

"How many people work here?"

"Besides Mr. Hyde, four. Me, Sue—she's out front now—Sapphire and Ronnie. Me and Sue are usually paired up, Sapphire and Ronnie, same. We trade off every other week working days and nights. This week we're on days, next week we'll work nights. We don't get bored that way, and then everybody can kind of, like, have a life, you know?"

"That does sound cool," Warrick said. "We just work the night shift."

"But it's day," Patrick said, shrewdly.

Sara said, "We like to think of it as flex hours. How much do you make, working here, Patrick?"

"Eight-fifty an hour. Me and Ronnie, I mean, 'cause we're both assistant managers. Sapphire and Sue are makin' seven-fifty an hour."

"Not bad pay," Sara said, "for sitting here getting stoned."

Patrick tried to parse that—nothing judgmental had been in Sara's tone, but she was with the cops—but finally he said, "I only do that if it's real dead."

"Which is a lot of the time."

Patrick's shrug was affirmative.

Warrick, feeling Sara was getting off track, asked, "Do you remember, exactly, when Mr. Hyde has been out of town?"

"Oh, hell—all his trips are marked on the calendar."

Warrick traded glances with Sara, then asked, "What calendar is that, Patrick?"

"This one," the kid said, pointing to the July Playmate, who loomed over the desk.

"Mind if I have a look?" Warrick asked.

"No, but . . . don't you need a warrant or something?"

Warrick's reply was casual. "Not if you don't mind."

"Oh, well. Sure. Go ahead."

Flipping the pages with a pen, Warrick read off the dates and Sara copied them down. When they finished, she used the little camera from her purse to take shots of the calendar, just in case.

Patrick became a tad nervous, when Sara started shooting the photos, and Warrick put an arm around the young man. "Patrick, I'm going to make you a deal."

"A deal?"

"Yeah, if you don't tell Mr. Hyde that we were here asking questions, I won't bust your ass."

"Bust my ass . . ."

"You know—for felony possession."

"Felony? I've only got half a . . ." Patrick froze as he realized what he was saying. His eyes looked pleadingly from Warrick to Sara. "I mean . . . I thought you guys were cool. . . ."

Warrick's voice went cold. "Patrick, have we got a deal?"

Reluctantly, Patrick nodded. "Yeah."

Outside in the sunshine, Warrick said to Sara, "There's something not right here."

"More than pot smoke smells in there," Sara agreed. "The manager's never around, doesn't worry about business, and lives in an expensive new house in an upscale neighborhood."

"And he's gone from time to time—just short hops."

"Like maybe the Deuce *isn't* retired, you mean?"

"That does come to mind. We better go do some research about Mr. Barry Hyde."

That was when Grissom swung in, in the Tahoe; and on the way back, Warrick driving, they told their supervisor what they'd learned—and what they thought.

"I want that list of dates," Grissom said, "when Hyde was out of town."

Other than that, however, Grissom said nothing.

Which always made Warrick very, very nervous.

Culpepper was waiting in Grissom's office, the FBI agent having helped himself to the chair behind the desk, his feet up on its corner. "Hey, buddy, how're you doing?"

Feeling his anger rising, Grissom breathed slowly and stayed calm. "Why, I'm just fine, Special Agent Culpepper—and how are you?"

Brass came into the office, saw the FBI agent, and said, "Our government tax dollars at work."

Culpepper's feet came off the desk and he sat up straight, but he said nothing for several endlessly long moments. At last, he said, "I hear you guys got something on the Deuce."

Grissom kept his face passive, though he wondered where Culpepper got his information. "You heard wrong."

"I've been waiting here for half an hour. Where were you, Grissom?"

"Lunch. I don't remember having an appointment with the FBI."

"I heard you were so dedicated, you don't even find time for lunch."

"Today he did," Brass said. "With me. We would have invited you, but you didn't let us know you were coming."

Grissom said, "Was there a purpose to your visit, Culpepper, or are you just fishing?"

The FBI agent's smile was almost a sneer; he straightened his tie while he stalled to come up with an answer. "I stopped by to tell you that we heard the Deuce has left the area."

Grissom allowed his skepticism to show through a little. "If you think he's gone, why are you still nosing around here?"

"Just covering all the bases, buddy. Like you, this is my turf—keeping my fellow law enforcement professionals informed. You should know that."

"Covering your what?" Brass asked.

Culpepper rose and came around the desk, stopping in the doorway. He beamed at Grissom. "Too bad you didn't come up with anything, buddy. I figured if anybody would catch this guy, it would be you. They say you're the number two crime lab in the country . . . not counting the FBI, of course."

"Yeah," Brass said, "your lab's got the reputation we're all longing for."

Culpepper made a tsk-tsk in his cheek. "Must be hard not being number one."

"We try harder," Grissom said.

The FBI agent nodded. "You'll need to. Good luck, gentlemen—keep the good thought."

And Culpepper was gone.

"Damnit," Brass said, leaning out into the hall, making sure the FBI agent wasn't lingering."How did he know?"

"Maybe he doesn't."

"Maybe he does."

Grissom shrugged. "You talked to the county clerk, the utilities, and I don't know how many other agencies."

"He's not helping us, is he? He's watching us. Why?"

"Easier than solving the case himself maybe—steps in and takes the credit." Grissom shook his head, disgusted. "What a backward motivation for this line of work. . . . Until just now, I was tempted to give him the list of dates Warrick gave me."

"Of times Hyde's been out of town this year?"

"Yeah. See what unsolved murders or missing persons cases match up to those dates."

"Give me that list, and I'll do what I can."

Grissom did.

"You think the killer's still active?" Brass asked.

Grissom got back behind the desk, sitting. "We know he is—he shot Dingelmann. Maybe he stopped doing mob-related work and his contracts are with individuals now. That could be the reason he hasn't turned up on the FBI's radar in the last four years."

"Are you convinced Hyde is the Deuce?"

"No. Too early. Hell of a lead, though. Warrick gets the MVP of the day."

On cue, Warrick appeared in the office doorway, Sara just behind him; Grissom waved them in.

"The esteemed Agent Culpepper looks steamed," Warrick said.

"Good," said Brass.

"Saw him in the parking lot," Sara said. "What did you say to him?"

Eyes hooded, Brass said, "We just did our best to share as much with him as he shared with us."

Warrick said, "Bupkis, you mean."

"Oh, we didn't give him that much," Brass said.

Shifting gears, Warrick fell into a chair across from

Grissom, saying, "Something stinks about that video store."

"Besides cannabis?" Grissom asked innocently.

Warrick and Sara smiled, avoiding their boss's eyes.

Brass picked up on the train of thought. "You're referring to that horde of customers we saw in there today."

"Even for an off time," Warrick said, "that was grim."

With a twinkle, Sara said, "And Patrick—who was very open, you know, to young people like us—admitted they don't ever do a lot of business."

"Yet the four kids that work there," Warrick said, "are pulling down decent money, and Barry Hyde doesn't seem to care about the lack of cash flow."

"Money laundry?" Brass asked.

Grissom ignored that, saying to the two CSIs, "Okay, let's take Barry Hyde to the proctologist. Sara, I want you to look into his personal life."

"If he has one, I'll find it."

"Photocopy these," Brass said, handing her his field notebook, indicating the pages, "and get that back to me. . . . This is what we do know about Hyde, from the phone calls I made around."

She scanned the notes quickly. "Not much, so far."

"It's a place to start," Grissom said. "Find out more. Warrick."

"Yeah?"

"Try coming at this through the business door."

"You got it."

Then Warrick and Sara went off on their respective missions, and Brass departed as well, leaving Grissom lost in thought, trying to figure out what the hell

Culpepper was up to. For someone supposedly sharing information because both groups were looking to bring the same animal to justice, Culpepper hadn't contributed a thing to their investigation—just a vague, unsubstantiated notion that the Deuce was no longer in the area.

How long he'd been pondering this, Grissom didn't know; but he was pulled out of it by a knock on his open door. He looked up to see Sara standing there.

"You look confused," he said.

"I am confused." She came in, plopped down across from him. "This Barry Hyde thing just keeps getting weirder and weirder."

"Weird how?"

She shifted, tucked a foot under her. "Let's take his college years, for example."

"Let's."

She flashed a mischievous smile. "You can get a lot of stuff off the Internet these days, Grissom."

"So I hear. Some of it's even legal."

"Legal enough—lots of records and stuff you can go through."

"Less how, more what," he said, sitting forward. "Did you find Barry Hyde's college records?"

"Sort of," she said, wrinkling her nose. "Barry Hyde has a degree in English from the University of Idaho."

"Our Barry Hyde?"

She nodded, going faster now, in her element. "Only thing is, I went to the University of Idaho website and they have no record of him."

"You mean they wouldn't give you his records?"

"No. I mean they have no record of his ever having been a student there."

"Maybe he didn't graduate."

"You don't have to graduate to get into the records, Grissom. He didn't matriculate."

"Anything else?"

"Oh yeah. Everything for the last five years is fine. Barry Hyde's a sterling citizen. Bank loans paid on time, credit cards paid up, member of the Rotary, the Henderson Chamber of Commerce, the guy even pays his traffic tickets."

"Good for him."

"But before that? Hyde's military record says he was stationed overseas, but I found a medical file where he claimed to have never been out of the country. The whole thing's nuts. Information either doesn't check out, or is contradicted somewhere else. This guy's past got dumped into a historical Cuisinart."

"Or maybe," Grissom said, eyes tightening, "it came out of one."

14

Exiting the break room with a cup of coffee, Catherine almost bumped into O'Riley, who was bounding up to her, a file folder in hand.

"Well, hello," she said.

Grinning, O'Riley said eagerly, "I've got a buddy in LAPD. Tavo Alverez."

"Good for you, Sergeant."

"Good for all of us—he tracked down Joy Petty."

"Great! Walk with me . . . I've got to catch up with Nick. . . ."

O'Riley did. "Tavo stopped by the Petty woman's place in Lakewood—she's unemployed right now, but I guess she's mostly a waitress. Unmarried, lives with a guy, a truck driver."

"Okay, she's alive and well—but is she Joy Starr?"

"Oh yeah, sure, she admitted that freely. Tavo said she seemed kinda proud of her days in 'show business,' once upon a time. Joy Starr, Monica Petty, Joy Petty—one gal."

Catherine stopped, their footsteps on the hard hallway floor like gunshots that trailed off. Her gaze locked with O'Riley's less-than-alert sagacious stare. "Now that we've confirmed that, we need to have Joy Petty interviewed in more depth."

He shrugged his massive shoulders. "I can work this through Tavo—he's a good guy."

"Can you fly over there, or even drive?"

"I think we're better off usin' Tavo. I mean, he's willing, and he's tops."

"Then get back in touch with him," Catherine said, walking again, heading toward the lab where Nicky worked. "We need Joy Petty interviewed in detail about her relationship with Marge Kostichek."

"Okay, but Tavo phoned me from the site of a homicide, to give me that much. I mean, it is L.A.—they do have a crime of their own go down, sometimes."

"Stay on him, Sarge."

"Will do. Here." He handed her the folder. "Background check on Gerry Hoskins."

"Good!"

Another shrug. "Seems to be a right guy, got his own contracting business—you know, remodeling and stuff."

"Thanks, O'Riley. Fine job."

He smiled and headed off. Catherine caught up with Nick in the lab where he was already poring over the fingerprints.

"What do we know?" she asked as she came up next to him.

"It's looking like Gerry Hoskins is in the clear." Nick sat on a stool before a computer monitor whose screen displayed two fingerprints, one from Joy Starr's note to Fortunato, the other from Hoskins's fingerprint card. "This is not his print."

Catherine nodded and held up the file folder. "O'Riley just gave me this. Hoskins's background check."

"What's it say?"

She opened the folder, gave its contents a quick scan, saying, "Carpenter, got his own business, lived in Scott's Bluff, Nebraska till, seven years ago. Got divorced, moved here, been relatively successful, moved in with Annie Fortunato . . ." She did the math. ". . . five and a half years ago."

"Okay," Nick said, "one down."

Catherine filled him in on what O'Riley had told her about Joy Petty.

"An in-depth interview with her could really fill in some blanks," Nick said.

"We won't know until O'Riley's guy gets back, and that could be hours. For now, we stay at it."

The next print he brought up belonged to Annie Fortunato.

"The wife's prints don't match the forged note, either," Nick said.

Silently, Catherine gave thanks; she had hoped that Annie Fortunato was innocent. Grissom could preach science, science, science all he wanted: these were still human beings they were dealing with.

And the CSIs were human, too—even Grissom. Probably.

"This print, though," Nick said, bringing up a third one, "is a very definite match. Textbook."

Catherine leaned in. "The former owner of the strip club?"

"Yeah—Marge Kostichek." Nick's smile was bittersweet; he shook his head. "I'm almost sorry—the salty old girl is a real character."

"Character or not," Catherine said, studying the screen, "she wrote that note to Malachy Fortunato."

Nick's eyes narrowed. "I don't think it really was written for Malachy to read, do you?"

"No. Our friend Mr. Fortunato was probably tucked away under that trailer, by then—a fresher corpse than when we found him, but a corpse."

"But why would Marge sign Joy Starr's name to a note like that? What motive would the old girl have for killing Fortunato?"

"*Having* him killed," Catherine reminded him. "Working strip clubs in a mobbed-up town like Vegas used to be, Marge might well have access to somebody like the Deuce."

Nick just sat there, absorbing it all; finally he said, "I think we need a search warrant."

"Oh yeah."

Hopping off his stool, Nick asked, "We better round up O'Riley—seen him lately?"

"Just," Catherine said. "He's probably back in the bullpen by now. . . . You get your field kit organized, and I'll go tell Grissom what we're up to—and see if he can't find a judge to get us that warrant."

Ten minutes later, Catherine and Nick were moving quickly into the detectives' bullpen. Two rows of desks lined the outer walls and another ran down the center, detectives in busted and battered swivel chairs behind gray metal desks about the color of Malachy

Fortunato's desiccated flesh. The skells, miscreants, and marks that made up their clientele sat in hard straightback metal chairs bolted to the floor, to prevent their use as weapons.

O'Riley was nowhere to be seen; his desk—the third one from the back on the far wall—looked like an aircraft carrier. His in-out baskets served as the tower, his phone perched on the corner like a parked fighter, and the desk top was as clean as a deserted flight deck.

Nick ran a finger over the surface and said, "I wonder if he does windows?"

Catherine called to Sanchez, the detective at the desk behind O'Riley's. "Where's he hiding?"

Without looking up from his one-finger typing, Sanchez said, "Do I look like his mother?"

"Just around the eyes and when you smile."

The detective graced her with a sarcastic smirk and resumed his hunt-and-pecking.

"Leave him a note," Nick said to her. "And we'll page him from the car."

There wasn't so much as a Post-it on that spotless desk top. She turned to Sanchez. "You got a . . ."

A small pad came flying at her and she caught it.

"Thanks." She wrote the Post-it, stuck in right on the phone, then, without looking, tossed the pad over Sanchez's way, heading out of the bullpen with Nick on her heels. When driven by a sense of urgency like this, Catherine felt frustrated by the minutiae of daily existence.

They were halfway to the suspect's house when Catherine's cell phone rang. "Willows," she said.

"It's O'Riley. I got your page, and I got your note.

I'm on my way. Somebody had to pick up the search warrant, y'know."

"Ah. You're leaving the courthouse?"

"Yeah, what am I . . . maybe five minutes behind you?"

"Yep. You want us to wait for you, Sarge?"

Nick stopped for a red light. "O'Riley?"

She nodded.

"Has he got the warrant?"

She nodded again.

"Tell him he better hurry if he wants to be there when we question her."

O'Riley's voice said in her ear, "I heard that. You tell him to wait till I get there."

And O'Riley clicked off.

Matter of factly, Catherine said to Nick, "He wants us to wait for him."

"Damn."

"It's procedure, Nick. His job—not ours."

"But it's our case. . . ."

As the light turned green and Nick eased the Tahoe into the intersection, he shook his head. Ahead of them the sun was just dipping below the horizon leaving behind a trail of purple and orange that danced against fluffy cumulus.

"He wants us to wait for him," Catherine repeated, not liking it any better than Nick, but accepting it.

Nick shrugged elaborately. "I don't see why. The old girl likes me. We'll just chat with her until O'Riley shows. Loosen her up."

Catherine said nothing.

Five minutes later, Nick pulled the Tahoe up in

front of Marge Kostichek's tiny paint-peeling bungalow. Darkness had all but consumed dusk, but no lights shone in the windows. For some nameless reason, Catherine felt a strange twinge in the pit of her stomach.

Nick opened the door of the SUV and unbuckled his seatbelt.

"Let's wait for O'Riley," she said reasonably. "How long can it take him to get here?"

"Why wait?"

"We should wait for O'Riley. We don't have a warrant."

But then they were going up the walk, and were at the front door, where Nick knocked. He threw her one of those dazzlers. "It'll be fine."

This is wrong, Catherine thought; she was the senior investigator on the unit—she should put her foot down. But the truth was, she was as anxious as Nick to follow this lead; and she knew that once O'Riley got here, she herself would take the investigative lead, anyway.

So why this apprehension, these butterflies?

No answer to Nick's knock, so he tried again and called, "Ms. Kostichek? It's Nick from the crime lab!"

Through the curtained window, Catherine saw a figure move in the gloomy grayness, someone with something in his or her hand—*was that shape . . . a gun?*

She shoved Nick off the porch to the left, her momentum carrying her with him just as a bullet exploded through the door and sailed off into the night. Another round made its small awful thunder and a second shot drilled through the door, at a lower trajectory, and spanged off the sidewalk.

Catherine and Nick lay sprawled in the dead brown bushes to the left of the front door.

"You all right?" she asked.

Shaken, startled, Nick managed, "I think so. How did you . . ."

She rolled off the shrubbery, pistol in her hand—she didn't even remember drawing it—and she said to Nick, "Head for the truck—I got your back . . . stay low." She lay on the lawn, gun trained on the front door.

Nick, shaken, was clearly afraid, but concerned for her. "I'll cover you. Never mind the Tahoe—just get the hell out of here."

"Damnit, Nick—we don't leave, we contain the scene. Get behind the truck, and call this in. Now, *move!*"

This time Nick didn't argue—he rolled out of the bushes, got to his knees, then blasted off like a sprinter coming out of the blocks, keeping low as he raced across the front yard.

Another shot splintered through the door and Catherine wanted to return fire, but who would she be shooting at? She couldn't blindly shoot at the house.

"Put your weapon down!" she yelled, remaining on her stomach, on the grass, handgun aimed at the doorway. "Come out with your hands high, and empty!"

Nothing.

Nick was already behind the Tahoe, his own pistol in hand. A distant siren wailed and Catherine knew help was on the way. Some neighbor had called 911.

"Come on, Cath," Nick yelled. "I've got you . . ."

But a bullet cracked the night and shattered its way

through the window and smashed the driver's side window of the Tahoe.

Nick ducked and Catherine took the opportunity to roll left, come up running, and plaster herself against the side of the house. Her heart pounding, gunshots echoing in her ringing ears, she glanced out front to make sure Nick was all right. She couldn't see him.

"Nicky—you okay?" she yelled.

"Peachy!"

The siren grew. Sliding along the clapboard side of the bungalow, she made her way toward the back. Only two windows were on this side of the house, the living room picture window, and one in what might be a back bedroom. She tried to see in the edge of the shattered picture window, around the border of the curtain, but it was just too damn dark. She was moving along the side of the house when she heard a car squeal to a halt in front—O'Riley.

"What the hell!" O'Riley was saying, and Nicky's voice, softer, the words not making their way to her. Then another three shots cracked from out front—O'Riley drawing fire now.

She took a hesitant step around the corner. If she could slip in through the back door, maybe she could get the drop on the old woman—if that was who'd been firing on them. Ducking down below a window, Catherine took a second step, then the back door flew open and she froze as a tall figure—male figure—in head-to-toe black bolted out the door and sprinted across the yard. Her pistol came up automatically, but she saw no weapon in the man's hands and did not fire.

She took off after him.

The perp ran with the easy grace of an athlete, but Catherine managed to keep pace with him for half a block before he vaulted a chain link fence, stopping for a split second on the other side, then speeding across the yard, jumping the fence on the other side before disappearing into the night.

"Damnit," she said, stopped at the first fence. She holstered the weapon, and walked back to the house, still trying to catch her breath.

When she got back out front, she found O'Riley pacing in the yard, talking to two uniformed officers, whose black-and-white at the curb, with its longbar, painted the night blue and red.

"Where's Nick?" she asked him.

O'Riley pointed. "Inside. . . . The woman's dead."

"What?"

He shook his head. "It's ugly in there, Catherine—double-tapped, just like Fortunato and Dingelmann."

She filled him in quickly, about the perp's escape, and he turned to the uniformed men, to start the search, and she went inside to help Nick process the scene.

Marge Kostichek lay facedown on the shabby living room rug, a large purple welt on her left cheek, her eyes mercifully closed. A gag made from a scarf encircled her head, blocking her mouth. A large crimson stain stood out where her mouth was. So much blood was on the floor, it was hard to find a place to stand without compromising the evidence.

"It's him," Nick said, his complexion a sickly white. "He got to Kostichek before we could. He even cut off her fingertips, like Fortunato. Two of them anyway—

we must have interrupted him." He swallowed thickly. "Judging from the gag, I think she bit through her tongue."

They heard another vehicle squeal to a halt outside. Within seconds, Grissom—his black attire not unlike the perp's—stood in the doorway.

"What were you doing here without O'Riley?" he demanded.

"O'Riley was on his way with the search warrant," Catherine said, covering. "We had no way of knowing the Deuce would be here."

"Tell me," Grissom said, and Catherine filled him in, in detail.

Then Grissom took a deep breath. "All right," he said. "Let's do the scene and see if maybe we can find a way to get this guy."

Catherine pointed to the floor. "If he's still using the same gun, these shell casings will be a great start."

Expressing his agreement with a nod, he jerked his cell phone out and punched speed-dial. ". . . Jim, get over to Hyde's house, now. Someone just killed Marge Kostichek. . . . I know—maybe he's on his way home right now. . . . Not yet, we're doing that now." He hit END, then turned to Catherine and Nick. "Find us what we need."

Catherine was already bagging shell casings.

Grissom, clearly pissed, said, "I don't like murders on my watch."

At the front doorway, O'Riley—keeping out of the way of the crime scene investigation—called Catherine over. Grissom came along.

O'Riley said to them, "I got a little good news—my man Tavo in L.A. just interviewed Joy Petty."

Catherine and Grissom exchanged glances, the latter prompting, "And?"

"Seems the Kostichek woman took Joy in as a runaway, raised her like a daughter. Joy says her 'mom' considered Malachy Fortunato a 'bad influence'—you know, a married man, a degenerate gambler, with the mob nipping at his heels. After Malachy disappeared, Joy says she was afraid the mob had killed him, so she took off, to protect herself."

Grissom asked, "Where is Joy now?"

"Still there at the stationhouse with Tavo—my LAPD contact."

"Have him take another run at her—but this time tell her about Marge's murder."

Catherine glanced at Grissom quizzically.

"Yeah?" O'Riley said. "Why?"

But now Catherine had caught up with her boss, saying, "Because Joy might stop protecting her mom, if she knows her mom is dead . . . particularly if she knows *how* her mom died."

O'Riley looked from one of them to the other. "No details spared?"

"None," Grissom said. "The LAPD uses digital tape for their interviews, right?"

"I think so. I mean, we do."

"Good. Tell your man Tavo I'm gonna want this interview sent up to our server, toot sweet, so we can download it."

O'Riley nodded and ambled out.

Grissom pitched in with them, as they looked for

footprints first. Nick used the electrostatic dust print lifter and pulled up a running-shoe print from the linoleum floor in the kitchen. Next they photographed the body, the living room, the kitchen and an open drawer that Catherine found in a back bedroom.

With Grissom's help, they fingerprinted everything the killer might have touched. While Nick did the flat surfaces, Catherine used Mikrosil to print the doorknobs, but she had seen the killer wearing gloves when she chased him. She didn't expect to get much and they didn't. She bagged all of Marge's shoes so they could later prove that none of them matched the print they got from the kitchen. Catherine found nothing in her search of the backyard or the alley. Then, shining her mini-flash on the top of the chain link fence, she saw something glimmer.

Moving closer, she found a few strands of black fiber and a small patch of blood. She snapped some photos and then, using a pair of wire cutters, snipped two of the ends off the top of the fence and deposited them in evidence bags.

She shared this with Grissom, who had spent much of his time in the house supervising their work, but also snooping around on his own.

"Come with me," Grissom said, and in the kitchen he pointed out a knife almost out of its holder on the counter, and, on the floor, a few drops of blood and some strands of gray hair.

Then Catherine followed Grissom into the living room, where he pointed out a suspiciously clear area on the cluttered writing desk—had something been taken?

Now Grissom was staring, apparently at the wall.

"You think you know how this went down," Catherine said, knowing that look.

"Yes," he said.

The Deuce knew they would never let up now. All he could do was cover his tracks as much as possible. He'd seen the article in the Las Vegas Sun *and knew they had stumbled onto Fortunato's mummified body. If the cops had that, how long until they found the woman?*

The old woman didn't think he knew about the younger one, but he did. It was his business to know. The stripper had been sleeping with the mark, so damn right he knew about her. According to the phone book, the old woman, Kostichek, still lived where she always had. That made it easier. He had no idea where the stripper was, but he would find out. That was part of the reason for his visit to the old woman.

He parked a couple of blocks away in the parking lot of a grocery store, no point in getting careless now. Taking his time, he walked a block and a half before cutting up the alley behind her house. Even though the sun had started to set, it still beat down on him, his black clothes absorbing the heat like a sponge, and he felt the sweat beginning to pool at the small of his back, behind his knees, and under his arms. A lighter color would have been cooler, but he knew he'd be here past dark and he might want to leave without being seen, so he wore the black.

He came up behind the house, pulling on black leather gloves as he edged closer. Looking around carefully, he tried to make sure no one saw him as he took the silencer from his pocket and screwed it on the handgun. Then he knocked lightly on her back door, stepping to one side so she would have to open both the inside door and the screen to see him. Reaching around, he knocked again, louder this time.

"Jesus jones, I'm coming!" she yelled.

The woman opened the door, said, "Who's there?" and then opened the screen and saw him.

She tried to pull the door shut, but he was much stronger, and jammed himself into the frame. Ducking back inside, she tried to close the inner door in his face, but again he overpowered her. She fell back against the stove, turned and reached for a knife from the block on the counter. He pressed the silenced snout of the automatic to her cheek and she froze.

Raising the noise-suppressed weapon, he cracked her across the face and she collapsed to the floor. Grabbing her by the hair, he dragged her, struggling, into the living room.

"Where is she?" he asked, crouching over her.

The old woman seemed confused. "Who?"

"The stripper—where is she?"

"Go to hell!"

Casually, he pulled a pair of garden clippers from his pocket. "I'm going to find out anyway. You can make this easy, or hard."

Her eyes filled with tears, but her jaw set and she said nothing.

"Hard it is," he said. Putting down the clippers, he picked up one of her scarves off the back of a chair. He gagged her with it, then picked up the clippers and closed them around the pinky of her left hand.

Tears running down her cheeks now, her sobs fighting to get out through the gag, she closed her eyes.

"This little piggy . . ." He tightened the clippers' grip on her finger, blood leaked out around the edges. "Are you sure it has to be this way?"

She said nothing, sobs still wracking her body.

". . . goes to market." The clippers closed with the angry crack of her fingertip snapping off.

Her scream was louder than he would have expected with the gag and she tried to crawl away, but he cuffed her alongside the head, grabbed a handful of hair and jerked her back. She wailed now, her right hand coming up to cup the left one as she watched blood stream down her hand.

Only risk was, he knew, she might pass out from pain and shock . . . but she was a tough old bird.

Batting away her good hand, he closed the clippers on her ring finger. "This little piggy stayed home . . . ready to tell me? Just nod."

She shook her head, defiant, but this time she screamed into the gag before he did it. That didn't stop him. He heard the same crack and watched the fingertip fall to the floor.

"Ready now?"

The old woman curled into a ball and tried to protect her hand, but he jerked her hand up, closed the clippers around the middle finger. Her eyes went wide and wild, and, using her good hand, she pointed toward the desk.

"What?" he asked.

She couldn't speak; the gag was bloody. She'd bit through her tongue, so taking the gag off would not aid clarity.

"You're telling me the information is in the desk?"

Weakly, she nodded.

He went to the desk and looked back at the old woman. He picked up piles of mail until lifting one rubber-banded stack of letters made the woman nod. Joy Petty, *the return address said. Sticking the stack inside his shirt, he returned to the woman. She tried to crawl away but couldn't. Right on top of her, he fired a shot into the back of her head, then one inch below it, a second.*

He had just removed the noise suppresser when a car door slammed outside and he saw a man and woman coming up the front stairs. They came to the front door and the man knocked. At first he did nothing. The man knocked again—and announced himself as the police!

Moving slightly to to his right, the killer fired through the door. Then a second shot. He moved back left, saw the woman aiming at the house and the man take off across the front yard. He fired once more at the running man, then the woman yelled—identifying them as police . . . big surprise.

He heard the man shout something from behind their black SUV. Firing through the front window now, he blew out the truck's driver's side window. An encroaching siren, told him there was no point in hanging around here waiting for them to surround him. He pulled on his hood, got to the back door, opened it quietly, then taking a deep breath, took off at a sprint across the backyard.

He thought he heard footsteps advancing behind him, but he couldn't be sure. He vaulted a neighbor's chain link fence, the top of it cutting into his hand. The sudden pain stopped him, but only for a second. Seeing a silhouette running toward him, he turned and took off across the yard jumping the front fence, and then he was gone.

After two hours, they had worked the scene thoroughly, pausing only to watch as the EMTs loaded Marge Kostichek's body onto a gurney and wheeled her out.

Grissom, at the writing table, had found two more

bundles of letters from Joy Petty, which Nick bagged, saying, "This guy is starting to piss me off."

"Nobody likes to get shot at, Nick," Grissom said.

"But it's like he's always one jump ahead of us."

Catherine said, "He just reads the *Sun,* is all."

But a cloud drifted across Grissom's face.

Catherine said, "What?"

"Nothing," he said. "Just a feeling."

She gave him a small wry smile. "I thought you didn't believe in feelings—just evidence."

"This feeling grows out some piece of evidence," he said, "or anyway, something I already know, that I just haven't given proper weight. But I will."

O'Riley bounded in. "My buddy Tavo called. He got a videotape statement of Joy Petty saying that Marge Kostichek hired the Deuce to kill Malachy Fortunato."

Grissom and Catherine exchanged wide-eyed glances.

"Just that simple?" Nick asked.

"It's not all good news," O'Riley said. "Joy Petty's in the wind."

"What?" Grissom snapped.

O'Riley shrugged. "She asked to use the john. She wasn't a suspect, she wasn't even a witness—just a citizen cooperating of her own free will. She smelled the danger. She's gone."

"Have they checked her house yet?"

"Yes. All her clothes were gone, she even took her cat. Like she'd been ready for this day for years."

She had been, Catherine thought.

Grissom asked, sharply, "Well, are they looking for her? She's an accessory after the fact."

"Oh, yeah. I mean, I don't know what kind of priority they put on this—it's not their case. This was just a favor Tavo was doing me."

"Get your friend on the phone now, Sergeant," Grissom said. "We're heading back to home base and in half an hour, I want to be able to download that interview. We need to see this for ourselves."

"I'll try."

"Don't try. Do it."

In just under forty-five minutes, Grissom had assembled Catherine, Nick and O'Riley in his office.

On the computer screen was the image of an interrogation room. Across the table from the camera sat a fortyish woman with shoulder-length black hair, brown eyes and a steeply angled face.

Though the interrogating officer wasn't in the picture, his voice now came through the speaker. "State your name."

O'Riley whispered, "That's my buddy Tavo."

The woman on screen was already saying, "Joy Petty."

Grissom shushed O'Riley.

The off-camera Tavo asked, "Your address?"

She gave an address in Lakewood.

"You are here of your own volition without coercion?"

She nodded.

"Say yes or no, please."

"Yes, I'm sorry. Yes, I'm here of my own volition, without no coercion."

As they watched, the woman before them grew

more agitated. She took a pack of cigarettes from her purse.

Tavo must have been looking at his notes, because she had it lighted before he said, "No smoking, please."

With a smirk, she stubbed the cigarette out in a black ashtray in front of her.

"You've used other names during your life, correct?"

"Yes. Joy Starr, Joy Luck, and several more other stage names. They called me Monica Leigh in the *Swank* layout; that's a magazine. The name I was given at birth was Monica Petty."

Without even thinking about it, she lit another cigarette and took a deep drag. Tavo said nothing. She took a second drag, blew it out through her nose and finally realized she was smoking where she shouldn't be and blotted out the second butt in the ashtray.

Half-annoyed, half-curious, she asked, "Why is there a goddamnn ashtray if we're not allowed to smoke?"

"It's just always been there," Tavo told her.

For several minutes Tavo elicited from her the story of Marge Kostichek taking in her in as a runaway, raising her like a daughter (albeit a daughter who worked in her strip club). Catherine wondered if a sexual relationship might have developed between the women, but the officer didn't ask anything along those lines.

Finally, Tavo lowered the boom. "Ms. Petty, I'm afraid I have bad news for you."

"What? What is this about, anyway? What is this really about?"

"Marge Kostichek was murdered this evening."

"No . . . no, you're just saying that to . . ."

Tavo assured her he was telling the truth. "I'm afraid it was a brutal slaying, Ms. Petty."

Her lip was trembling. "Tell me. Tell me. . . . I have a right to know."

Tavo told her.

"Ms. Petty—do you know who killed Malachy Fortunato in Las Vegas in nineteen hundred eighty-five?"

"I . . . I know what they call him."

"And what is that?"

"The Deuce. Because of those two head wounds, like Marge got."

"The Deuce is a professional killer?"

"Yes. I don't know his name, otherwise."

"Do you know who hired him?"

". . . I . . . know who hired him, yes."

"Who?"

The woman seemed fine for a moment, then she collapsed, her head dropping to the table as long, angry sobs erupted from her. Tavo's hand came into the picture, touched her arm. The gesture seemed to give her strength and she wrestled to control her emotions.

"I've . . . I'm sorry." A sob halted her, but she composed herself again and said, "I loved him, but Malachy was not a strong man. He didn't have the strength to choose between his wife or me. And neither of us would give him up, either. He had a tender touch, Malachy. But he was selfish, and weak, too—that's what led him to embezzle from the Sandmound, you know . . . the casino where he worked."

Tavo said nothing, letting her tell it in her own time, in her own way.

"I stripped at a bar called Swingers. I'd been there since the owner, Marge Kostichek, took me in when I was fifteen. Marge knew that once the mob found out Mal was embezzling they'd kill him, and anybody who had anything to do with him. So, she beat them to the punch.

"She hired this guy who did these mob hits. I don't know how she knew about him, how to contact him; I heard Swingers was a money laundry for some mob guys . . . I just heard that, you know . . . so maybe that was how. Anyway, hiring this guy cost her most of the money she'd saved over the years. The rest she gave to me along with a bus ticket to L.A."

"Excuse me, Ms. Petty—I want to remind you that I did advise you of your rights."

"I know you did. See, I didn't know Marge did it, till years later. I thought . . . I thought the mobsters had Malachy killed. And Marge told me I was in danger, too, and put me on that bus. And I went willingly. I was scared shitless, believe me."

"So . . . you stayed in touch with Marge over the years?"

"Yes—we wrote to each other regularly. She even came out to visit a few times."

"Have you been back to Las Vegas?"

"I'm not that brave."

"So how did you come to find out the truth?"

"Maybe five years later, when she visited me. I was in Reseda at the time. We spent a long evening, drinking, reminiscing . . . and she spilled her guts. I think she felt guilty about it. I think she'd been carrying it around, and she told me how about, and cried and cried and begged me to forgive her."

"Did you?"

"Sure. She did it to save me, she thought—those mobsters mighta killed me, too, *and* Mal's wife . . . I mean, if they thought one of us was in on it, the embezzling?"

"I see."

"Do you? End of the day, I loved her a hell of a lot more than I did that candy ass Malachy. . . . Listen, Officer—I need to use the restroom."

And that was the end of the taped interview.

O'Riley covered for his pal Tavo in L.A. "Hey, she wasn't under arrest or anything. She came in voluntarily. He let his guard down. By the time he got a female officer to check the john, and hunted down his partner, they were fifteen minutes behind her, easy."

"Plenty of time," Nick said, "for Joy to pack up and get out of Dodge . . . but why? Why did she run?"

Grissom was staring at the blank screen.

"Running is all she knows how to do," Catherine said, with an open-handed gesture. "That's what she's done her whole life. It started at fifteen when she ran from her parents, and she's never stopped since."

"And Marge Kostichek was just trying to help the poor girl," Nick said, bleakly.

"You don't win Mother of the Year," Grissom said, "by hiring a hitman to commit first-degree murder."

15

ABOUT THE TIME O'RILEY AND NICK FOUND MARGE Kostichek's body, Warrick was hunkered over a computer monitor in the layout room at work. His eyes burned and his temples throbbed and his neck muscles ached. A while back Sara had stopped by to tell him about the bewildering background search on Barry Hyde's personal history, and Warrick had told her that Hyde's business life was proving equally messy and mysterious.

"No matter what I learn," he'd said to her, "something else suggests the opposite."

"I know the feeling," she'd said.

Now, an hour later at least, things were messier and more mysterious. Although the business spent money buying the latest video releases, A-to-Z did little advertising and had the worst rental rates around. Patrick the pot-smoking manager had copped to the store's light traffic, and yet every month Hyde paid what Warrick considered an exorbitant rent in addition to buying more and more movies. Where did the money come from?

He turned away from the monitor's glow, rubbing his eyes, wondering where he would search next.

That was when Brass stumbled in, exhausted and a little disheveled, looking for Grissom.

"Not sure where he is," Warrick said. "One minute he was here, then O'Riley called from Kostichek's house."

"What was it?"

"Frankly, sounded like your ballpark—I think Marge got sent to that big strip club in the sky."

Brass's well-pleated face managed to tighten with alarm. "You don't think it's the . . ."

"Deuce if I know," Warrick said.

Brass slipped into a chair next to Warrick, slumping. "The more we work on this, the more bizarre it gets."

With a slow nod, Warrick said, "Tell me about it. It's like that damn video store—hardly any business, you wouldn't think much cash flow, and yet Hyde seems to have plenty of dough."

The cop grunted a humorless laugh. "What do you make of Hyde traveling all the time?"

"If he's the Deuce, maybe he's got gigs all around this great land of ours."

Brass shrugged. "So we just trace where he went. And see who got murdered, or disappeared, there."

"I'm all over that—for what good it's doing. No record of Barry Thomas Hyde on any passenger manifest for any airline . . . ever."

"Some people hate to fly. Maybe he drives."

Warrick shook his head. "Last month, when he was

traveling, his car was in a Henderson garage getting serviced."

"What about ren—"

"No rental records. And he doesn't have a second car—I mean, he's unmarried, no record of a divorce or kids, either."

"What are you telling me?"

"That the guy leaves town regularly. He doesn't fly, drive his own car to get there, or even rent a car."

"Bus? Train?"

"No records there, either. For a guy who gets around, there's no sign he ever left home."

Brass smirked. "Just that calendar and that pothead's word."

"Why would Hyde tell his video store staff he was gonna be out of town, if he wasn't?"

"Well, then he's got another identity."

"Our maildrop guy, Peter Randall, maybe? That's the only thing that makes sense—particularly if he's still taking assignments as the Deuce, despite the lack of bodies that've turned up in the past few years."

Brass stared into nothing; then he shook his head, as if to clear the cobwebs, and turned to Warrick and asked, "What about hotels?"

"Well, that's going to take forever to check in detail, you know, to try to see if he was registered anywhere . . . I mean, he never told Patrick where he was off to . . . but I can tell you this: Hyde never charged a hotel or motel room to any one of his three credit cards, and never wrote 'em a check either."

Brass sighed heavily—then he rose, stretched; bones popped. "Something very wrong here—very wrong . . . When Grissom gets back, have him page me."

"You got it."

Brass walked out of the office, got about four feet, and his cell phone rang. The conversation was a short one, Brass sticking his head back inside the layout room moments later, his expression suddenly alert.

"C'mon," Brass said, waving impatiently. "You're with me."

"All right," Warrick said, and in the corridor, falling in next to Brass, he asked, "What's up?"

Brass wore a foul expression. "Barry Hyde's number, I hope."

Sara awoke with a start. She had fallen asleep at her computer and evidently no one had noticed. She sat up, made a face then rolled her neck and felt the tight stiffness that came when she slept wrong. Reaching back, she kneaded her neck muscles, applying more and more pressure as she went, but the pain showed little sign of dissipating. Standing up, her legs wobbly, she got her balance and went out into the hall to the water fountain. Then she wandered from room to room looking for the rest of the crew, but found no one.

At least not until she stepped into the DNA lab, where she discovered skinny, spiky-haired Greg Sanders, on the phone, a huge grin going, his eyes wide.

"You're going to do what?" he asked. "You . . . you're such a bad girl. . . ."

Clearing her throat, Sara smiled and, when he spun to face her, gave him a little wave.

The grin turned upside down, as he said, "Um, we'll

continue this, later. I've got to go." He hung up without further comment.

"Serious, meaningful relationship?" she asked.

"Hey, it's not as kinky as you think."

"No, Greg, I'm pretty sure it is. Where is everybody?"

He shrugged. "Catherine and Nick are at a murder scene. I think Grissom went to join the party, and Warrick left with Brass, like, I dunno, ten minutes ago."

She felt very awake, suddenly. "Murder scene?"

He held up his hands. "I don't know the details."

She sat down on an empty stool. "What do you know?"

On his wheeled chair, he rolled over to another work station, saying, "I know the cigarette butt Catherine brought in, from the mummy site, is too decomposed, and too old, to give us any workable DNA after all that time."

"Okay. That's the bad news part—how about some good news?"

"If you insist. How about that other cigarette butt? The one they brought in from Evidence—it was old, too, but somebody bagged it years ago."

"What about it?"

"It doesn't match the mummy's blood . . . or the wife's DNA, either." Warming to the topic, Sanders grinned at her in his cheerful fashion and pulled a sheet of paper out of a folder. "Take a peek."

She rolled on her stool over next to him. "DNA test results," she said, reading, pleased. "So, the cigarette butt came from the killer?"

"Hey, I just work here. I don't know whose DNA it is—it just isn't the wife's or the mummy's."

"Does Grissom know about this? Anybody?"

"No." Sanders shook his head. "I haven't had a chance to tell them."

"I know," she said. "You were busy—had phone calls to make."

"Listen, I get break time like anybody—"

She leaned in and smiled her sweetest smile. "Greg—I'm just teasing you. From what I heard, sounded like you enjoy it. . . . Anyway, I'll pass the news along. You're going to be popular."

He shrugged and smiled. "Good. I like being popular."

"So I gathered."

And she left the lab.

Warrick sat in the darkened car next to Brass. The unmarked Taurus was parked at the intersection of Fresh Pond Court and Dockery Place, with a good view of Hyde's house and its putting-green front yard. The car windows were down, the evening nicely cool, the night a dark one, not much moon. Patrol cars were parked on Eastern Avenue, South Pecos Road and Canarsy Court, observing the sides and back of the house, to make sure Hyde didn't sneak in on foot.

The Hyde residence stood dark and silent, a ranch-style tomb. The neighbors' houses showed signs of normal life, the faint blue glow of televisions shining through wispy curtains in darkened rooms; others were well-lit with people occasionally crossing in front of windows, somewhere a stereo played too loud, and a couple of houses away from Hyde's, somebody had his garage door open, fine-tuning the engine of a Kawasaki motorcycle. At this hour the guy was pushing it—it was almost ten P.M.

"You think Hyde's really the Deuce?" Warrick asked.

Brass shrugged.

"If he is, you think he'd come back here, right after murdering somebody?"

Within the dark interior of the car, the detective gave Warrick a long appraising look. "You know, Brown, sometimes it's better not to think so much. Just wait for it and react. If he comes, he comes. Don't try to out-think these mutts. Leave it to them and they'll do it. That's when we pick them up."

Warrick knew Brass was right; but it frustrated him.

They sat in silence for a long time; how long, Warrick didn't know—he thought he might even have dozed off a couple of times. Stakeout work was boring, even when there was an undercurrent of danger, and it made Warrick glad he wasn't a cop. The neighbor with the motorcycle either got tired or somebody called to complain, because he stopped working on the machine and shut his garage door. One by one the lights in the windows around the court went out.

"Maybe he's made us," Warrick said, "or one of the squads."

Brass shrugged. "Wouldn't surprise me. He didn't stay alive in that business this long being careless. I doubt if he spotted us, though—there hasn't been a car on this street since we got here."

Just then a vehicle turned toward them off South Pecos Road. Its headlights practically blinded them and they slid down in their seats. Then the vehicle—a big black SUV—pulled to a stop almost even with them.

"Grissom," Brass said, sounding a little peeved.

The black Tahoe idled quietly next to them and Grissom rolled down his window. "So?"

"Nothing," Brass said. "House has been dark and quiet since we got here."

"All right. When you get back, Jim, you need to see an interview the LAPD sent over—Joy Petty confirming Marge Kostichek hired the Deuce."

Brass blew out air. "Jesus—so she was an old loose end getting newly tied off."

Grissom didn't respond to that, saying, "I'm going back to the lab. Warrick . . ."

Brass shushed him and pointed to Hyde's house where a light had just come on in the living room. Grissom eased the Tahoe over to the far curb, parked it and returned to the Taurus on foot, quietly slipping into the backseat.

The walkie seemed to jump into Brass's hand. "Light just came on in the house."

The reports came back quickly. No one had seen anything.

"Damnit," Brass said. He sighed. "All right—I'm going to go take a peek in the window. You two stay here."

"No way, Jim," Grissom said. "We're not going to let you go up there alone."

"Let's not completely blow our cover," Brass said. "It could just be a timer."

"And," Warrick added, "Hyde might be a professional killer who has already done one murder tonight, and forty-some others over the years—that we know about. You really want to go up there alone?"

Brass scowled at Warrick. "Are you trying to tell me how to do my job?"

Letting out a long tired sigh, Warrick said, "No, I just asked a question. Do you really want to go up there alone?"

Brass thought about it; finally he said, "All right—one of you."

Warrick opened the door and jumped out, beating Grissom to the punch. The pair made their way cautiously up the street, moving through yards and trying to avoid the circle of light thrown off by the only street light, back on the corner. Warrick stayed behind the much shorter Brass, keeping low. At the edge of Hyde's yard they ducked in next to the garage.

"You only go as far as that end of the garage," Brass whispered, pointing.

"What are you going to do?"

"I'm going around the back, and come up the other side, and try to see in the window."

Warrick nodded. "I'll follow you to the back of the garage. When you go up the far side, I'll move up to the front."

"Okay," Brass said, and pulled his revolver from his hip holster. He eased to the back of the garage and Warrick, his own pistol in hand, crept along in Brass's shadow. At the corner, in darkness out of the range of the street light, the detective gave Warrick a little wave and edged around the corner. Taking position, Warrick watched as Brass moved across the huge backyard. The detective was halfway across when a high-mounted motion light came on, putting Brass in the spotlight. . . .

Warrick dipped into shooter's stance, pistol leveled at the back door, centered above a wide octagonal deck. Initially, Brass froze; but the deer-in-headlights moment passed, and he dove to his right, rolled, and came up running toward the far side of the house, in darkness again.

Ready to shoot, Warrick searched for a target, finding none, and not unhappy about it. Brass, now on the far side of the house, would be making his way toward the front and expecting Warrick to be there to cover him.

Spinning, Warrick sprinted back to the front. He turned and, at the garage door, stayed close as he slithered to the far end. Peeking around the corner, Warrick saw nothing and wondered if something had happened to Brass. Fighting panic, he saw Brass's face slide out from behind a shrub at the corner of the house. Warrick's trip-hammer heartbeat slowed only slightly, as he watched the detective trying to see inside.

The CSI watched intently, as Brass crawled beneath the window, stopping to peer over the edge of the frame. Just when he thought they were going to pull this off without a hitch, Warrick felt a hand settle on his shoulder. He jumped and turned, bringing his pistol up as he went.

Grissom just looked at him. "Damnit, Gris," Warrick half-whispered, keeping his voice down at least, as the adrenaline spiked through his system. Turning back, he realized he couldn't see Brass now, and—panic rising again—wondered where the detective had gone. As he prepared to stick his head around the corner, Brass came the other way, suddenly appearing three inches in front of him, and Warrick jumped again. *Damn!*

"Hyde's not home," Brass said, his voice low, but no longer a whisper.

"Not home," Warrick echoed numbly—but as much as he wanted this son of a bitch, he couldn't help feeling relieved.

Brass was saying, "Those lights gotta be on a timer. No sign of him in the living room, and the lights are still off in the rest of the house."

Spinning back to Grissom, Warrick asked, "And just what the hell were you doing?"

"Neighbors called in a prowler," he said. "Henderson PD is coming—silent response."

The words were no sooner out of his mouth than three police cars rolled into the court, cherrytops making the night psychedelic, spotlights trained on the three of them. No sirens, though—that might disturb the neighborhood.

Officers piled out, using their doors for cover as they aimed their pistols at Brass and Warrick.

"Drop your guns," one of them ordered, and then another one or two yelled pretty much the same thing.

Carefully kneeling, Warrick and Brass set their guns on the ground in front of them.

"Is our cover blown yet?" Grissom asked.

As Brass explained the situation to the Henderson Police Department, Warrick and Grissom stood staring at the big, expensive and apparently very empty house.

"He's making us look like fools," Warrick said.

Grissom didn't reply immediately; but then he said, "When we're done here, we'll swing by the video store."

"He could be there."

"Yes he could."

Brass returned, shaking his head. "They're a little pissed."

Warrick said, "I guess we coulda given 'em a heads up."

"It's not ideal interdepartmental relations," Brass admitted. He looked at the disgruntled uniforms, who were milling out by their black-and-whites, cherry-tops shut off. "They also informed me that Barry Hyde has been a model citizen since moving to Henderson . . . and if in the future we want to do some police work in their fair city, they would like us first to ask their permission."

"They said that?" Grissom asked.

"I'm paraphrasing, but the message was the same. So—let's go home."

Warrick said, "Gris wants to drop by A-to-Z Video on the way back."

"Hell no," Brass said.

"Maybe I want to rent a movie," Grissom said.

Brass seemed to struggle for words. Finally he managed, "You know, Warrick, after your boss finishes this case, it's possible you and I are both going to be looking for work."

"Maybe they could use us in Henderson," Warrick suggested. "Looks like a nice town to work in. But till then, what do you say we go scope out the vids?"

Brass shook his head again. "Might as well. It'll give me something to look at while I'm on suspension."

16

About the time night shift actually started—after she had already put in over four hours that included getting shot at and working a particularly unpleasant crime scene—Catherine Willows nonetheless exuded vitality as she made a bee-line for the DNA lab. From behind her, Sara's voice called out: "Hey, wait up!"

She slowed, turning to see Sara hustle up, a report in hand. "If you're headed for DNA, I may have something for you."

As they walked, Sara handed her the report, saying, "I told Greg I'd give this to you. It's the DNA results from your Fortunato evidence."

Catherine took it, but asked, "What's the news?"

"Blood was the mummy's. Cigarette taken from the Fortunato backyard sixteen years ago contains DNA that doesn't match either the late husband or his living wife."

Catherine smiled wickedly. "Could be the Deuce's."

Sara flashed her cute gap-toothed grin. "Could be. But why are we still headed to the lab?"

" 'Cause this isn't what I was going there for."

Quickly Catherine filled Sara in, slightly out of order: telling her Marge Kostichek had been murdered, apparently by the Deuce, then about the tight scrape she and Nick had been in. And finally she brought Sara up to speed on Joy Petty and the Kostichek woman hiring the murder of the mummy.

Sara, clipping along beside her, said, "And here I thought sure Fortunato was a mob hit."

"We all did," Catherine said, with a sour smirk. "Grissom told us not to assume anything, yet we all bit. Maybe that's why this woman is dead now."

"And I take it you've already dropped off the Kostichek crime scene evidence to Greg. . . ."

"Yes, and maybe we'll match up that ancient cigarette DNA—when I chased the son of a bitch tonight, he cut himself on a chain link fence."

Sara, mimicking the milk ad, asked, "Got blood?"

"Oh yeah," Catherine said, and strode into the lab, Sara right behind her.

Sanders almost jumped off his stool. "God! Don't you guys ever knock?"

Catherine leaned on his counter. "That murder crime scene stuff I dropped off? You said you'd get to it ASAP."

"And I will."

She just looked at him. Then she said, "Maybe it's time to define 'ASAP.' "

The normally cheerful lab rat scowled at the two women. "Listen, I'm so far behind it'll be, like, Monday before I can get to it. I got overload from Days to deal with—day shift has, like, two murders, a rape and—"

"Days?" Catherine asked. "You're giving priority to dayshift?"

His brow lifted and half his mouth smirked. "You ever had Conrad Ecklie on your ass?"

"I'm not interested in your personal life, Greg."

He lowered himself over a microscope. "I'll laugh next week, when I have the time."

Leaning near the door, Sara said, "Speaking of time, Cath—while you're waiting for that DNA evidence, we could check the phone records around here . . . for personal calls."

Greg glanced up.

"You know," Sara continued, with a shrug, "as responsible public servants, we need to make sure the taxpayers are being well-served."

Sanders stroked his chin as if a beard were covering his baby face. "For two such dedicated public servants, I might be able to squeeze it in."

"Thanks, Greg—you're the best."

The Taurus and Tahoe pulled into the parking lot and glided side by side into stalls in front of the video store. Warrick climbed down from the driver's seat of the Tahoe, and Brass got out of the Taurus, where Grissom had ridden in the front passenger seat. The CSI supervisor—after taking a long, deep breath, letting it out the same way—followed, joining the two men on the sidewalk.

The normally cool Warrick seemed just a little nervous to Grissom; the lanky man was bobbing on his feet, as he looked in the storefront window and said, "The cashier tonight must be Sapphire—that means the assistant manager on duty is Ronnie. These people have never seen us before, Gris—how do you want to play it?"

It only took Grissom a moment to decide. "Jim and I'll head straight to the back room—you stay out front and keep an eye on the cashier."

A nod. "You got it."

"Gil," Brass said, his face creased with worry, "I've got to tell you, I think this is the wrong play. There's something going on here that we don't understand, yet. You really think sticking our hand into a blind hole makes sense? We could pull out a bloody stump."

"Hyde has to be somewhere," Grissom said. "He's not at his residence—this is his business. What else do you suggest?"

Without waiting for an answer, Grissom pushed open the glass door and went inside.

"May I help you, sir?" a cheerful voice asked from the cashier's island.

Moving into the brightly illuminated world of shelved videos and movie posters, Grissom said, "Just looking," and kept moving toward the back of the store. He felt Brass behind him, maybe two steps.

Warrick strolled in a few seconds behind them, and walked straight to the cashier.

"Hi," he said in a loud voice. "How are you?"

"Fine."

"Have you got the director's cut of *Manhunter?*"

As Warrick and the cashier chatted, Brass said to Grissom, "You're the evidence guy, for Christ's sake! What can we do here that will hold up in court?"

Still ignoring his colleague, Grissom pushed open

the swinging door, despite the PRIVATE sign tacked to it, and almost immediately a figure from inside blocked the way: a kid not any older than the last one they'd met here.

"Hey! Can't you read?"

As the kid pointed to the PRIVATE sign, Grissom took a step back and appraised the youth, who wore a blue polo shirt with A-to-Z stitched over the breast, a pudgy kid with dirt-brown hair and dirt-brown eyes set deep inside a pale face.

"You can't come back here!"

The kid said this loudly—too loudly, as if it were for someone's benefit other than Grissom and Brass.

Grissom leaned in, almost nose to nose with the kid. "We're looking for your boss—Barry Hyde."

"Uh, uh . . ."

From inside the office, a voice called, "I'm Barry Hyde! . . . Let the gentlemen in, Ronnie."

Shaken, Ronnie stepped aside, and Grissom stepped into the small office, Brass following glumly.

Getting up from a desk at the right, where a security monitor revealed four angles of the store (including Warrick and the cashier talking), the man rose to a slim six-foot-one or so. That thin build was deceptively muscular, however. The man—who wore no name tag—was in a black polo shirt and black jeans—wardrobe, Grissom noted, not far removed from his own. He was in his fifties, but youthfully so.

And the man's right hand was wrapped in a large gauze bandage.

"I'm Gil Grissom from—"

"Do you always barge into private places unannounced, Mr. Grissom?" Hyde asked, superficially pleasant, but with an edge.

"From the Las Vegas Criminalistics Bureau," Grissom finished. "This is Captain Brass. We'd like to ask you a few questions."

"We should have knocked," Brass mumbled. "Sorry."

"Apology noted," Hyde said. "And I always like to cooperate with law enforcement, but I'm sure you'll understand if I ask see to your credentials."

"Certainly," Brass said, and they complied with the request.

Hyde studied Brass's badge and Grissom's picture ID a few beats longer than necessary, Grissom thought; a smirk lurked at the corner of Hyde's mouth. This man was not afraid of them, or thrown by their presence: he seemed, if anything, amused!

Handing than credentials back, Hyde gave them a curt nod. "Fine, gentlemen. Now. What may I do for you? And let me assure you that any adult material we rent is clearly within community standards."

Grissom smiled, just a little. "Mr. Hyde, I notice you're wearing a bandage on your right hand—it looks fresh. Would you mind telling us how you injured yourself?"

The mouth smirked, but the forehead tensed. "Is there a . . . context to these questions?"

Brass said, "Could you please just answer."

Hyde's smirk evolved into a smile consisting of small even teeth—something vaguely animal-like about them. He held up the hand in front of him, the bandage like a badge of honor. "Shelving units. Ronnie . . . that's the young man you were intimidating just now . . . Ronnie and I were rearranging some shelves and one of them cut my hand."

"Could I take a look at the injury?"

"Why, are you a doctor?"

"Well, yes . . . in a way."

"I'm going to say no," Hyde said, firm but not unfriendly. "I only just now got the bleeding stopped, and got it properly bandaged. I'm not going to undress the wound so you can look at it, for some unspoken reason. Out of the question, gentlemen."

Grissom fought the irritation rising in him. It must have shown, because Brass jumped in with his own line of questioning. "Mr. Hyde, can you tell us where you were, earlier this evening?"

"I could, but you're going to have to be frank with me, gentlemen, if you want my cooperation."

Grissom laid it out: "This is a murder investigation."

That might have given the average person pause, but Hyde snapped right back: "And that gives you the right to be rude?"

Grissom said nothing.

"Please, Mr. Hyde," Brass said, reasonably, "tell us where you were earlier this evening."

"Any particular time?"

Brass shrugged. "Let's say since five."

"A.M. or P.M.?" Hyde asked, his eyes on Grissom, that tiny half-smirk tugging at his cheek.

"Make it P.M.," Brass said, and took a small notebook from his pocket.

"All right." Now Hyde shrugged. "I've been here at the store."

"Since five?"

"Earlier than that even," said Hyde. "Since around four."

Their earlier visit to A-to-Z had been mid-afternoon; had they just missed their man?

"Witnesses to that effect?" Brass asked casually.

"Ronnie and Sapphire. They both came in at four today."

"Isn't that early?" Grissom asked. "I mean, you open at ten, and go to midnight. I thought the shifts would be divided in half."

A smile split the pockmarked face, a stab at pretended cordiality. "That would make sense, wouldn't it? But today Patrick and Sue had plans—they're something of an item . . . not ideal, a workplace romance, but it happens, and I just hate to be a hard-ass boss."

Pothead Patrick had indeed said good things about their boss; but Grissom didn't mention the other assistant manager—Warrick had negotiated the kid's silence, earlier. Or was there a surveillance tape that Hyde had looked at? Had the killer been reviewing security tapes, too?

Hyde was saying, "The lovebirds left an hour early, and Sapphire and Ronnie came in to cover."

Brass asked, "Did your other two employees see you, today?"

Hyde shook his head. "No, they left right at four, and I wandered in a few minutes after."

"Did you know about their plans?"

"They had permission. Like I said, I try to be a good boss to these kids."

Grissom found himself fascinated by this specimen:

if Hyde was the Deuce, Grissom was looking at a classic sociopath. If they could bust this guy, and convict him, he would make a great subject for one of Grissom's lectures.

Brass was asking the guy, "Did you go out to eat or anything? Run errands maybe?"

"No, it's just as I've told you." His tone was patronizing, as if Brass were a child.

Hyde continued: "I was here all evening. Ask my kids, they'll tell you. Oh, Ronnie did go out and get Italian—pizza for them, salad for me. I believe it was about nine o'clock. The three of us ate." An eyebrow arched. "The pizza box, and the little styrofoam salad box, are in the Dumpster out back . . . if you would care for further confirmation."

Grissom had rarely encountered this degree of smugness in a murder suspect before.

Brass asked, "Where did Ronnie go to get this Italian?"

"Godfather's . . . it's a bit of a drive, but that's Ronnie's favorite pizza."

Brass wrote that down, dutifully.

Grissom asked, "You didn't eat any pizza?"

"No. It was sausage and pepperoni—I'm a vegetarian."

"Oh. Health reasons, Mr. Hyde, or moral issues?"

"Both. I try to stay fit . . . and of course I take a stand against wanton slaughter."

Grissom admired Hyde's ability to say that with a straight face. "What's your stand on dairy items?"

"What does that have to do with a murder investigation?"

Grissom shrugged. "I'm just wondering. I have an interest in nutrition. Mind humoring me?"

"Not at all—I'm lactose-intolerant. No cheese on my salad—just good crisp healthy veggies. But I do like some sting in my dressing."

Grissom said, "Thank you."

Brass gave Grissom a sideways you're-as-nuts-as-this-guy-is look, and returned to his questioning. "When was the first time you visited Las Vegas, Mr. Hyde? Prior to moving here, I mean."

Hyde considered that. "Six years ago, I believe—just a month or so before I moved here. I fell in love with the place—was here for a video store owners convention—and moved out here."

"Never before that?"

"Never. I don't have any particular interest in gambling. It was the climate—the beauty of the desert sunsets. That sort of thing."

"All right," Brass said, making a note. "Do you know a woman named Marge Kostichek?"

No hesitation. "No—should I?"

"How about a Philip Dingelmann?"

"No."

"Malachy Fortunato?"

"No . . . and I have to say, I'm growing weary of this game. Who are these people, and why would you think that I'd know them?"

Brass smiled—as enigmatic as a Sphinx. "Why, they're our murder victims, Mr. Hyde."

The smirk lost its sarcasm; the eyes hardened. "And you are suggesting I knew these people?"

Brass said, "We're asking."

Hyde seemed to get irritated, now; but Grissom wondered if it was just another chess move, more cat and mouse.

"You think I've killed these people, don't you? What preposterous, presumptuous . . . this interview is over, gentlemen."

"All right," Brass said.

But Hyde went on: "I've tried to assist you, cooperate with you despite your rudeness, and now you repay my good citizenship by accusing me of murder."

Good citizenship? Grissom thought.

"And within the walls of my own establishment, no less." He went to the door, pushed it open, and waited for them to leave.

Brass began to move, but Grissom gently held him back, by the arm. To Hyde, Grissom said, "Talking here at your . . . establishment . . . might be more comfortable for you."

"Than what? The police station?"

Neither man said a word.

Releasing the door, Hyde returned to his desk, sat, and said, "All right—continue your interview." He gestured to the telephone nearby. "But if you accuse me of murder, if you even imply it, I'll end this interview, phone my attorney and file charges for harassment."

Grissom noted that the security cam system did not include the office or back room.

"You mentioned gambling, Mr. Hyde," Brass said. "So you don't gamble?"

"I said I had no great interest in it. I live at the doorstep of the gambling capital of the United States, if not the free world. Of course I've tried my luck from time to time."

"Ever at the Beachcomber?"

Grissom could sense the wheels turning behind the controlled if smug facade; but Hyde gave up nothing.

He said, "I've been there. I've been to most of the casinos on and off the Strip, for dining and entertainment, if not always gaming. I've lived here for over five years."

"We'll get to that," Brass said. "You ever use the ATM machine at the Beachcomber?"

Grissom thought he saw Hyde give the slightest flinch. It happened so fast he couldn't be sure. . . .

Hyde said, "I don't believe so."

"But you're not sure?"

"No, uh, yes, I'm sure."

That was the closest to flustered Hyde had been, so far.

Brass said, "There's a security tape that shows you using the ATM machine there almost seven weeks ago."

A disbelieving smile twisted the thin lips. "Shows me? I hardly think so. . . ." This was almost an admission of his avoidance of the casino security cameras, and Hyde quickly amplified: "I've never used my ATM card. . . ."

After his voice trailed off, Hyde seemed lost in thought.

"What?" Grissom asked.

Nodding, Hyde said, "You must have seen the man who stole it."

Brass cocked his head as if his hearing were poor. "How is that?"

"On the tape. The casino security tape—you must have seen the individual who stole my ATM card."

Brass sighed. "You're telling us someone stole your ATM card?"

Hyde nodded. "Yes, around the first of May."

"And when did you report the theft?"

"Just now, I'm afraid," Hyde said, with what seemed an embarrassed shake of his head. "Right after the card was stolen, I got called out of town on business and then I simply forgot about it."

Grissom said, "You forgot your ATM card was stolen?"

Brass didn't wait for a response, asking, "How was it stolen?"

"I don't really know."

Grissom felt the irritation rising again; the man's contempt for them was incredible. "You don't know," he said.

Hyde shrugged. "One day I went to use it . . . in my wallet . . . and it was just gone."

"Then you *lost* it," Brass said, apparently trying not to lose it himself. "Mr. Hyde, that's not the same thing as having it stolen."

Hyde looked at them with undisguised disdain. "I never found it, and the bank never called to say that they had it. So it must have been stolen. . . . I probably left it in a machine when I used it, and someone else simply took it."

Now it was Grissom's turn to feel smug. "How do you suppose this guy got your PIN then?"

Hyde's smile managed to turn even more condescending. "The number was written on the back of the card, at the end of the signature box. I'm afraid I have a terrible memory."

Brass said, "You've been doing pretty well with it tonight."

"Numbers, names, that sort of thing, I'm hopeless. So I just wrote the PIN on the card. You know, to this day, I can't remember my social security number."

Grissom had to wonder if that was because he'd had more than one.

"Then you forgot to report the card's loss," Brass said.

"Yes—precisely. What a fool." Hyde put his hands behind his neck, elbows winged out, as he leaned back, clearly enjoying himself.

Brass flipped a notebook page. "Let's talk about before you moved here, five years ago."

"Let's."

"Where did you live before you moved to Henderson?"

"So many places."

"For instance."

"Coral Gables, Florida . . . Rochester, Minnesota . . . Moscow, Idaho—I even lived in Angola, Indiana, once upon a time."

"Let's talk about Idaho—when did you live there?"

"During college. More years ago than I would like to admit."

Grissom figured there was a lot this guy wouldn't like to admit.

Brass was asking, "So, you went to the University of Idaho?"

Hyde nodded. "Graduated with a degree in English." He removed his hands from behind his head and gestured to the posters. "For all the good it's done me."

"You seem to have done all right for yourself," Brass commented.

" 'Education,' " Grissom said, " 'is an admirable thing.' "

" 'But it is well,' " Hyde said, picking up where the criminalist left off, " 'to remember from time to time that nothing that is worth knowing can be taught.' "

"Oscar Wilde," Grissom said, trading a tiny smile with Hyde.

"Speaking of education," Brass said, unimpressed, "can you explain why the University of Idaho has never heard of Barry Hyde?"

He seemed surprised. "No, I can't. I suppose it's possible they've lost my transcript. It has, after all, been quite a few years . . . and a lot of these institutions, when they switched over to computerized systems, well . . . I must have gotten lost in the technological shuffle."

Brass asked, "Is there anyone at the university you knew back then we could talk to now?"

"You must be kidding. My old college chums?"

"Yeah—let's start with 'chums.' "

"I have no idea. I haven't been back since I graduated. You might find this hard to believe, but I was painfully shy and kept to myself."

"And instructors?"

Hyde mulled that over momentarily. "I don't know if they are still there, but Christopher Groves and Allen Bridges in the English department might remember me."

Though not one to make assumptions, Grissom felt sure these were the names of two deceased faculty members.

Brass, jotting the names on his pad, glanced at Grissom. "You got anything else, Gil?"

"Couple questions," he said, lightly. "Were you in the service, Mr. Hyde?"

"The United States Army, Mr. Grissom—why?"

"I was wondering where you were stationed."

Not missing a beat, Hyde said, "I received basic training at Fort Bragg, North Carolina, advanced training in communications at Fort Hood, Texas, and then spent nine months at Ansbach, Germany."

"It's odd," Grissom said, "that your doctor's report says that you've never been overseas."

Hyde's eyes narrowed. "Do you make a habit out of invading the privacy of upstanding citizens, Mr. Grissom?"

"Not upstanding citizens, no."

A sneer replaced the smirk. "Well, in that case, you must have stumbled across the records of a different Barry Hyde." He glanced at his watch—a Rolex—and said, "Now, if you gentlemen will excuse me—while talking with you has been more interesting than I could ever have hoped, it's time to close . . . this conversation, and my store."

He rose, held open the door for them and they went out into the store, where he wordlessly led them to the front door—Warrick was gone, the cashier closing out the register. This door Hyde held open for them, also, nodding, smiling.

Grissom turned to him. "See you soon, Mr. Hyde."

Hyde laughed—once; there was something private about it. "I doubt that very much, Mr. Grissom." He went back inside and locked the door. They watched as he took the cash drawer from Sapphire and retired to the back of the store.

"What did he mean?" Brass asked. "We got a flight risk here?"

"Maybe."

"Cocky son of a bitch."

They found Warrick sitting behind the wheel of the Tahoe. "I got chased out," he said. "Any luck?"

"He was less than forthcoming," Grissom said.

Brass snorted. "That's being generous. What did you learn, Brown?"

"Once you were in back, I showed my ID to Sapphire and Ronnie. They were pretty cooperative—both said Hyde's been here all night, since just after four. Of course when Ronnie went out for pizza, around nine—that left Hyde in the back office, and Sapphire up in the cashier's slot, a post she couldn't leave. They ate carry-out pizza when Ronnie got back, and that's about it."

"Actually," Grissom said, "Hyde ate salad. No cheese, just veggies . . . Which may break this case wide open."

"Huh?" Brass said, blinking.

Getting it, Warrick was grinning. "We'd be shit out of luck, if Hyde was in on that pepperoni pizza."

Brass was lost. "What are you guys *talking* about?"

Warrick cackled and said, "No animal DNA in salad."

"Meet you at the Dumpster," Grissom said to Warrick, and headed to the back of the building.

17

In the layout room, Grissom had arrayed various crime scene photos—of the mummy case, at left, and the Dingelmann shooting, at right—on two large adjacent bulletin boards. He had sent Nick to round everybody up, and Catherine—sipping coffee and eating a vending-machine Danish—was at one of the tables. Nick was already back, sitting next to her, sipping a Diet Coke. Along the periphery, blank computer monitor screens stared at them accusingly—as if it was time to put these cases to bed.

Grissom agreed.

Warrick stumbled in, a coffee in one hand, his other rubbing his face; then the hand dropped away and a tired and puffy set of features revealed themselves, including bloodshot, obviously bleary eyes. "So, boss—what's up?"

Looking equally exhausted, Sara tumbled in on Warrick's heels. She carried a pint of orange juice and half a bagel with cream cheese.

Grissom filled everybody in on anything they might have missed, and Nick had the first question.

Nick said, "Okay, Marge Kostichek hires the Deuce to remove Malachy Fortunato, for reasons that are clear, by now, even to those among us who tend to lag behind. . . ."

"Ease up on yourself, Nick," Sara said.

Nick grinned at her, but the grin was gone by the time he posed the rest of his question to Grissom: "But why kill the lawyer—Dingelmann?"

"Because," Grissom said, "Hyde recognized him."

"Pardon?" Nick said.

"If you study the casino tape, the body language is unmistakable—Dingelmann recognizes the man at the poker machine . . . and the man at the poker machine recognizes him."

"Not a contract hit, you're saying," Catherine said. "Something more spontaneous."

"No, no," Nick said, shaking his head, grinning in disagreement, "silenced automatic, two shots in the back of the head? The Deuce is a hired assassin. . . . He kills for money."

"That's one reason he kills," Grissom said, patient. "But why did he murder Marge Kostichek?"

Sara shrugged. "Every cornered animal protects itself."

"Exactly," Grissom said, pointing a finger at her. "Put the pieces together, boys and girls. We have a hired killer with a very distinct signature."

Nods all around.

Grissom continued: "A signature that hasn't been seen for over five years."

"Not," Warrick said, "since he moved to Henderson."

"So he *is* retired," Sara said.

Nick was shaking his head again. "But what about the traveling?"

"For now, never mind that," Grissom said. "Trips or not, five years ago he came here to make a new life—to live under a new name. The contrived background Warrick and Sara uncovered confirms that."

"And Philip Dingelmann," Catherine said, "was a face out of his old life . . . the mob connections he's turned his back on, for whatever reason."

Grissom smiled. "That's a big 'bingo.' For five years, Hyde's been living quietly in Henderson, running his video store, at an apparent loss, and his only recreation, that we know of anyway, is to come in, twice a week, and gamble a little."

"At the Beachcomber," Warrick said. "At off times. So nobody from his past life might recognize him."

"Right," Grissom said, pleased.

"That's crazy," Nick said, not at all on board. "Even with its family-values facelift, Vegas still has mob roots—plus people from all over the country come here, vacationing. Why would somebody who's tucked himself out of the way, in Henderson, Nevada, come to Sin City twice a week?"

"He can't help himself, man," Warrick said. "He's an adrenaline junkie. All those years doing what he did? Couple days a week, he gets a little taste, gets that buzz that lets him survive in the straight world. Gambling does that for some people."

Grissom said, "It's no accident that more wanted

felons are arrested every year at McCarren than at any other airport in the country."

Warrick nodded. "Even in this Disneyland-style Vegas, it's still *the* place where you can find the biggest rush in the shortest amount of time."

"So," Catherine said, almost but not quite buying it, "the mob lawyer just happened to walk into the casino where Hyde was gambling?"

Grissom pointed to a photo of the dead lawyer in the Beachcomber hallway. "Dingelmann was a registered guest at the hotel, yes. Catching some R and R before an upcoming big trial."

"Coincidence?" Sara asked, almost teasingly.

"Circumstance," Grissom said. "There's a difference."

Nick, still the most skeptical of them, said, "And Hyde just happened to have a gun and a silencer with him? Give me a break."

Grissom came over to where Nick and Catherine sat; perched on the edge of the table. "Look at when Hyde gambled. He always picked a time when business was slow. He knew someday, somebody might recognize him . . . and he'd have to be prepared. *That's* why he carried the gun and the noise suppresser."

"Hell," Warrick said. "Maybe that was a part of the buzz."

"Tell us, Grissom," Catherine said. "You can see this, can't you? Make us see it."

And he did.

The .25 automatic, in the holster at the small of his back, brought a feeling of security . . . like that credit card commercial—never leave home without it. On several occasions, he'd almost made it out the front door without snugging the pistol in place, and each time, almost as if the gun called to him, he'd turned around and picked it up.

You just never knew, maybe today would be the day he'd need it. He'd survived this long by being cautious—never scared, just cautious. Dangerous situations required care, planning, consistency. A careful man could survive almost anything.

Over the years, he'd done a number of jobs near Vegas, and he'd always loved the town—Vegas getaways had been something he looked forward to. Now, Vegas getaways from Henderson were twice-a-week oases in a humdrum existence. He derived great pleasure coming to the football field–sized casino at the Beachcomber, but he felt secure: at five-thirty on a Monday morning, only a couple hundred players would be trying their luck.

In a room this size, this time of day, the gamblers were spread out, making the casino seem nearly deserted. Tourists—the few that ventured this far off the Strip—wouldn't be here at this hour unless they were lost or drunk. These were the hardcores, mostly locals, who never gave him a second glance.

Occasionally, a bell would go off, a machine would ding ding ding, or he might hear a muffled whoop from the half-dozen schmucks gathered around the nearest craps table; but basically, the casino remained as quiet as a losing locker room. He might have preferred a little more action, more glitz, more glamour—but he still had that habit of caution even as he took risks.

He always played at this time of day, fewer people, less noise, hell, even the cocktail waitresses didn't bother him now that they knew him to be a recluse and a shitty tipper. He played on Mondays and Wednesdays, Senior Days at the

Beachcomber, when a registered player's points would be multiplied by four.

Though only fifty, his ID claimed he was fifty-six, and the silver hair at his temples made it easier to sell the lie. Right now he had the slot card of a nonexistent registered player plugged into a poker machine closer to the lobby than he would have liked. Normally, he'd play further back in the casino, away from the lobby, but his luck had been bad, and a few months ago, this particular machine had been kind. So, he'd positioned himself here, facing the lobby (his shoulder turned away from the security camera, of course).

He punched the MAX *bet button, dropping his running total from twenty-five to twenty. He'd started the session with two hundred quarters when he'd slipped a fifty into the machine only a half-hour earlier. Looking at his hand, he saw a pair of threes, one a diamond, the other a club, plus the six, nine, and jack of diamonds. Sucker bet, he told himself, even as he dropped the three of clubs and tried to fill the flush. He hit the* DEAL *button and was rewarded with the three of hearts. Naturally.*

He cursed under his breath, bet five more quarters, and wondered if his luck could possibly get any worse. Over a month since he won any real money, and he wondered what the hell it would take to turn things around. He looked up to see one of last night's holdouts finally trudging toward the elevators, calling it a night. The guy wore a dark suit, his geometric-patterned tie loose at the neck, puffing like a tan flower from his chest.

The video poker hand came up: two kings, a jack, a queen, a seven. He kept the two kings, dropped the others.

When he saw the man's face, he knew his luck wouldn't be changing today, not for the better anyway. He fought the urge to duck under the machine, but it was too late, the suit looking right at him now, recognizing him—Dingelmann.

The lawyer. His *lawyer, in another life. . . .*

And right now the ever so cool-in-court counselor's eyes were growing wide in surprise and alarm.

Unconsciously, the player's hand moved toward the back of his slacks, under his lightweight sport coat. He stopped as the lawyer took off at a brisk pace, heading for the bank of elevators to the left and, no doubt, the phone that waited upstairs in his room.

Can't do him here, *the player thought,* way too fucking public. Be patient, patience is the key. *He rose, took a step, the plastic chain attaching him to his player's card reining him in, drawing him back.*

He pulled the card, and barely aware of it, looked down as the poker machine started burping out coins. He glanced at his hand, four kings. Damnit. Without another thought, he left the machine and followed Dingelmann. As they neared the elevators, the lawyer's pace quickened and a couple of night owls turned, trying to figure out if the guy was loony or just drunk.

The stalker kept his face blank, though his mind raced, nerve endings jangling, long-lost emotions roiling in his gut. The lawyer, almost running now, got to the elevators, punched the UP *button repeatedly and just before the killer could get to him, a car came, Dingelmann entered, and the doors slid shut.*

Pounding his fist on the door, he watched as the elevator indicator reported its rise to the second floor; he jabbed the UP *button, as the indicator registered the third floor. A car stopped, its door sliding open, but before he stepped on, he looked up at that indicator, which had paused at the fourth floor.*

He jumped into the empty car and slapped the four but-

ton. By the second floor, beads of sweat were blossoming on his forehead and he was pacing like a caged animal. As the elevator passed the third floor, the pistol seemed to jump into his right hand, his left digging the noise suppresser out of the pocket of the linen sport coat. The door dinged at the fourth floor, and he stepped out, screwing the two pieces together.

He listened for a moment. He'd been up into the hotel a couple of times before, with hookers, and he remembered that a steel-encased video camera hung high on the wall at the far end of the hall. The doors for each room were inset into tiny alcoves, making the hall appear deserted; but the Deuce knew better.

Moving quickly, keeping his head down (even though the camera was thirty yards down the hall), he went from door to door. Finally he found Dingelmann, frightened and fumbling with his key card at the door to room 410.

The Deuce pressed the silencer into the back of the lawyer's head and heard the man whimper. A squeeze of the trigger and a round rocketed into Dingelmann's skull, slamming him into the door, and he slumped, slid, to the floor—already dead.

Then, just to make sure, and out of ritual, he fired one more round into the lawyer's head.

A sound behind him—a yelp of surprise—prompted the Deuce to spin, bringing the pistol up as he did, never forgetting the eye of the security camera. Before him, a skinny, dark-haired waiter carrying a tray full of food gasped a second time as he dropped the tray. The metal plate covers and silverware clanged as they hit the floor, spaghetti exploding across the hallway.

Even before the clatter died away, he and the waiter took off running in opposite directions, the waiter toward the elevators, the Deuce directly at the video camera at the far end of the hall. As he took off, his right foot slipped in the lawyer's blood, and his feet nearly went out from under him. Regaining his balance, he flung himself down the hall, the blood smearing off with his first two steps.

As he sprinted he brought his arm up, destroying any chance the camera had of capturing his face on video. He shoved through the fire exit door into the stairwell and tore down the steps two at a time. As he rushed down, his mind worked over the details. Many things yet to be done.

At the first floor exit he stopped. He unscrewed the silencer, slipped it into a pocket. The pistol went into another and he checked himself carefully for splatter. He found a small scarlet blob on the toe of his right running shoe. Using a handkerchief from his pants' pocket, he daubed the spot away, got his breathing under control, stuffed the handkerchief back in his pocket, wiped the sweat from his brow with his left hand, and finally took in a deep breath, then slowly let it out through his mouth. He was ready. He eased the door open and stepped out.

Across the lobby, at the front desk, he saw the waiter screaming at a female desk clerk, and pointing in the general direction of the elevators.

The Deuce, deciding to avoid the lobby as much as possible, turned into the casino, walked past a scruffy-looking blonde girl, probably all of twenty-one, who now occupied his poker machine. The tray was still full of coins from his four kings. Silently cursing, he hoped she pissed it all away.

Avoiding security cameras altogether, often hugging walls, he kept moving, walking not running, not too slow, not too fast, then hustled through the door into the back parking lot, to his car. No rush now—he eased the car out of the parking lot, jogging from Atlantic to Wengert, then finally onto Eastern for the ride home.

The Deuce was free—the lawyer was dead—and Barry

Hyde could only wonder whether today had been an example of good luck or bad.

Nick asked, "Then why aren't we busting the guy now?"

"On what evidence?" Grissom asked.

"The videotape," Sara said.

"Can't get a positive ID from that."

Warrick asked, "What about the ATM transaction?"

"Hyde claims his card was stolen. Brass is checking into that now."

"We can match his fingerprints to the shell casings," Catherine offered.

"That's a big one," Grissom said, nodding. "But we have no murder weapon. And nothing that ties Hyde to the murders of Fortunato and Kostichek except the signature."

Greg Sanders leaned in. "Excuse me—oh, Catherine?"

"Yeah?"

"Thought you might like to know—your cigarette butt from Evidence matches the blood you took from the fence."

"All *right!*" she said, jumping to her feet. All around the room, smiles and nods appeared.

Greg wandered on in, eyes dancing, his grin wide even for him. "That 'ASAP' enough for you?"

"Absolutely," she said, sitting back down.

"But like they say at the end of the infomercials," the lab tech teased, holding up a forefinger, ". . . that's not all!"

Everyone looked at him.

Enjoying center stage, Sanders said to Grissom, "Thanks for the take-out salad."

Willing to play along—for a moment—Grissom asked, "You enjoyed it?"

"I think *you* will—the saliva matches the DNA from the blood and the cigarette."

"Salad?" Sara asked.

"From the Dumpster behind A-to-Z Video," Grissom said. "Hyde even invited me to help myself to his garbage."

"Nice guy," Sara said.

Catherine smiled. "What CSI would pass up an all-you-can-eat buffet?"

"Well, I stepped up," Grissom said, "with Warrick's help—and now we have Barry Hyde's DNA at the scene of the Fortunato killing . . . ten years before he claims he ever came to Vegas . . . and we've got that same DNA from the fence he vaulted, behind Marge Kostichek's house."

"What more do we need?" Nick asked.

Grissom said, "Right now, nothing—we've got what we need for the warrant that'll get us even more evidence."

"At his residence," Nick said, finally a believer.

"And the video store," Catherine added.

"I'll call Brass," Grissom said. "With any luck, we'll have a warrant in half an hour . . . Nick, Sara, Warrick—get your equipment together, full search. We're rolling in five minutes."

They all seemed to launch at once. The exhaustion left their faces, and they moved now with enthusiasm and a grim sense of purpose. Grissom watched, a faint smile not softening the hardness of his eyes.

As he was heading out, Warrick turned to Grissom and the two men's eyes locked. "Gris, Barry can run . . ."

"But he can't hide," Grissom said.

18

MAINTAINING A LOW PROFILE IN THIS HIGH-RENT NEIGHBORhood would have been damn-near impossible; so Jim Brass didn't even try. In the early morning sunshine, dew still dappling, the cramped court looked like the Circus Circus parking lot: the two Tahoes and Brass's Taurus were parked in front of the Hyde residence, and two Henderson PD black-and-whites were pulled into the driveway across the street (Brass had not been about to repeat his *faux pas* with the local police, not only alerting them but calling them in).

Neighbors—some in bathrobes, others fully dressed—came out to gawk as the CSI group, led by Grissom and Brass, stepped from their vehicles, a little army removing their sunglasses and snapping on latex gloves. For July, the morning was surprisingly cool, and Warrick and Nick wore dark windbreakers labelled FORENSICS—this was in part psychological, a way to inform the onlookers that this was serious business, and they should keep back and stay away. As the team approached the house, each CSI carried his or her own equipment, each already handed a specific assignment for the scene by Supervisor Grissom.

Warrick would track down the shoes, Nick dust for prints, and Sara handle the camera work. Catherine would join Grissom as the designated explorers, their job to search out the more obscure places, seeking the more elusive clues. Brass—the only one not in latex gloves—would take care of Hyde.

As they marched up the sidewalk to the front door, an aura of anxiety burbled beneath the professionalism.

"Think he might start something?" Nick asked, obviously remembering the close call at the Kostichek house.

At Nick's side, Warrick shook his head, perhaps too casually. "Why should he? Sucker thinks he's Superman. We ain't laid a glove on him yet."

Brass heard this exchange, and basically agreed with Warrick—but just the same, he approached the door cautiously. He held the warrant in his left hand, his jacket open so that he could easily reach the holstered pistol on his hip. Behind him, Grissom motioned his crew—their hands filled with field kits and other equipment, looking like unwanted relatives showing up for a long stay—away from the door, corralling them in front of the two-car garage.

With a glance over his shoulder, Brass ascertained the CSIs were out of the line of fire; then he slowly moved forward. The front door—recessed between the living room on the left and the garage on the right—reminded the detective of the room doors at the Beachcomber, providing a funny little resonance, and a problem: if something went wrong, only

Grissom—barely visible, peering around the corner like a curious child—would see what happened.

Nick's words of apprehension playing like a tape loop in his brain—"Think he might try something?"—Brass, within the alcove-like recession, stepped to the right of the door, took a deep breath, let it out . . . and knocked, hard and insistently.

Nothing.

He waited . . .

. . . he pressed the doorbell . . .

. . . and still nothing.

Glancing back at Grissom—who gave him a questioning look—Brass shrugged, turned back, and knocked once more.

Still no response.

Grissom moved carefully forward to join the homicide cop, the rest of the crew trailing behind.

"I don't think our boy's home," Brass said.

Grissom reached out and, with a gentle latex touch, turned the knob.

The door swung slowly open, in creaking invitation, Brass and Grissom both signaling for the group to get out of the potential line of fire.

"Open?" Brass said to Grissom. "He left it open?"

"Cat and mouse," Grissom said. "That's our man's favorite game. . . ."

They listened, Brass straining to hear the slightest sound, the faintest hint of life—Grissom was doing the same.

Long moments later, they traded eyebrow shrugs, signifying neither had heard anything, except the sounds of a suburban home—refrigerator whir, air-conditioning rush, ticking clocks. Drawing his pistol, Brass moved forward into the foyer of the modern, spare, open house—lots of bare wood and stucco plaster and stonework.

Grissom said to Warrick, "Tell those uniformed officers to watch our back. Then join us inside."

"On it," Warrick said, and trotted toward Henderson's finest.

Then Grissom and the other CSIs joined Brass, inside.

A wide staircase to a second-floor landing loomed before them; hallways parallel to the stairway were on its either side, leading to the back of the house—kitchen and family room, maybe. At right was the door to the attached garage, and at left a doorless doorway opened onto the living room.

The loudest thing in the quiet residence was Brass's own slow breathing, and the shoes of the team screaking on the hardwood floor.

In a loud voice—startling a couple of the CSIs—Brass called out, *"Barry Hyde—this is Captain James Brass, Las Vegas PD! We have a search warrant for your home and its contents! . . . Sir, if you are here, please make yourself known to us, now!"*

The words rang a bit, caught by the stairwell, but then . . .

"Simon and Garfunkle," Sara said.

Brass looked at her.

"Sounds of silence," the CSI replied, with a shrug.

Brass eased forward and turned left into the living room, his pistol leveled—a big, open, cold room with a picture window, a central metal fireplace, and spare

Southwestern touches, including a Georgia O'Keefe cow-skull print over a rust-color two-seater sofa.

"Clear!" Brass called, when he came back into the foyer, Warrick had already joined Nick, Sara, Catherine and Grissom, who were fanning out—firearms in hand, an unusual procedure for these crime scene investigators, but the precaution was vital.

Opening the door to the attached garage, Nick flipped the light switch and went in, pistol at the ready. After a quick look around, he yelled, "Clear."

They went from room to room on the first floor—Brass, Nick, and Warrick—checking each one. Grissom and Catherine—weapons in their latexed hands—stood at the bottom of the open stairway, to make sure Hyde didn't surprise them from above.

When Brass, Nick and Warrick returned to the foyer, they all shook their heads—nobody downstairs. Brass then led the way up the stairs, with the same combo of guns and caution, and they inspected the second floor the same way.

"It's all clear," Brass said, returning to the top of the stairs, holstering his handgun. "Barry Hyde has left the building."

"Okay," Grissom said, obviously pleased to be putting the gun away, "let's get to work. You all know what to do."

Sara unpacked her camera, Nick his fingerprint kit and they went to work as a team. Catherine and Warrick disappeared into other parts of the house.

Adrenaline still pumped through Brass as he came down the stairs. "Couldn't the son of a bitch have done us the courtesy of just opening the door and getting indignant about his rights and his goddamn privacy?"

"You're just longing again," Grissom said, "for those days when you could shoot a perp and then say 'freeze.' "

"That approach has its merits."

"So is he not home . . . or is he gone?"

"I said he might be a flight risk."

Grissom nodded, starting up the steps. "I'll check his clothes, his toiletries—see if there are any suitcases in the house."

Brass moved into the living room, where Sara was snapping photos that would comprise a three-hundred-sixty-degree view of the room, working from that central fireplace. As she moved on to another room, Brass poked around. The front wall consisted of one huge mullioned window looking out onto the street, and that lone sapling in the front yard.

A television the size of a compact car filled most of the west wall to Brass's left. A set of shelves next to the TV was filled with stereo equipment, several VCRs, a DVD player, and a couple of electronic components Brass didn't even recognize. On shelves over the television sat a collection of DVD movies, most of which Brass had never heard of. *I have to get out more,* he thought.

Opposite the entertainment center sat a huge green leather couch and a matching recliner squatted along the shorter southern wall. Next to the recliner and at the far end of the couch were oak end tables supporting lighter-green modernistic table lamps with soft white shades. A matching oak coffee table, low-slung in front of the couch, displayed a scattering of magazines with subscription stickers to BARRY HYDE and a few stacks of opened mail and loose papers.

Grissom came in, saying, "No clothes seem to be missing, but it's hard to say. Closet with suitcases seems undisturbed, and all the normal toiletries—toothbrush and paste, aftershave, deodorant—seem to be at home."

"So maybe he's just out for breakfast. Or putting bullets in somebody else's brain."

"You find anything yet?"

Brass pointed at the line of movie cases on top of the television. "I found out I haven't seen a movie since John Wayne died."

Without sarcasm, Grissom asked, "And this is pertinent how?"

The detective shook his head. This was one of the reasons he liked Grissom: the scientist had little use for the outside world, either. His universe consisted of his calling and the people he worked with; beyond that, not much seemed to get Grissom's attention.

"Nothing pertinent about it," Brass said. "Just a social observation."

Kneeling, Grissom started going through the material on the coffee table. Brass plopped down on the couch, watching as the criminalist leafed through Hyde's magazines. Several were vacation guides, one was a *Hustler*, and the last one a copy of *Forbes*.

"Varied reading list," Grissom said.

"Travel, sex, money," Brass said. "American dream."

Loose papers, in with the mail, included various reports from the video store, a folded copy of a recent *Sun,* and an A-to-Z memo pad—an address in black ballpoint scrawled on the top sheet.

Holding up the pad, Grissom asked, "Familiar address?"

"Marge Kostichek?"

"That's right. Why do you think Barry Hyde has Marge Kostichek's address in his home? In the same stack including a newspaper with an account of the discovery of a certain mummified body?"

"I could maybe come up with a reason."

"But if he's expecting us—if he knows he's on the spot—why leave this lying around?"

Brass considered that. "More cat and mouse?"

Grissom's eyes tightened. "Maybe he hasn't been home since we talked to him. Get Sara, would you, Jim? I want a picture of this."

Outside a horn blared, and both men looked through the picture window to see a huge semi-truck, out in the suburban street, apparently somewhat blocked by the two curbed SUVs. The driver of the van blew the horn again, and the Henderson cops—who were parked in the driveway of the home across the street—were approaching.

Sara's voice came from the kitchen. "What's going on out there?"

Brass and Grissom looked at the moving van, then at each other. From Grissom's expression, Brass found it a safe bet that the criminalist had a similar sick sinking feeling in *his* stomach. . . .

"Let's go outside and talk," Brass said, rising from the sofa, his voice lighter than his thoughts.

Grissom got up, too, saying, "You guys keep working."

The CSIs did, but in strained silence; something in Grissom's voice had been troubling. . . .

Following Grissom outside, Brass felt a headache, like a gripping hand, taking hold of him. Every time they got a goddamn break in this case, it evaporated before they could play it out! And he knew, damnit, he just knew, it was happening again. . . .

The coveralled driver—heavyset, about twenty-five, with sweaty dark hair matted to his forehead and a scruffy brown mustache and goatee—had already climbed down out of his cab to talk to the Henderson uniformed men. The latter moved aside as Brass and Grissom came quickly up, meeting the driver in the street, in front of the van. Another guy—a mover—was still seated up in the cab; he had the bored look of the worker at the start of a thankless day.

Brass flashed his badge. "What are you guys doing here?"

Not particularly impressed by the badge, the mover said, "What do you think? We're here to move furniture."

"What furniture?"

He pointed to the Hyde residence. "*That* furniture."

"There must be a mistake," Brass said.

Fishing a sheet of paper from his pocket, the mover said, "Fifty-three Fresh Pond Court."

Brass and Grissom traded a look.

"Show me," Brass said.

Rolling his eyes, the mover handed the sheet of paper over to Brass.

"This seems to be in order," Brass said, reading it, giving Grissom a quick look, then handing the paper back.

Grissom asked, "How were you supposed to get in? Was someone supposed to meet you here?"

The mover shrugged. "Guy on the phone said the police would be here to let us in . . . and here you are."

"When did this work order come through?"

"Just now—I mean, they called the twenty-four-hour hotline. It was a rush job. They paid extra—through the nose, better believe it."

"Son of a bitch," Grissom said, and sprinted toward the nearest Tahoe.

Brass yelled at the mover, "Get that truck out of here—now!"

"But . . ."

"There's a murder investigation going on. You touch that furniture, you're in violation of a warrant."

"Maybe I oughta see—"

"Get the hell out of here!" Brass blurted, and the mover jumped. Brass planted himself and glared at the guy and, finally, the man climbed back into the truck and ground the gears into reverse. As the moving van backed slowly up the court, Grissom was cranking the Tahoe around; then he pulled up next to Brass.

"You coming?" Grissom asked. He seemed calm, but Brass noted a certain uncharacteristic wildness in the CSI's eyes.

Brass jumped into the passenger seat and the SUV flew out of the court, going up on a lawn to get around the semi. As they hurtled down the adjacent Henderson street, Brass—snapping his seatbelt in place—asked, "You want me to drive?"

"No."

"Want me to hit the siren?"

"No."

Accelerating, Grissom jerked the wheel left to miss a Dodge Intrepid. Brass closed his eyes.

As the criminalist ran a red light, Brass flipped on the flashing blue light—still no siren, though. Right now Grissom was jamming on the brakes, to keep from running them into the back end of a bus.

Brass was glad it was such a short hop to A-to-Z Video.

The SUV squealed into the lot and slid to a stop in front of the video store. Grissom was out and running to the door before Brass even got out of his seatbelt. Working to catch up, the detective pulled even just as Grissom pushed through the door and said, "Where's Barry Hyde?"

The cashier said, "Mr. Hyde isn't here right now."

Grissom cut through the store, down the middle aisle, Brass hot on his heels.

Pushing open the back-room door, Grissom demanded, "Where is he?"

Patrick, the hapless assistant manager, merely looked up, eyes wide with fear, and he burned his fingers on his latest joint. With a yelp of pain, the kid jumped out of his chair and backed into a corner.

"Barry Hyde," Grissom said. "Where is he?"

"Not . . . not here. I told you guys before, he won't be back until Monday!"

Grissom pushed through a connecting door into the back room. Brass tagged after. Shelves of videos, stored displays, empty shipping boxes, and extra shelving, but no Barry Hyde. The criminalist and the cop went back through the office, where the assistant manager stood in trembling terror, the scent of weed heavy.

"Sometime soon I'll be back," Brass said, "and if there's any dope on these premises, your ass'll be grass."

Patrick nodded, and Brass went after Grissom, who had already moved out into the store.

As Grissom headed toward the cashier's island, and Brass labored to catch up, a tall blond man in a well-tailored navy blue suit stepped around an endcap, and held out a video box.

The smiling cobra—Culpepper.

"You like Harrison Ford movies, Grissom?" the FBI agent asked casually, his voice pleasant, his smile smug.

"Why am I not surprised to see you here," Grissom said, with contempt.

"This is a modern classic, Gil," Culpepper said. "You really should try it—cheap rental, older title, you know."

And Culpepper held out the video: *Witness*.

Brass frowned, not getting it.

"I haven't seen it," Grissom said. "Is it about a freelance assassin in the Federal Witness Protection Program?"

Oh shit, Brass thought, as it all clicked.

"No," Culpepper said. "But that would make a good movie, too—don't you think?"

Grissom's voice was detached and calm, but the detective noted that the criminalist's hands were balled into fists, the knuckles white. "You weren't looking for your Deuce, Culpepper—you already had him . . .

you've had him for almost five years. You were just hanging around criminalistics, to see what we knew, learn what we found, so you could keep one step ahead."

Leaning against the COMEDY shelf, a self-satisfied grin tugging at a corner of his cheek, Culpepper said, "I really can't say anything on this subject. It's sensitive government information. Classified."

"You can't say anything, because then I could have you arrested for obstruction."

Culpepper's smile dissolved. "You're a fine criminalist, Grissom. You and your team have done admirable work here—but it's time to pack up your little silver suitcase and go home. This is over."

Grissom glanced at Brass. "Those short trips Hyde was making, Jim—he wasn't doing hits. The Deuce really was retired—and Barry Hyde was off on short hops, testifying in RICO cases and such. . . . Right, Agent Culpepper?"

"No comment."

"You people made a deal with a mad dog, and now you're protecting him, even though he's murdered two more people."

Now Culpepper turned to Brass. "Maybe you can explain the facts of life to your naive associate here. . . . When cases are mounted against organized crime figures—the kind of people who deal in wholesale death, through drugs and vice of every imaginable stripe—deals with devils have to be made. Grown-ups know that, Grissom—they understand choosing between the lesser of evils."

"Compromise all you want, Culpepper," Grissom

said. "Evidence makes no compromises—science has no opinion beyond the truth."

The agent laughed. "You ever consider goin' into the bumper-sticker business, buddy? Maybe you could write fortunes for fortune cookies? You have a certain gift."

"I like the job I'm doing just fine. I'm just getting started on this case. . . ."

"No, Grissom—stick a fork in yourself. You're done."

Grissom's eyes tightened; so did his voice. "When I'm done, Culpepper, you'll know it—you'll be up on charges, and Barry Hyde will be on Death Row."

"Barry Hyde?" Culpepper asked, as if the name meant nothing. "You must be confused—there is no Barry Hyde. Within days the house on Pond Court'll be empty, and in a week, A-to-Z Video will be a vacant storefront."

"Call Hyde whatever you want," Grissom said. "I've got enough evidence to arrest him for the murders of Philip Dingelmann, Malachy Fortunato and Marge Kostichek."

"There's no one *to* arrest. Barry Hyde doesn't exist—it's sad when a man of your capabilities wastes time chasing windmills."

"Barry Hyde's a sociopath, Culpepper," Grissom said. "What's your excuse?"

With a small sneer, Culpepper leaned in close and held Grissom's gaze with his own. "I'm telling you as a brother officer—let it go."

"You're not my brother."

Culpepper shrugged; then he turned and walked quickly out of the store.

Grissom watched the exit expressionlessly, as Brass moved up beside him, saying, "Real charmer, isn't he?"

"Snake charmer."

"Is he right? Are we done, you think?"

"Culpepper doesn't define my job for me—does he define your job for you, Jim?"

"Hell, no!"

"Glad you feel that way. Let's get back to work."

They drove back to the house in silence; both men were examining the situation, from the ends of their respective telescopes. The moving van still sat blocking the court, and Grissom had to park around the corner. As they walked past the truck, Brass was concerned to see no one up in the vehicle. "Where are they?"

Grissom shook his head and headed toward the house. The other Tahoe and Brass's Taurus were still parked out front; the Henderson cops leaned against their squads, sipping something from paper cups. Trotting up the driveway, Grissom led the way through the front door. They found the two movers sitting on the stairs sipping similar cups.

Grissom and Brass nodded to the movers, who nodded back.

"Honey, I'm home!" Grissom announced, voice echoing a bit, in the foyer.

Sara came in from the kitchen, the camera still in her hands. "Where have you been?"

"The neighborhood video store."

Brass said, "Hyde's flown the coop."

Grissom asked her, "Where's everybody?"

With appropriate gestures, she responded. "Nick's printing the bathroom, then he'll be done. Catherine's doing the garage. Warrick found three pairs of running shoes and bagged them. I think he's . . ."

"Right here." Warrick walked down the stairs, stopping just above the two movers. "You guys want some more lemonade?"

They both shook their heads, sliding to one side, so Warrick could come down the stairs between them.

Warrick stood before Grissom and said, "I'm sure one of those pairs of shoes is the right one, Gris. He had three identical pair—really liked 'em."

"Anything else?" Grissom asked.

Nick ambled in from the bathroom. "I've got plenty of prints . . . plus, I found this on the desk in Hyde's office." He held up a plastic evidence bag with a pile of letters inside. "Letters from Petty to Marge Kostichek—which he obviously stole from Kostichek's."

Brass gave Grissom a hard look. "I hope the LAPD catches up with the Petty woman—or that she really knows how to run away and start over. If Hyde has any friends in L.A., we could be looking for another body."

Grissom asked the movers to wait outside, which they did. Then—with the exception of Catherine, who wasn't finished out in the garage—Grissom gathered everyone around him in the foyer and explained the video store encounter with Culpepper.

"Prick," said Warrick.

"You're saying he just made Hyde disappear," Sara said.

"After we talked to Hyde last night," Grissom said, "that was it. Hyde made a call, and they whisked him out of town. He didn't even stop back at home, for fear he'd run into us."

Brass said, "And now they'll start him over, somewhere."

Sara looked dazed. "How can they do that?"

Brass smiled, wearily. "The feds play by their own rules. They don't give two shits about ours."

"So, that's it?" Nick asked, truly pissed. "We bust our butts, and the FBI pulls the rug out from under us? It's just . . . over?"

"I know Gil wants to pursue this," Brass said, "that's my desire, too. But maybe we have to face facts—we've been screwed over by people who were supposed to be our allies. How do we fight Uncle Sam?"

"Let's back up," Grissom said. "Before we march on Washington, let's review what we have, other than a lot of circumstantial evidence. If Barry Hyde walked into this house, we could arrest him—but could we convict him?"

"We could now," Catherine said.

Everyone turned to see her standing in the doorway to the attached garage. An evidence bag dangled from her right hand, inside of which was tucked a 1930's vintage Colt .25 automatic.

Brass felt a smile spreading. "Is that what I think it is?"

"It's not a water pistol. And, if the boss will allow me to make an educated guess, I'm predicting the barrel on this baby will match the bullets we took from Marge Kostichek. And the primer markings on shell casings found at all three murders should tie Mr. Barry Hyde up in one big bloody bow."

Astounded but pleased, Grissom took the bagged weapon, asking her, "Where did you find it?"

"I'll show you."

Catherine led the way into the garage. She stopped in front of a fuse box on the back wall, while the others gathered around her in a semicircle. The gray metal box looked like every other fuse box in the world, with conduit running out the top, disappearing inside the false ceiling of the attic above.

"I noted a fuse box in the basement," she said. "So I wondered why he would have a fuse box in the garage, when there's no heavy duty tools and only two one-hundred-ten outlets."

"Nice catch," Grissom said.

She opened the little gray door, revealing no breakers, no fuses, no anything except the end of the hollow conduit. With her hands in their latex gloves, she removed the gun from the evidence bag to carefully slip it inside the conduit, to demonstrate where she had found it; then just as carefully rebagged the evidence.

Sara, grinning, shaking her head, said, "Almost your classic 'hide it in plain sight.' "

"And the feds lifted him out of this life so fast," Warrick said, "he didn't have to take his favorite toy with him."

"We should look for the black ninja outfit," Sara said. "He obviously made a quick stop here after he killed Marge Kostichek, before going back to the video store."

Everyone was smiling now, proud of Catherine, proud of themselves. That left it to Brass to bring them back to reality.

"Okay," Brass said, "so we have the evidence. But we still don't have Barry Hyde. He's in the FBI's loving arms, helping them bring the really big bad guys down."

"Please," Sara said, making a face. "I may want to eat again, someday."

Grissom did not seem put off by Brass's little speech. "Let's get back to work. Sara's right, let's look for those clothes. . . . We've got a killer to catch."

"But Brass said this was over," Nick said.

"We need to gather our evidence," Grissom said, calmly, "analyze it, prepare it for use in Hyde's eventual prosecution. And, of course, Sara's going to play the major role."

"I am?" she asked, bewildered.

"Don't be modest," Grissom said, with a tiny enigmatic smile. "Let's finish up here, guys—then we'll go back and I'll tell you how we're going to nail Barry's hide to our non-federal wall."

19

Befitting the bitter December weather, the Federal Courthouse in Kansas City might have been fashioned from ice by some geometrically minded sculptor, not an architect working in glass and steel. The interior of the structure, however well-heated, remained similarly cold and sterile. No straight-back wooden chairs for the jury boxes in this building, rather padded swivel chairs and personalized video monitors—though the latter were seldom used, as lawyers so frequently arranged plea bargains before trials began. The justice meted out here seemed to contain no compassion, no humanity, also no punishment in some cases—just judgments as icy as the steel and glass of a structure that seemed a monument to bureaucracy . . . and expediency.

In a courtroom on the second floor, Gil Grissom—in a dark jacket over a gray shirt with black tie, a gray topcoat in his lap—sat in the back row, his eyes on the three-sided frame screen whose white cheesecloth concealed the witness box. Another set of screens blocked any glimpse of the witness's entrance by way of the judge's chambers. Onlookers took up only a third of the gallery.

The twelve jurors—evenly divided between men and women—sat blankly, though the unease of several was obvious; one individual looked as if he'd rather be in a dentist's chair. Behind the bench, the judge was moving his head from left to right, and front to back, apparently trying to work a kink out of his neck.

At the prosecutor's desk a wisp of a woman in a gray power-suit sat next to a bullish federal prosecutor. At the defense table, a nationally known attorney—at least as well-known as the late Philip Dingelmann, whose murder had finally hit CNN, the day the owner of A-to-Z Video disappeared—wore a gray suit worthy of a sales rack at Sears. He had the wild long hair of an ex-hippie, the tangled strands now all gray; he was a character—the kind of lawyer Geraldo loved to book.

Right now he was sucking on a pencil like it was a filterless Pall Mall, speaking in quiet tones to his client. The lawyer had made his bones defending pot farmers and kids charged with felony possession. When the drug of choice shifted to cocaine and the cartels moved in, the attorney had changed—and grown—with the times.

Back here in the cheap seats, Grissom could see only the lawyer's profile, and that of his client, Eric Summers, whose black hair, with its hint of gray, was tied in a short ponytail, his face angular, clean-shaven, with a sharp, prominent chin. Despite his conservative dark suit and tie, this defendant in a major RICO case looked more like a middle-aged rock star, and why not? His forays into the distribution of controlled substances, escort-service prostitution and big-time dot-com scams—the local papers referred to him as "a reputed leader among the so-called new breed of K.C. gangsters"—had allowed him to enjoy a rock-star lifestyle.

Up front, just behind the prosecutor's table, a blond head bobbed up, in conferral with the female prosecutor. Grissom leaned forward, to get a better view—Culpepper, all right.

The witness was escorted in, shadows playing behind the cheesecloth curtain—probably a federal marshal back there, with him—and then the witness took the chair of honor. The bailiff, on the other side of the screen, swore the witness in, referring to him only as "Mr. X."

Grissom sat forward, not breathing, not blinking, focused solely on the two words that would now be spoken—the words he had shown up to hear, the sound that would make worthwhile his CSI unit finding time for this case, over these last six months, despite whatever demands other crimes might make. It might even justify the overtime Sara Sidle had maxed out on. . . .

And the witness promised to tell the truth, and nothing but, in the traditional fashion: "I do."

Grissom smiled.

The voice was an arrogant voice, self-satisfied . . . the distinctive voice of Barry Hyde.

And Grissom could breathe again. He even blinked a few times. Hours of work, weeks of tracking, months of waiting, had come down to this. Outside were freezing temperatures, an inch and a half of snow, and his colleagues—Warrick Brown, with Sara Sidle, guarding the building's side entrances, Jim Brass covering the back, Nick Stokes standing watch out front.

Grissom and Catherine Willows—in a black silk blouse, black leather pants, a charcoal coat in her lap—sat in the courtroom watching the proceedings, just two interested citizens. Next to Catherine sat Huey Robinson, a Kansas City detective, black and burly, big as a stockyard, barely fitting into his pew. O'Riley knew Robinson—they had been in the army or Marines or something, together—and Brass had recruited the hard-nosed cop, in advance, from the local jurisdiction.

That minor debacle with the Henderson PD had reminded Jim Brass that a little interdepartmental courtesy went a long way; and Grissom had seen from Culpepper's example how a show of contempt for another PD's concerns could rankle.

Sending Grissom, his unit and Brass to Kansas City for this trial had been expensive; but Sheriff Brian Mobley had been so furious with Culpepper that he'd have spent half a year's budget, if it meant settling scores with the conniving FBI agent.

So with Mobley's help, all the jurisdictional *i*'s had been dotted, and the *t*'s painstakingly crossed. For this exercise to work, everything would have to be by the book.

And right now the object of that exercise was testifying behind a cheesecloth curtain—a vague shadow, but a specific voice.

"It's him," Grissom whispered to Catherine.

Catherine nodded as she looked around the gallery, slow-scanning the faces for possible undercover FBI agents, mixed in with the citizens.

The judge said, "Your witness, Mr. Grant."

Rising slowly, milking the dramatics, the prosecutor said, "Mr. X, you performed a certain task for Mr. Summers, did you not?"

"Yes, sir."

"What was that task?"

"I killed people."

The prosecutor turned to the jury box, letting that sink in; then said, "On more than one occasion?"

"Yes. Three times."

"Did he pay you to assassinate one of his competitors—a Mr. Marcus Larkin?"

"He did."

The prosecutor started to pace in front of the white curtain. "When was this, Mr. X?"

"Just about eight years ago. . . . It'll be eight years, February."

For three and a half hours in the morning, the prosecutor led Barry Hyde through a description of the assassination of Marcus Larkin, a local pimp and drug dealer. When the judge called the lunch break, Grissom and Catherine ducked out of the courtroom, leaving the building, to prevent Culpepper from seeing them. Kansas City cop Robinson—who was unknown to the FBI agent—stayed behind to keep an eye on things.

Catherine suggested grabbing Hyde at the lunch break, but Grissom knew that could put them at odds not just with the FBI, but with a pissed-off federal judge.

"Better we wait," he told her, in the corridor, "till Hyde's testified and the judge doesn't have any further use for him."

So they sat in the rental van, eating sub sandwiches for lunch. The car heater thrummed, throwing out more hot air than the attorneys inside, though never enough to satisfy these desert dwellers, who were literally out of their element in this cold, snowy clime.

"There's Culpepper," Catherine said, pointing to the FBI agent, as he strode up the Federal Courthouse's wide front walk. They watched him disappear into the building.

"That's our cue," Grissom said.

"Yeah. Remember, we got deliveries to make first."

Grissom carried the sandwiches and Catherine the tray of cups of hot coffee—the latter at least a token effort toward thawing the CSIs assigned to standing outside in a wind chill barely above zero.

They came to Sara's station first. In her black parka with the hood pulled up and drawn tight, only her nose seeming to peek out, she looked like a reluctant Eskimo. Hopping from foot to foot, she wore huge black mittens that made her hands look like useless paws.

"Oh, God," she said when they approached. "I thought you'd never get here. I'm freezing. Do people really live in this crap?"

"Stop whining," Grissom said. "How did you survive in Boston?"

"Alcohol—lots and lots of alcohol."

Catherine said, "You'll have to settle for caffeine," and handed Sara a cup of coffee.

"Th–th–thanks."

"Go sit in the van for a while," Grissom said, and he handed her the keys. "This may go all afternoon. The prosecutor took most of the morning, and the defense will take even longer. When you get warmed up, relieve Nick out front."

"I'll never warm up," she groused, accepting the keys and putting them into her pocket.

"This isn't any colder than Harvard yard, is it?"

Sara flipped him off, but the mittens ruined the gesture. He held a sandwich out and she took it and trudged toward the rental vehicle.

"She did a hell of a job on this," Grissom said, watching the young woman trundle off.

"Yes she did," Catherine said.

For these past months, on top of all of her other duties, Sara had kept tab on every mob-related federal trial across the country in an effort to determine when and where Barry Hyde would surface, to testify.

"Somebody better take this post," Catherine said.

"Right."

"Are you staying here or am I?"

"You." He took the tray of coffee cups from her.

"Power corrupts, you know," she said.

"Absolutely," he said.

As he moved off, she called, "Don't be a stranger. Feel free to stop back." She pulled up the hood of her gray coat and jammed her gloved hands into her pockets.

But Grissom was actually on his way to relieve Brass, who in turn took over for Warrick. After an hour, Nick had replaced Catherine, and Warrick had taken over for Grissom, in the back of the courtroom. With a still-shivering Catherine beside him, Grissom finally got back inside the court around three-thirty, easing into their seats beside Detective Robinson.

The defense attorney was attacking Mr. X's credibility. "Mr. X, isn't it true that you would be on Death

Row if the government had not intervened and cut a deal with you?"

Behind the curtain, the shadow bounced a little as Hyde chuckled. "No, that's not true. The authorities attempted for years to catch me. Truth is, most federal officers couldn't catch a cold."

This elicited a nervous laugh from the gallery, and a banging of the gavel from the judge—also a warning from His Honor to Mr. X. Frowning, Culpepper turned his head away from the witness stand—almost far enough to spot Grissom. . . .

Catherine glanced at Grissom, who shook his head. *Didn't see us,* he mouthed.

Culpepper was facing front again.

"I turned myself in," Mr. X went on. "I wanted out of that filthy life. You see—I've been born again."

That caused Catherine to smile and shake her head. As for Grissom, despite his antipathy for Hyde, he was enjoying watching the defense attorney search hopelessly for a ladder to help him climb out of the hole he had just dug himself.

Realizing too late his error, the defense attorney finally muttered, "No further questions, Your Honor."

The prosecutor sat back, relaxing just a little.

Grissom rose and moved to the door, Catherine and Detective Robinson falling in behind him.

The judge asked, "Any redirect, Mr. Grant?"

"None, Your Honor."

Pushing the door open, Grissom stepped into the corridor just as Culpepper was getting to his feet. Throwing on his overcoat, Grissom strode quickly down the hall, pulling the walkie-talkie from his pocket. He pushed the TALK button and spoke rapidly. "It's going down now. Everybody inside. Second floor Judge's chambers."

He turned a corner to the right and practically sprinted down the hall so he could be at that door when Hyde came out. Behind him, he heard Catherine and Robinson pounding along step for step.

Opening the door, stepping into the hall, was a marshal, maybe fifty years old with a crewcut on a bowling ball head, and a shabby brown suit jacket a size or two too small. Barry Hyde emerged next, wearing an expensive gray suit and a matching Kevlar vest. Behind Hyde came a second marshal, this one younger, probably in his early thirties, longish brown hair combed straight back, his charcoal suit a better fit than his partner's.

Grissom stepped in front of them, holding up the folded sheets of paper. All three men froze. The older marshal eyeballed Grissom, the younger one reflexively reaching under his jacket.

"Las Vegas Metropolitan Police—I have a warrant."

"Mr. Grissom, isn't it?" Hyde asked, the pockmarked face splitting into a typically smug smile. "How have you been? Couldn't you find a warmer place for your winter vacation?"

"Sir," the older one said to Grissom, giving Hyde a quick glare to shut up, "I'm afraid you've wandered off your beat. . . ."

"This warrant is legal, Marshal." He held it up for the man to see.

But it was the younger marshal who leaned in for a look.

"Wrong guy," he said. "That's not our witness's

name. . . . Now, if you'll excuse us." His hand remained under his coat.

Catherine and Robinson formed a wall behind Grissom.

Then Culpepper's voice came from behind Grissom. "Aw, what the hell is this nonsense?"

But the young marshal was curious, despite himself. "What's the charge?"

"First-degree murder—three counts."

The two marshals exchanged glances, and Hyde's smug grin seemed to be souring.

"You have no legal grounds, Grissom," Culpepper said, moving into the midst of it, anger building to rage. "No jurisdiction . . . This man is a federal witness granted immunity for his crimes."

Warrick, Nick, Sara, and Brass all seemed to appear at once—in their heavy coats, they looked ominous, a small invading army.

Grissom was well-prepared for this assertion from Culpepper; and for all to hear, he said, "This man has no immunity for murders he committed after making his agreement with the government—specifically, the murders of Philip Dingelmann and Marge Kostichek."

The marshals exchanged frowning glances, and Hyde's smirk was long gone.

Brass slipped between Culpepper and the rest of the group.

Handing the warrant to the older marshal, Grissom said, "Read it over, Marshal—I think you'll find everything in order."

The older marshal pulled a pair of half-moon reading glasses from his inside suit-coat pocket, and read.

Steaming, Culpepper said to the marshals, "If you two surrender my witness to this asshole, your careers are over."

People down in the main corridor were clustered there now, watching the goings-on in this side hallway.

Robinson, his basso profundo voice resonating throughout the corridor, introduced himself to Culpepper, displaying his badge, and saying, "If you do not surrender this prisoner to these officers, you will be accompanying me, them and the prisoner to the Locust Street Station."

Brass added, "After which, you can come home with us, to Las Vegas, where you'll be charged with obstruction of justice."

Culpepper's lip curled in a sneer. "Officer Robinson, this is a federal courthouse—and you're in way over your head."

Ignoring this, Robinson moved in beside Grissom, his Kansas City cop's glare firmly in place as he stared at the younger marshal, to whom he also displayed his shield. "And you, sir, would be well served to get that hand out from under your coat."

The younger marshal looked over at his partner who nodded. Slowly, the empty hand came out of the coat and dropped to his side.

"Thank you, sir," Robinson said.

Anger had turned Culpepper's face a purplish crimson; looking past Brass, at the marshals, he said, "We need to get the witness out of here. March him the hell out."

Robinson turned toward him, but Brass was closer, and held up a hand, as if to say, *Please . . . allow me.*

Grabbing Culpepper roughly by the arm, Brass said, "You want to be the next FBI agent to go down for obstruction? I got no real problem helping you do that."

Culpepper glared at him, but said nothing, his glibness failing him at last.

The older marshal said to Grissom, "You really think this man," he glanced at Hyde, "killed Philip Dingelmann?"

"It's not an opinion," Grissom said. "I have the evidence to prove it."

"I'll die of old age before you prove it," Hyde said, blustering now, his smugness, his self-confidence a memory. "You haven't got anything!"

"We have something," Brass interjected. "We have the death penalty."

Hyde managed a derisive grin, but the bravado had bled out.

"You're almost right, Barry," Grissom said to the object of the tug of war. "We don't have much. Just you on casino videotape, bullets and shell casings matching your gun, with your fingerprints; then there's your footprints, matching DNA from the Fortunato and Kostichek murder scenes . . ."

Hyde's face drained of color.

". . . but why spoil your attorney's fun? We should leave something for the discovery phase."

"This time you may want to go to a different law firm," Brass advised him, "than Dingelmann's."

Culpepper's hand dropped to his pistol and he said, "This is my witness. This is an illegal attempt to hijack a protected government witness—all of you step aside."

Culpepper didn't see the older marshal draw his

weapon, but he certainly felt the cold snout of it in his neck. "Put the gun away, Agent Culpepper—Jesus, didn't you assholes learn anything from Ruby Ridge?"

The FBI agent's face turned white and he was trembling as he moved his hand away. Brass moved toward Culpepper, fist poised to coldcock him; but Grissom stepped between them.

"Calm down, everybody," Grissom said. Then he turned to the devastated FBI man.

The younger marshal holding on to his arm, Hyde said, "You're in charge, Culpepper—remember, you're in charge!"

"Agent Culpepper," Grissom said, "either we're going to walk out of here with Hyde in our custody, or you can go downstairs with us and face the media. How do you think you're going to explain to the American people that you're aiding and abetting a murderer? Obstruction is nothing compared to accessory after the fact."

Culpepper seemed to wilt there in front of them.

Hyde said, "Goddamnit, Culpepper—they're bluffing!"

Time seemed to stop as the two men stared at each other, like gunfighters on a Western street; but Grissom had already won, without using any weapon but his wits.

"Fine," the agent said to Grissom. "Take him."

Hyde, realizing he'd just been sold out, tried to make a break for it, yanking himself free from the younger marshal's grip, running toward the gathering crowd at the end of the hallway. But he didn't get six feet before Warrick and Nick grabbed him on either side. Before he could do more than wrestle around a little, Robinson had his hands cuffed behind him.

"Smart decision, Agent Culpepper," Grissom said. "It's just sad when a man of your capabilities goes tilting at windmills."

"Go to hell, Grissom."

Grissom cocked his head. "Is that any way to talk to a 'brother' officer?"

Culpepper muttered, "Next time," then turned on his heels and headed quickly down the corridor, almost on the run—away from the crowd.

And his witness.

"Culpepper!" Hyde yelled. "What, you're gonna leave me hanging?"

"Actually," Brass said, "it's lethal injection."

"Cul-pepper!" he wailed.

But Culpepper was gone.

Ambling up to Grissom's side, Catherine said, "You know for somebody who smiles as much as he does, Culpepper doesn't seem to have much of a sense of humor."

"He's lucky I didn't cap his ass," Robinson said, "goin' for that gun . . ."

The older marshal extended his hand to Grissom. "Nice piece of work, even if we were on the receiving end of some of it. . . . I'm sorry, what was your name?"

Warrick—who had one of Hyde's arms—said, "Why, that's the Lone Ranger," and Nick—who had Hyde's other arm—grinned big.

Smiling, their boss said to the marshal, "Gil Grissom, Las Vegas Criminalistics Bureau."

As they shook hands, the marshal said, "It's been a

pleasure, Mr. Grissom." He nodded toward Hyde, who stood between Warrick and Nick with his head low. "We've been babysitting that stuck-up prick for too long. It'll be good to see him pay for his crimes, for a change."

"See what we can do."

Then the marshal turned to his young partner, saying, "Come on, Ken—we better get goin'. We're gonna be filling out reports on this one for the next hundred years."

Not as enthusiastic as his partner, the younger marshal followed the more experienced man up the hallway with a frown, apparently trying to assess how much damage he had just done to his career.

Brass moved in front of Hyde, gave him a nice wide smile. "You have the right to remain silent . . ."

"Well," Catherine said to Grissom. "You got him—you happy?"

"*We* got him," Grissom corrected. "And, yes, I'm very happy."

"You don't look happy."

"Well, I am."

The killer had been stopped, he was thinking; but what a swath of carnage this sociopath had cut. . . .

As Nick and Warrick led the prisoner toward the elevator—with Robinson accompanying them—Brass, Sara, Catherine and Grissom all fell in behind.

As they waited for the elevator, Catherine asked Grissom, "So—what do we do now?"

Everyone except Hyde looked Grissom's way.

Bestowing them all a smile, Grissom said, "Let's go back where it's warm."

Author's Note

I would like to acknowledge the contribution of Matthew V. Clemens. Matt—who has collaborated with me on numerous published short stories—is an accomplished true crime writer, as well as a big fan of *CSI*. He helped develop the plot of this novel, and worked as my researcher.

Criminalist Sergeant Chris Kauffman CLPE, Bettendorf (Iowa) Police Department, provided comments, insights and information that were invaluable to this project. Books consulted include two works by Vernon J. Gerberth: *Practical Homicide Investigation Checklist and Field Guide* (1997), and *Practical Homicide Investigation: Tactics, Procedures and Forensic Investigation* (1996). Also helpful was *Scene of the Crime: A Writer's Guide to Crime-Scene Investigations* (1992), Anne Wingate, Ph.D. Any inaccuracies, however, are my own.

Jessica McGivney at Pocket Books and Michael Edelstein at CBS were remarkably helpful, providing support and guidance. The producers of *CSI* were gracious in providing scripts, background material and episode tapes, without which this novel would have been impossible.

Finally, the inventive Anthony E. Zuiker must be

singled out as creator of this concept and these characters. Thanks to him and other Season One *CSI* writers—including Josh Berman, Ann Donahue, Elizabeth Devine, Andrew Lipsitz, Carol Mendelsohn, Jerry Stahl, and Eli Talbert—whose scripts provided information and inspiration.

MAX ALLAN COLLINS has earned an unprecedented nine Private Eye Writers of America "Shamus" nominations for his "Nathan Heller" historical thrillers, winning twice (*True Detective,* 1983, and *Stolen Away,* 1991).

A Mystery Writers of America "Edgar" nominee in both fiction and nonfiction categories, Collins has been hailed as "the Renaissance man of mystery fiction." His credits include five suspense-novel series, film criticism, short fiction, songwriting, trading-card sets and movie/TV tie-in novels, including *In the Line of Fire, Air Force One,* and the *New York Times*–bestselling *Saving Private Ryan.*

He scripted the internationally syndicated comic strip *Dick Tracy* from 1977 to 1993, is co-creator of the comic-book features *Ms. Tree, Wild Dog,* and *Mike Danger,* has written the *Batman* comic book and newspaper strip, and the mini-series *Johnny Dynamite.* His graphic novel, *Road to Perdition,* has been made into a DreamWorks feature film starring Tom Hanks and Paul Newman, directed by Sam Mendes.

As an independent filmmaker in his native Iowa, he wrote and directed the suspense film *Mommy,* starring Patty McCormack, premiering on Lifetime in 1996, and a 1997 sequel, *Mommy's Day.* The recipient of a record five Iowa Motion Picture Awards for screenplays, he wrote *The Expert,* a 1995 HBO World Premiere, and wrote and directed the award-winning documentary *Mike Hammer's Mickey Spillane* (1999) and the innovative *Real Time: Siege at Lucas Street Market* (2000).

Collins lives in Muscatine, Iowa, with his wife, writer Barbara Collins, and their teenage son, Nathan.